The Icing on the Cupcake

The Icing on the Cupcake

a novel

Jennifer Ross

Ballantine Books Trade Paperbacks   New York

A 2010 Ballantine Books Trade Paperback Original

Published in the United States by Ballantine Books, an imprint of The Random House Publishing Group, a division of Random House, Inc., New York.

BALLANTINE and colophon are registered trademarks of Random House, Inc.

ISBN 978-0-345-49296-8

Printed in the United States of America on acid-free paper

www.ballantinebooks.com

9 8 7 6 5 4 3 2

Book design by Elizabeth A. D. Eno

To my cupcake lovers—Cole, Lyrah, and Treat

The Icing on the Cupcake

Prologue

For Vivian death was a social event. There were letters of acknowledgment to write—"Your flowers were so pretty, the arrangement was so thoughtful." Invitations to pity dinners to accept and then log into the calendar.

In the first week after the funeral she had been out to dinner three times. She had twice that many invitations for the next week and more pouring in for the third. Either people were terribly sympathetic or they never did like her late husband much.

She had her opinion.

"Dear Anna, of course I'll come to dinner at your house. What a thoughtful gesture. Unfortunately, I won't be able to make it to the charity ball." Vivian wrote.

That wouldn't look right. She shouldn't be seen with a glass of champagne in her hand and in a long evening dress for at least six months, given the forty-six years she was married. Grief had rules and regulations.

Vivian did things appropriately. She swam in the manners of society. There was only one event in her life that flew in the face of decorum. Of course, that event defined the rest of her existence. It set in motion a series of events that dictated what her life would be like. But what's done is done. One has to turn one's mistakes into triumphs or at the very least not wallow in them.

The question now was how would Vivian repair the damage she had wrought throughout her life? She was beginning to form a plan.

She started tentatively. Each day since her husband's death she sat at her desk, took out a piece of stationery and started to write a letter. After a couple hours she invariably crumpled that paper and threw it in the trash, always troubled by the same thought, *How does one reconnect with the daughter one abandoned when she was five? Does Hallmark make cards for that?*

Vivian imagined a sad-looking Snoopy lying on the top of his doghouse on the front of the card. Inside it would say, "Sorry I abandoned you for forty-six years but I'm here now. Hug."

She looked down at the letter she was writing. She had gotten as far as "Dear," but that didn't say reconciliation to her. It was too boilerplate. She crumpled up the page and threw it in the wastebasket.

She pressed her forehead against the palm of her hand until she could feel the pain and guilt that had been throbbing around her eyebrows slowly ebb away.

Chapter 1

You never know what party will be the one. The one that people talk about for days, weeks or even years to come. The one that other parties are judged against. The one that people say, "Wait, were you there? Tell me what happened!"

Ansley wouldn't have thought this lowly kegger at Baylor University would signal a pivotal point, a sea change in her life as well as fodder for cocktail parties for months to come. She didn't know, but she should've seen it coming.

Parish, her fiancé, picked her up at her sorority house and drove her to the party, which was only a mile away, in his new silver BMW 700 Series. It was a graduation gift. They both were graduating from the university in a few days.

Driving to the party, Parish was quiet, but Ansley had more than enough to say. They had been engaged for two months and the wedding was a year away, but Ansley had already decided to have a Vera Wang dress custom-made, hire Bronwen Weber to design the wedding cake because she made beautiful and tender yellow cakes. Yellow cakes were the hardest to keep moist, Ansley knew. She was a baking expert. She had been whipping batter since she could pull a step stool up to the counter. Ansley bet Bronwen folded whipped cream into her batter, added a couple tablespoons of potato starch and a combination of oil and butter to keep the cake from getting dry. Well, that's what she would do. She was toying with where to have the reception. They could do something traditional and moneyed like the Fairmont or the Adolphus, or they might opt for something totally radical and have it at the zoo or their favorite dive bar, with the corrugated steel fencing around the patio.

"Maybe the botanical garden," Ansley said. "Or we could hit up one of our parents' rich friends and do it on their grounds. My momma is close with the Hunts."

"We're not deciding this right now, are we?" Parish asked.

"No, but soon," Ansley said as she changed the CD from some rap that Parish claimed he liked to Gil Gilberto. She had a thing for Brazilian music. It made her feel a little wild.

Parish gripped the steering wheel tighter. He hated it when she changed the music without asking. He thought it was rude. He was right, but Ansley reasoned that she could be a little rude with the man who loved her unconditionally. In marriage, you let a few of the niceties slide, she thought. You get to be more your authentic self.

Ansley's authentic self wanted her way all the time. She usually got it.

Ansley leaned over and kissed Parish's cheek to soothe him about the music. He smiled slightly.

"So, what do you think?" Ansley asked.

"Of your musical choice?"

"Botanical garden? Bar?"

"What about Neiman's? That's your favorite place in Dallas," Parish said as he parked right in front of the Greek Revival frat house.

"Sure, we can set up a lounge area in the Chanel section and get them to give people free makeovers at the makeup counter. Half my sorority sisters wear the wrong shade of lipstick," Ansley said sarcastically. But really, she knew that it was her choice. If he wasn't going to seriously discuss it, fine. She'd get back to him when she made a decision.

Parish opened her door and she grabbed his hand as they headed to the party.

They walked into the frat house. It looked like Tara with its huge white columns and manicured rolling lawn, but as soon as one stepped inside, that comparison evaporated. The place was a hodgepodge of eras. There was a mid-century-modern coffee table in the shape of a kidney bean and a sofa that was weighed down with blue and white pinstriped throw pillows from the eighties. The living room was littered with people. Parish waved to someone and headed toward the fireplace. Ansley walked to the kitchen. She didn't want to be trapped in a conversation about what companies were offering high-paying positions and what law schools were hard to get in. Ansley knew what she was going to be doing—getting married, entertaining and raising a family.

Her whole life she dreamed of getting married. Ansley had been raised to believe that one of the highest honors a woman can achieve is to marry right out of college and never have to work. If she chose to work for a charity or start a clothing line, that was fine. But she would never have to pull down a serious paycheck. Parish was the answer to her life's goal. In Texas, most men his age were thinking marriage. But Parish was more stylish and romantic about it, and he was hers.

Also, Parish always had a certitude about him. He wasn't one of the men on campus who played the field and equivocated for months before choosing a girl. A week into her sophomore year she was formally introduced to him. He said, "Ansley. I've always liked that name for my little girl." He proclaimed his love for her to his friends, to her friends and to all concerned parents six months after they met. For Valentine's Day, he bought her a platinum necklace, one that didn't bear a cheesy heart, like the ones most fraternity boys bought. Instead, it was a square pendant with a child's profile etched on it because he said the child represented what he hoped their future together would hold.

Not many people could say that everything they had planned for their lives since they were ten was exactly what happened to them, but Ansley could. Her life was going exactly as she'd hoped. Everything had always fallen into precise place. She had followed every Dallas girl's dream life, down to being a natural blonde. College, engagement and love were all happening like clockwork.

Ansley sauntered back to the kitchen. This is where the women were. Clumps of three or more girls stood together drinking beer out of red plastic cups. Ansley saw two of her sorority sisters—Patty and Claire—talking to a girl from another sorority. They were each rubbing one of her shoulders, comforting her like she was a three-year-old who had scraped her knee. Ansley headed over.

"What happened?" Ansley asked in a soothing, sympathetic voice.

"I thought he was going to do it. I thought he was going to

propose. He made a reservation at Jeffrey's in Austin and booked a hotel room in case we got too tired to drive home. He told me to wear something sexy," the girl sputtered, and broke into tears. Her face quickly turned red and blotchy.

"Did he break up with you?" Ansley asked, in fact-finding mode.

"No, he told me we'd try to make long distance work. The dinner was to celebrate his new job," she whined.

"You will be in Dallas and he'll be . . . ?" Ansley asked.

"In South America," she said, and couldn't talk anymore. The crying became silent and heaving.

"You're never gonna get engaged to him now," Ansley pronounced. She crossed her arms over her chest and shook her head no, emphasizing the finality and severity of her words.

Her sorority sisters, who stood on either side of the girl, looked horrified. They patted her back hard as if they were counteracting Ansley's harsh words with their hands.

"You can absolutely get engaged. You're going to go see him in September, right?" Patty said.

"September is a long way away," Ansley scoffed.

"You have email and video phone," Claire countered Ansley.

The girl looked up hopefully. She sniveled as her crying lessened.

Ansley smiled at her. The girl smiled back. Ansley did a visual appraisal of the girl, starting with her feet and moving slowly up to her face. The girl was cute. She was maybe five foot two inches. Her legs were chunky. She had very little differentiation between her ankles and calves. She had perky breasts, a flat stomach and toned arms. Her neck was a bit thick. Her brown hair was cut into a long bob. She had freckles, a narrow face and a humped nose. She was clearly cute, not pretty.

"There's no chance in hell. As soon as he gets down there and starts visiting the beaches and the bars he'll forget about you. You're cute, but not gorgeous enough to wait for. In two years he'll bring his Spanish-speaking wife to Dallas. Start thinking about getting a job now."

The girl grunted like she had been hit in the stomach.

Patty took a step toward Ansley and whispered, "Why did you do that?" Patty was the sorority sister Ansley got along with the worst. Not only were Patty and Parish friends, which drove Ansley crazy, Patty always championed the underdog and Ansley had no use for those people. She once told Patty the world needed the underdogs to be underdogs because they made it clear that people like Ansley and Patty were superior.

"She needed to know the truth," Ansley said without a hint of empathy and loud enough for the girl to hear.

Her sorority sisters looked at her like she was the devil. Ansley didn't care. It was better that the girl face facts. This way she won't waste years pining after a guy who is obviously trying to let her down gently. In Ansley's mind, she was being helpful.

The girl was crying so hard now that it was hard to understand what she was saying. Patty kept saying, "It's okay. It's okay."

Ansley scanned the room for the next group to join. She saw Parish watching her from the doorway. She smiled and walked over to him.

"Missed me?" Ansley said as she wrapped her arms around him and cuddled up to his chest.

"Not exactly," Parish said.

"You were thinking dirty thoughts," Ansley said, and giggled, "Your face was so serious when you were looking at me I knew you had to be concentrating on not getting a boner."

"I wasn't thinking anything sexual," Parish said, and pulled Ansley's hands off of his shoulders.

Parish looked at her with eyes filled with sincerity and then he looked at the girl whom Ansley reduced to a puddle in the corner.

"I can't believe you made her hysterical. That poor girl," Parish said.

"She needed to know that he wasn't going to marry her. She has to start looking for a new one," Ansley said in a sweet teacherly voice.

"A new one?"

"A prospect, a potential husband," Ansley explained as she laced her fingers in his hair.

"How good a prospect was I?" Parish asked with a slight smile on his face.

"The best. That's why I wanted you."

"But you love me?"

"Of course I do."

"It seems like quite a coincidence that I'm a huge catch and you love me," Parish said as he leaned against the door frame and watched the party.

"Well, I love you because of all the things that make you a huge catch, so it's not chance at all. It's because of who you are," Ansley said.

"You make a good point," Parish said.

"Are we debating something?"

"We're deciding something," Parish said. He was paying attention to the other people in the kitchen. He was studying them.

Ansley turned to see what he was looking at. He was staring at couples—couples holding hands, kissing, arguing. He was in sociology mode. Parish was always trying to figure out what made other people tick. It was one of the things Ansley loved about him. She thought that it was a skill that would help him excel in business. He was very smart socially.

"They look cute, don't they," Ansley said as she looked at a couple who were nuzzling each other. The guy sat down and the girl gave him an impromptu shoulder massage.

"They like each other," Parish said.

"They do," Ansley said, slightly annoyed by how obvious his observation was.

"I don't like you," Parish said. "You're mean to people."

Ansley laughed from shock. Whenever she was surprised or angry, her first instinct was to break out in giggles.

"I am not mean," Ansley said.

"You made that poor girl cry uncontrollably," Parish said, and motioned to the woman who was still sniveling on the opposite side of the room.

"She needed to know," Ansley said.

"Why? Why did she need to know? And even if she did 'need to know,' why did you have to tell her in such a nasty way?" Parish asked. The veins in his neck popped out as he spoke. His jaw muscles clenched. He was really upset.

"Well," Ansley stalled. Their relationship had made a seismic shift in the last few seconds and she wanted to shift it back. She knew that the next few words out of her mouth had the power to push them further apart or sew them back together. "I was trying to be honest."

Parish shook his head, "You don't even know when you're being mean."

"I know you're being mean right now," Ansley said.

"Why do I bother?" Parish said as he rolled his eyes toward the ceiling and threw his hands up in dismay.

"Screw you," Ansley said, annoyed at his superior attitude. She backed away from him.

Parish started laughing hard.

"What are you laughing at?"

"Your first instinct is to be mean," Parish choked out the words between laughs.

"Why is that funny?" Ansley asked, uncomfortable with all the people looking at them.

"It's not. That's the thing," Parish said. "I've been thinking about this for a long time—I was going to be nice and wait until we were alone, but you'd never do that, would you? Our engagement is off. Whenever you're ready, give me my grandmother's ring back. I wouldn't ask, except it's a family heirloom."

"Are you crazy?" Ansley screeched in shock. "How could you be so stupid? Here, take your old-fashioned 'heirloom' one-carat clunker back right now. You'll regret this, I promise." The whole room was looking at them now.

"Please," Parish said in a serious voice.

Ansley stared at him. She'd gone on offense to protect her pride, but really, she wanted to hold on to that beautiful ring forever. But she didn't think she had a choice. If she fought him about giving the ring back, more people would listen to their fight and it would become a bigger deal. No, she needed to give the ring back and talk to him once he'd calmed down and possibly sobered up. She didn't know if he'd had a couple of shots before he came into the kitchen but she was hoping he had. It would explain his behavior.

Parish closed his hand around the ring, stiffly hugged Ansley and whispered in her ear, "Good luck." He walked out of the kitchen, and Ansley found out later he smiled and waved at people as he headed straight to his car and drove off. One of his frat brothers joked that he seemed happier than he had in weeks.

Ansley stood in the same place. She didn't know what to do. Should she turn around and pretend like nothing had happened? Should she go after Parish?

She stood in the same spot too long. Patty and Claire came up to her and wrapped their arms around her. The vultures of comfort said, "It's okay. It happens to the best of us."

Ansley knew they were enjoying her pain as they talked. They were savoring her humiliation. She looked at both of them and smiled. "Everything is fine. We fight like this all the time—it's just for fun. He'll be back in ten minutes."

"Sure," they both said as they led Ansley to the kitchen table. One sat with her while the other got her a shot of tequila and a beer.

She could hear people whispering and she knew they were talking about her. She knew this was a night no one would ever forget.

• *Heartbreak with a Strawberry on Top* •

½ cup sugar
¼ cup (or ½ stick) unsalted butter, room temperature
1 egg, room temperature
6 ounces vanilla yogurt
1 teaspoon vanilla extract
1½ cups all-purpose flour
2 tablespoons potato starch
1½ teaspoons baking powder
¼ teaspoon fine ground salt, either sea salt or iodized
¼ teaspoon baking soda
½ cup diced fresh strawberries

To Make the Cupcakes:
1. Place baking stone in middle rack of oven. Place mixing bowl in freezer for 5 minutes.
2. Preheat the oven to 400° F. Line a 12-cup muffin tin with paper liners.
3. Cream the sugar and butter together with an electric mixer until light and fluffy, about 3 to 5 minutes.
4. Add the egg and beat for 2 minutes.
5. Add the yogurt and vanilla. Beat until smooth.
6. Whisk the flour, potato starch, baking powder, salt and baking soda together.
7. Add the flour mixture to the batter. Mix until just blended.

8. Fold in the diced strawberries using a rubber spatula.
9. Pour the batter into the paper-lined cupcake holders. Fill three-quarters of the way to the top.
10. Turn heat down to 350. Bake for 20 to 25 minutes, or until a toothpick comes out clean after it is placed in the middle of a cupcake.
11. Cool for 5 minutes. Place on baking racks.

Yield: 12 cupcakes

Frosting

2 tablespoons butter, room temperature
1 cup powdered sugar
2 fresh strawberries, about 2 tablespoons mashed

To Make the Frosting:
1. Cream the butter, powdered sugar and mashed strawberries with an electric mixer until creamy and smooth, about 3 to 5 minutes.
2. Chill frosting for 15 minutes or until thick.
3. Frost cooled cupcakes.

Chapter 2

In his defense, Parish hadn't intended on publicly embarrassing Ansley. He hadn't intended on breaking the engagement. In that kitchen something in him woke up; he realized he didn't want to spend the rest of his life with a woman who made him, and everyone else, feel bad.

Watching Ansley reduce that woman to a puddle of tears with a smile on her face made him think of a bully on a playground. He imagined Ansley doing the same thing to him at breakfast every morning and then to their kids. He didn't want the kind of life where he hid out in the bathroom to avoid his wife. He saw his father do that and knew it was a miserable existence.

He would've never gotten engaged to Ansley if he'd known she could be so mean. Their relationship, which was more than two years old, had been perfect until their engagement party. She was sweet to him, her sorority sisters, even the dorks on campus. She never had a bad thing to say about any-

one. She was the quintessential Southern girl—doting, seductive and domestically capable. Ansley was an amazing cook,
baker and party planner. She always acquiesced to what he
wanted. Heck, he'd thought she loved rap. It was only after the
engagement that she started the completely annoying habit of
changing the music the moment she got into the car.

The engagement party is where everything started to un-
ravel. It's where Ansley started to show her "authentic" self. In
retrospect, it didn't seem so surprising that Ansley wasn't as
perfect as she seemed. What was shocking was that it took two
years for her to show her true colors. But hey, she obviously
knew better than to relax before the ring was on her finger.

The engagement party was at her mother's house on a Fri-
day evening in late April. The weather was perfect—eighties
during the day and high sixties at night. The grass and all the
plants were still vibrant because the 100-degree Texas summer hadn't arrived yet to batter their reserves.

The party was organized and executed with military precision. Tables were set up in the backyard with lacy cloths and
crystal vases full of pink hydrangea. Paper lanterns were strung
around the trees. There were silver trays stacked high with cucumber sandwiches and scones. China bowls were full of clot-
ted cream and strawberries. Cute cupcakes with pert vanilla
frosting clustered on stacked platters. Ansley made those.
They were the food that the guests came back to again and
again. She had a talent. When you walked outside it felt like an
English tea party that happened to serve alcoholic tea. Ansley
presided over it in a strapless white dress with a full skirt. She
glowed. Her hair was loose and dipped down her back. It was
a cascade of honey.

As soon as Parish saw her he felt sure he had made the right decision. This was the woman he wanted to be with every day of his life. He wanted to go grocery shopping with her and do taxes with her. Parish walked up to her, dipped her and planted a huge kiss on her lips. She laughed and kissed him back. Then she whispered, "Check out Kate over there. She got fat."

"Okay," Parish said, and looked over to Kate, a friend of Ansley's from high school. The girl wasn't rail thin, but she wasn't fat. She had a little bit of a stomach and butt. To most guys' eyes she had an earthy sexuality that was hot.

Ansley took him by the hand and led him through the party. They moved from group to group effortlessly. Ansley was skilled in beginning and politely ending conversations. She was gracious to everyone. Parish watched her giggle with his grandmother. She got his mother to down one of the alcoholic teas. He had never seen his mother drink. But soon she was flush-faced and smiling lazily. She was telling stories about her sorority days that he hadn't heard and doubted he ever would've if she didn't have the alcohol to loosen her tongue. Ansley even flirted in a very chaste way with his father. Dad was smitten and wore the satisfied look of a man who feels attractive and appreciated.

It was, in short, a perfect evening.

They were getting close to the champagne toast. Everyone was giddy with alcohol and the romance of an engagement. Parish had lost track of Ansley. He searched for her in the yard and didn't see her, so he headed to the house. She was inside, her back to the door. He opened it and heard a hard meanness in her voice. He shook his head and listened again. He couldn't believe it was Ansley speaking. He had never heard her voice contorted in such an ugly way.

"I told you to use the cloth napkins. I don't even know where you found these. These are shit. Go get the ones you put outside," Ansley snarled at three servers. One scurried out the door.

The other two cowered by the counter.

"You need to make sure the sandwiches are cool when you serve them. A warm cucumber sandwich tastes like shit warmed over," she said, and grabbed one from the serving tray and took a bite. She spit it out.

"This is horrible. You need a whole new tray. Do you have one in the fridge? Go get it and throw these out. Tell your boss to deduct the warm ones from the bill. They were completely useless," Ansley said, and then under her breath but loud enough for the caterers to hear, she whispered, "Incompetent." Ansley turned and looked at a tray of her cupcakes on the counter. She grabbed a pastry bag and marched over to it. "You've handled these like they're potatoes. The frosting is ruined," she said as she retouched each one.

Parish ducked out of the kitchen without Ansley even knowing he was there. He wandered back to the party and thought about what he'd seen. She sounded terrible, but he told himself she had a reason to act that way. She'd asked the caterers to do specific things and they hadn't. She was keyed up about her engagement party. It was understandable that she was curt and emotional. He could let it slide this time. But it didn't stop.

Ansley increasingly made nasty comments about her friends to him. She was cruel to waiters. She exuded smugness. At any get-together she attended she took the role of de-meaning sage and gave girls advice on getting married whether they asked or not. She was lethal when she latched on to a girl.

Parish registered each morsel of cruelty and shoved them to the back of his brain. He tried to ignore an obvious fact—Ansley was a bitch. He rationalized, reasoned and came up with dozens of excuses involving why she would act as she had. His feelings for her were gradually eroding. Each time he saw her sneer at a waiter or condescend to a sorority sister she fell further away from his heart. He noticed he stopped wanting to hold her hand. When she reached for him his first instinct was to move away. By the night of the kegger, he'd had to consciously stop himself from pulling away when she kissed him in the car.

Ansley was physically beautiful. She was tall, thin, tanned, taut. Her eyes were large and soulful, surrounded by lush lashes. Her face was fresh. She always looked happy, like she was having the best time ever. It's what had made him want to be with her. He wanted to be where the fun was. Unfortunately, he figured out too late that Ansley's sunny looks didn't convey real happiness.

When Parish met Ansley he thought he wanted the prettiest sweetest girl he could catch. He wanted a girl who made other guys salivate. When people saw them walk into a room he wanted them to ask themselves how he had gotten this beautiful woman to be his.

Parish realized he wanted something else now. He no longer wanted the prettiest girl. He wanted the nicest girl with a pretty good ass. That wasn't asking too much, was it?

• *Wake Up and Smell the Scandal Carrot Cupcakes* •

3 eggs, room temperature
1 cup vegetable oil
1 teaspoon vanilla extract
6 carrots, coarsely grated
1 Granny Smith apple, peeled and coarsely grated
1½ cups sugar
2 cups all-purpose flour or 1½ cups all-purpose flour
    and ½ cup chestnut flour
2 teaspoons baking soda
2 teaspoons ground cinnamon
1 teaspoon finely ground salt, either sea or iodized
2 tablespoons potato starch
½ cup dried bing or tart cherries
½ cup chopped pecans
½ cup dark chocolate chips
½ cup sweetened flaked coconut

To Make the Cupcakes:
1. Place baking stone on the middle rack of the oven.
2. Preheat the oven to 400° F. Place 18 paper liners into cupcake trays.
3. In a bowl, whisk flour, sugar, potato starch, baking soda, cinnamon and salt together.

4. Stir in carrots, cherries, pecans, chocolate chips, coconut and apple.
5. Whisk eggs, oil and vanilla together in another bowl, then add to flour mixture until just combined.
6. Pour batter into lined cupcake tray, filling to the top.
7. Turn oven down to 350° F. Bake 30 minutes, or until springy to the touch.
8. Cool in pans for 5 minutes and then turn out onto a rack.

Yield: 18 cupcakes

Cream Cheese Frosting

½ cup softened unsalted butter
4 ounces softened cream cheese
1 teaspoon vanilla extract
2 cups powdered sugar

To Make the Frosting:
1. Cream butter, cream cheese and vanilla together with an electric mixer until fluffy, about 3 to 5 minutes.
2. Add sugar and beat until smooth.
3. Frost cooled cupcakes.

Chapter 3

Ansley woke up the next day with a mammoth hangover and the desire to bake.

Baking had always put things in perspective. Placing the eggs and butter on the counter to warm, measuring the dry ingredients into one bowl and getting the sugar and vanilla out—the routine of it calmed her. The anticipation of tasting the creamed butter and sugar with her finger excited her. Seeing the cupcakes rise in the oven gave her a sense of accomplishment.

Baking was a perfect microcosm of success. Making a tray of cupcakes made her feel she had done at least one useful thing in a day.

Ansley pulled a T-shirt over her cotton tank top and crawled downstairs to the sorority house's kitchen. As soon as she saw the marble countertops and KitchenAid blender standing at the ready by the sink she felt an ounce better. She opened the fridge and chugged a coconut water for her hangover. Then she got out a pound of unsalted butter and a dozen eggs and placed them on the counter to warm to room temperature. As she walked to the pantry to gather ingredients she replayed last night's events in her head.

In her memory, she saw Parish's face reddened with anger as his hands ran through his golden blond wavy hair. He was the modern-day Ashley Wilkes—porcelain features, blue eyes, rosy lips. He was almost too pretty to be a boy.

But the moment Ansley remembered, that beauty was overcome with disgust as he said to her, "I don't like you."

She flinched at the memory as she pulled the Dutch-processed cocoa powder and the flour out of the pantry, pomegranate juice out of the fridge, and walked them over to the counter, arranging them in a neat line.

"My fiancé doesn't like me," Ansley said aloud, and laughed. She could feel anxiety flooding her body. It is almost too obvious a fact that a fiancé who doesn't like you is probably not your fiancé anymore. Ansley pushed that thought out of her head.

She went back to the pantry to collect baking soda, sugar and salt. She brought them to the counter and arranged them in a neat line next to her other dry goods. Then she got all the measuring cups, spoons, and bowls she would need. She never liked to start baking until everything was laid out in front of her, and even then she would scrutinize her ingredients. Usually she'd find inspiration for a new flavor of cupcake by staring at the bag of flour, letting the focus of her eyes relax and her mind go. Something would pop into her head she had never thought of before.

This morning she was making red velvet cupcakes. As she stared at the flour the idea to add dark chocolate shavings with a little bit of powdered espresso sprang into her head. Coffee in any form heightens the flavor of chocolate, and since there was already cocoa in the cupcakes, why not add even more chocolate?

Ansley measured the flour, baking soda and salt as she thought of ways she could get back into Parish's good graces and get his grandmother's engagement ring back on her finger. She would bring him a cupcake and cry. He couldn't resist crying. She'd tell him she had been stressed out lately and that stress had made her act bad. She had been mean to people and she'd change. She was still the same girl he proposed to.

Using a fork, she stirred her dry ingredients together with the care of a chemist making a new experimental drug. She made sure to combine them for thirty seconds to ensure proper blending. She grated the dark chocolate with the measured and equal movements of a machine. Ansley was a deliberate baker. All the good ones were. Once they figured out what they would make, they approached it like a science. They were exacting because they knew an eighth of a cup more or less of flour could have disastrous effects on how moist a cookie was or how well a cake rose. Precision mattered. That's what Ansley liked about baking and business, her major. There wasn't a "we'll see how it works" or "let's improvise it from here" attitude. It was all about being confident and certain.

Once she talked to him, she was sure Parish would see it her way. She was starting to feel her usual aura of confidence. Baking always helped with that. She now believed that by lunch her engagement ring would be back on her finger. How could Parish resist her? No one could.

Ansley creamed the butter and sugar, which must be beaten together for at least five minutes until the butter changes to a lighter yellow color. This is the only chance in the mixing to aerate the butter, or create bubbles that make a lighter cake. Her mother always fretted about the temperature of the butter. If it was too cold, it wouldn't beat properly. If it was too warm it would melt and make a flat cake. The perfect temperature for butter is between 65 and 68 degrees. You must whip the butter on low so you don't overheat it. Ansley's mother would put the whole bowl in the freezer if she thought she was in the danger zone.

Baking was the first thing Ansley was good at. When she was plopping batter into cupcake trays she felt as if she were ten again. That was the first time her mother let her use "the book," a three-inch-thick leather-bound family treasure. For generations, her relatives had written only their best efforts into it—no recipes copied from other cookbooks or friends. The entries had to be original.

Lots of families have legends about an incredible pot roast or to-die-for cheesecake, recipes that were only kept in the cook's head or scribbled on scraps of paper that were sadly lost in the chaos of living. In Ansley's family it was all preserved. From her first relative to arrive in the United States in 1853 on, Ansley's family kept meticulous track of the divine things to come out of their ovens. Marielle Bufe had her husband create the leather book with more than two hundred pages because she knew that cooking was important and would matter through the generations.

On the first page of the book she laid out simple rules. One: The book was to be passed from mother to the daughter who cooked the most. If there was no daughter, then the first granddaughter. Two: Three people must agree a recipe is fit to be put in the book. Usually a grandmother, mother and daughter were the voting parties. If the daughter was too young, the cook waited until she was old enough to vote. If there was no daughter, another suitable female relative could be substituted. Three: Never let anyone borrow the book.

Ansley understood the power of baking after she made strawberry cupcakes for her ten-year-old slumber party. Every girl at the party loved them and wanted to be her best friend.

She took the confidence she gained from baking and applied it to all other areas of her life. She learned to dominate, in a very Southern way, every grade and group of girls she joined from then on. Her brazen appraisals of other women and attention-seeking attempts were never curbed. In her last year of college she had become unstoppable—and once she became engaged, many would say unbearable.

She added all her dry ingredients to the batter, beating until they blended, and was now using an ice cream scoop to precisely measure how much batter went into each cupcake tin. In cupcake making, uniformity was crucial. When one looks at a platter of cupcakes and sees row upon row of similar-sized cakes, it pleases the eye and somehow makes the cupcakes more enticing. When one sees a platter full of cakes of varying sizes it looks like a child's baking experiment. You don't trust it. You're cautious about biting into one. What if the inexperienced baker mixed up ingredients or cooked the cakes until there were as dry as bricks? Consistency was key. Ansley kept going with the ice cream scoop until all the tins were full. Then she held the tray four inches above the counter and dropped it. She had been taught that was how you got rid of bubbles in the batter. She placed the tray on a baking stone in the oven. She had found that allowing the oven to heat up with the baking stone inside it to be a move of cake-rising genius. When the cupcake tray was placed on the hot stone it activated the rising ingredients in the batter more fully than if the tray was placed on the oven rack. Cupcakes on the stone always domed beautifully.

When she turned back from the oven she saw Patty, Claire, Morgan and a half dozen other sorority sisters crowded into the kitchen. They all smiled sadly at her.

"Ansley, sweetie, go back to bed. We'll bring you breakfast," Patty said as she engulfed her in a hug. Patty was tall and weighed about twenty pounds more than Ansley thought she should. When Patty hugged her she was swallowed up in rose-scented flesh, and Ansley felt a hint of disdain. All the other sisters looked on with empathy.

Ansley wanted to swat those upturned lips off of their faces. She was always the one who gave that look of benign self-satisfaction to others—in fact, she was a master of the look. But she'd never been its recipient. She could tell that some of these girls, her "sisters," held smirks dangerously close to the surface of their faces.

"I'm making cupcakes for Parish," Ansley said as she started to put away the cake ingredients and line up the icing essentials—cream cheese, butter, powdered sugar and vanilla—on the counter.

"Oh, dear," Patty said as if Ansley's baking was the saddest thing she had heard in a long time.

Patty and Ansley were never close. Often Ansley felt like Patty wanted to smack her in the face and she couldn't figure out why. She had been the one to help get Patty accepted to the sorority after another girl wanted to blackball her because she was self-righteous and too much of a bleeding heart. But Ansley's support and Patty's father's promise to renovate the kitchen got her unanimous approval. Sure, Ansley didn't approve of the way Patty let her ample cleavage flap around like two baby seals wrestling. She had kindly suggested to her that she invest in better bras and foundation garments in general—"Wearing Spanx is nothing to be ashamed of," Ansley said to Patty once when the girl was wearing a form-fitting jersey dress. When Patty told her she was indeed at the moment wearing the modern-day girdle, all Ansley could come up with as a response was, "Really?"

"We had a fight. People in relationships do that," Ansley said as she plopped butter and cream cheese into the KitchenAid and turned it on to its fastest setting. Something she'd never subject butter to under normal circumstances. The blender whirred around so loudly the girls couldn't speak above it. For a couple blessed minutes, Ansley could think.

If Parish was serious about this, it would mean she was a single college graduate. She'd have to get a job and search for a husband. Nothing felt more pathetic to her than the life of a poor single twentysomething trying to find someone to love. It was the plot to an outdated sitcom. She wasn't the plucky cute girl who didn't mind bargain shopping until her prince came. She didn't want to work. She didn't want to date. She was screwed. The thought rose up and stood in the middle of her head, illuminated in neon. That realization was like a baseball bat to her stomach. She had to grab the counter to steady herself. She stared at her cupcake pans in the oven. The batter was slowly bubbling up and puffing out over the tins. She was glad she had buttered along the surface of the tins, not just the cupcake holder. It'll be much easier to take them out of the tray, she thought, and then felt the air sharply leave her lungs.

She knew she was on the verge of something like panic so she started to rattle off recipes in her head. For some reason all of them seemed to involve a pound of butter.

She turned off the mixer as her breathing returned to normal.

"He asked me to give you this," Patty said, and handed Ansley an envelope. "And also asked me to tell you not to come over. He'll call you when he moves back to Dallas next week." Ansley stared at the envelope and excused herself—she knew she had about ten minutes until the cupcakes would be ready to take out of the oven, and that would be enough time to read the letter if she moved quickly. She ran into the bathroom as her sorority sisters looked at her with more self-satisfied pity.

"See you in a moment, girls," Ansley said with as much false cheer as she could muster.

In the bathroom, she read Parish's letter.

Dear Ansley,

I need you to know that I loved you from the moment I saw you walk down the hallways of the business school to the moment I proposed to you. I know now, though, that it wasn't you I was in love with. You pretended to be someone else, someone nice. You're not. I recognize that now.

Maybe it's because you're not happy with yourself. I don't know. I just know that I can't be with you.

Find some happiness and peace with someone else.

Yours, Parish

"Yours"? Not even "Love"? Christ, this was bad. As she sat on the bathroom sink, tears began to form in the corner of her eyes. She was about to break down, but suddenly, an idea occurred to her. She began to smile, and as she dried her eyes, she heard the kitchen timer. It was time to take the cupcakes out of the oven. And also time for an announcement that would shock everyone.

Back in the kitchen, she put on a couple mitts and took the cupcake trays out of the oven. She immediately started to take the hot cakes out of the trays and placed them on baking racks. Her fingers were like Teflon, always had been, they didn't even feel the heat. She knew everyone was watching, waiting for her to break down; well, she wasn't going to give them what they wanted.

"Here, have one," Ansley said as she handed a cupcake to Claire and took one for herself. She needed to do something or she would break down and cry. She unfolded the paper wrapper and bit into it. She closed her eyes and slowly chewed, waiting to see what she thought worked and what didn't. She always did this with a new invention. The shreds of chocolate nicely complemented the cake, she thought—then she heard one of the girls scream. She opened her eyes and saw Claire's mouth spill out bits of red velvet and chocolate, or what looked like blood clots. Claire was always the first on board whenever food was being offered. That's why she started college at a size two and graduated at a ten.

"What did you put in here?" Claire screamed. "Is this blood?"

"It's food coloring, pomegranate juice and chocolate," Ansley answered, impatient.

"That does look pretty gross." Patty said.

"Come on, it tastes delicious," Ansley said as she picked up another cupcake and bit into it.

"It was good until I saw what I was eating. Now it's gross," Claire screamed again and ran to the kitchen sink to wash out her mouth, "I won't be able to eat a rare piece of meat for weeks."

"Oh, please," Ansley said as she finished her second cupcake defiantly, "Delicious."

Patty came up behind Ansley and put both her hands on Ansley's shoulders. She gave them a squeeze and started to do a slow massage. It felt sexual in an inappropriate, awkward way, like a gym teacher coming on to you.

"You were reading the letter, weren't you? It's okay," Patty said in a sickly sweet voice, "you can tell us all about it—we're your sorority sisters and we'll help you. We'll cheer you up, really. You can find a job and a new boyfriend. There are lots of guys other than Parish in Dallas."

"Who cares about guys in Dallas? I'm moving to New York," Ansley announced, hoping that would wipe the smirks hovering on many of the girls' lips off their faces completely.

Another collective intake of breath from the room of girls, and then a group, "What?"

Each girl at Sigma Phi is worldly enough and has enough money to have visited New York City several times for shopping trips. All talk about how great it is, how pretty Central Park is, how convenient it is to have all major jewelry stores located within a block of one another on Fifth Avenue. But each one of them secretly thinks the same thing, *It's a dirty, dirty place*, and every one of them finds such great comfort in coming home that they feel it's almost the whole purpose of the trip—to make them appreciate where they live even more.

"Yep, I'm going to live with my grandmother and find more tolerant friends. I'll write y'all." She smiled and turned to go upstairs, leaving behind gasps and Patty's surprised question, "You have a grandmother in New York?" Ansley just laughed to herself. She'd caused quite a stir, but this time it was her choice.

But as she finished packing her last bag, she started to second-guess herself. Was she really going to move to New York? Would her grandmother even answer a letter from Ansley, never mind let her live with her? Ansley involuntarily shuddered. She'd never wanted to leave Dallas—or Texas, for that matter. She loved the city with a passion usually reserved for a living and breathing person. The city was everything she ever wanted. Even her church was perfect—two hundred young congregants and it was gorgeous, with it's Spanish-influenced terra-cotta roof, and oaks dripping with honeysuckle. She could always find a place to park wherever she went. Every service she wanted—hair, nails, exercise—were all easily obtainable and hassle-free. Her family was all there. She called her mother several times a day and saw her almost as often. Her father was always good for a sip of whiskey and some sports talk. She loved waking up early, going to the gym for a kick-boxing class, showering, meeting the girls for breakfast, going to shop, meeting her mother for lunch, volunteering some and then meeting Parish for dinner. It was truly the lifestyle, the only lifestyle, she thought herself suited to.

Well, she'd shocked them at least, she thought as she looked around the room she had lived in for the past four years. She remembered when they all decided to have their rooms painted a pale pink and embrace the rose-patterned bedspreads and sheets that an alum had donated. The sorority sisters decided to make all the bedrooms girly to excess be-cause when were they going to have the chance to act like they were living in an all-girl slumber party again. Every week their housemother put a fresh bouquet of flowers in each of their rooms. Ansley's were lilies. She fingered their petals del-icately, knowing she'd never sleep in this room again.

"It's all for the best," she said to herself as she started to put her toiletries into her bag. Two thoughts replayed themselves in her head, *What the hell am I doing?* and *Do they have Twinkies in New York?*

• *Seeing Red and Tasting Chocolate,* *or Shot Through the Heart* •

1 ounce pomegranate juice

1 cup buttermilk, room temperature

2 eggs, room temperature

1½ sticks unsalted butter, room temperature (can substitute with 1½ cup Canola oil)

1 tablespoon red food coloring

1 teaspoon white distilled vinegar

1 teaspoon vanilla extract

2½ cups all-purpose flour

1½ cups sugar

1 teaspoon baking soda

1 teaspoon powdered espresso

1 teaspoon finely ground salt, either sea or iodized
2 tablespoons potato starch
1 teaspoon cocoa powder
2 tablespoons grated dark chocolate

To Make the Cupcakes:
1. Preheat the oven to 350° F. Place 24 paper liners in cupcake trays.
2. Cream butter in mixer for five minutes or until it changes to a pale shade of yellow.
3. Add sugar and beat for another two minutes.
4. Add eggs. Beat three minutes.
5. In a separate bowl mix together pomegranate juice, buttermilk, vinegar, food coloring and vanilla.
6. In another bowl, whisk together flour, baking soda, salt, powdered espresso and cocoa powder.
7. Alternate adding dry and then wet mixtures to batter.
8. Gently fold in grated chocolate.
9. Pour batter into paper liners. Fill two-thirds of the way to the top.
10. Bake 20 to 22 minutes, or until a toothpick comes out clean after it is placed in the middle of a cupcake.
11. Cool for 5 minutes before placing the cupcakes on baking racks.

Yield: 24 cupcakes

Cream Cheese Frosting

1 cup (or 2 sticks) butter, room temperature
1 pound cream cheese, room temperature
1 teaspoon vanilla extract
4 cups sifted powdered sugar

To Make the Frosting:
1. Cream butter, cream cheese and vanilla together with an electric mixer until smooth and fluffy, about 3 to 5 minutes.
2. Add sugar and beat until smooth.
3. Frost cooled cupcakes

Chapter 4

Vivian Osterhaut retained the bearing of a woman who either practiced ballet seriously in her younger life or had steel rods framing her spine. When she sat at her desk to write a letter her posture was so ramrod straight it made her seem much younger than her seventy years.

She sat at her primitive wooden table desk overlooking East 62nd Street. From the second-story window she could watch her neighbors walk by with their little dogs and children. She could look across the street at another impressive townhouse with customized wrought-iron work that swirled around in a pleasing abstract pattern rather than the typical straight lines. She liked to stare out the window when thinking. It cleared her head and refocused her, the equivalent of rebooting your mind.

She scribbled line after line on her thick stock stationery. She was on a roll. She addressed Agent #1432 appropriately, reintroduced her case and asked in very direct terms when the IRS's persecution of her will stop.

Her husband died six months ago and left her all his money in appropriately tax-sheltered vehicles. Ever since his obituary appeared in the *New York Times* (in fifteen column inches of glory, of course) the IRS had been pestering her. They started with thin envelopes. Polite letters asking about one or two items in the estate. Vivian had her people promptly send replies. The questions didn't stop. They escalated. It seemed like every answer she provided was the jumping-off point for a set of a dozen new questions. And now they've come to this. Telephone book–sized envelopes requesting volumes of information and citing law upon tax law. Vivian was tired.

She was tired of answering questions. She was tired of thinking about Charlie.

There were no shell corporations, fake mortgage statements or personal income mislabeled as corporate, as one letter claimed. She wasn't trying to pull a fast one. She was more than happy to fork over a large part of the estate to the IRS and move on with her life. Didn't they understand she'd earned this money? Did they ever meet Charlie Osterhaut? If they had they would gladly relinquish all her assets and even give her a bonus. He was a difficult man. She wrote, and signed, "With best wishes, Vivian. P.S. Unseasonably warm in New York. Lilacs will bloom early," to the IRS.

She meticulously folded the letter into thirds and placed it in the heavy matching envelope with the red floral pattern inside.

She pushed away from the desk to retrieve the mail that her maid had left on a sterling silver tray on a spindly table by the door. The room was spare in decoration but that was a statement itself. It was painted Swedish blue. All the furniture was composed of slightly curved lines and muted floral patterns and stripes that echoed the gray blue of the walls.

She took her stack of mail back to her desk and worked through it slowly. Many pieces were invitations to parties, benefits and luncheons. She studiously marked in her calendar which ones she'd attend and left a pile of the rejected ones for her assistant to deal with. She opened up a rather large envelope and discovered, instead of a printed card or thank you note–sized stationery, three pieces of paper, which were filled with text.

She skipped to the last page and saw her granddaughter's name at the bottom. Ansley. She hadn't heard from Ansley since, well, she'd never heard from Ansley. She'd gotten the general evolution of Ansley's life from the few friends she still had in Dallas. They kindly sent her pictures and kernels of information they obtained from their own granddaughters. Hattie, Vivian's daughter, never even sent a birth announcement.

The letter rambled—a trait Vivian didn't like. Go right to the heart of it. Be clear and concise, because people have other things to do. Ansley dithered on about college, business school and baking. She said she'd like to spend some time in New York to figure out what she wanted to do and she asked to stay with Vivian. That took some guts. Oh, how unhappy Ansley's mother, Hattie, would be if Ansley came to New York, she thought. This wasn't the kind of connection Vivian hoped to spark. But she had failed to write the letter she has spent the last few months trying to craft. The closest she'd come was, "Dear Hattie." That was it. She couldn't find the words to express all the repressed emotion and regret she felt.

Vivian stared out the window and saw a young woman with one of those tiny dogs with the shaggy brown fur. The dog relieved itself on the tree outside Vivian's house. The girl patiently waited. She didn't pick up the dog's poo. She never did. Vivian allowed it. She had her staff pick up the mess because the girl was probably about Ansley's age. If Vivian could see her every day, she felt that she had a gauge on what her granddaughter was up to. The girl moved like she half expected she'd be playing soccer in a second. There was an agility and spontaneity that younger women's bodies slowly relinquish the further they get away from team sports. *Does Ansley play team sports?* Vivian wondered.

Vivian has stared out this window for years picking out girls that would be around Ansley's age, reading their clothes and mannerisms in an effort to divine what her granddaughter would be doing.

Vivian pulled out a sheet of her weighty stationery. She wrote in clean crisp lettering, "Come in two weeks. Write back with your flight details and I'll send a car. Love, Vivian," and folded the paper as she had the one to the IRS. She put it in her to-go pile and picked up Ansley's letter again. She scrutinized it for what it didn't say.

Vivian may have been a New Yorker for forty-six years, but she was once a Dallasite through and through. She knew the culture, which hadn't changed that much in the past few decades. Ansley didn't mention a boy, and that was key. Vivian assumed Ansley was pretty. She'd seen pictures of her and she looked perky, blond and skinny. Vivian also assumed Ansley veered toward traditional because that's how her mother would've raised her. All this meant that Ansley should be getting married by now but she wasn't. Something had happened. Perhaps because she'd been embroiled in so many scandals herself, Vivian could smell a scandal a mile away.

"Well, she's coming to the right place," Vivian said to herself, and chuckled.

Vivian was sure that whatever happened must have sent Hattie into a drama-filled panic worthy of the best soap opera actresses. From the time Ansley could form sentences Hattie probably filled the girl's head with the importance of being a pillar in the community and that meant not making any waves, not causing scandals or acting in any manner that could be "talked about." She was sure that part of Ansley's education was cautionary tales of her grandmother and her escapades, all whitewashed in fairy tale language a child could understand. She imagined Hattie used phrases like "and then your grandmother became a bad woman," and "she proved that she wasn't a princess at all but really a witch." Hattie might have been only five years old when Vivian left, but Hattie was a very determined five-year-old. One might say she was a middle-aged woman trapped in a child's body. She drank Milk of Magnesia a couple times a week at her insistence. She scolded Vivian if she skipped church or said, "Jesus," as a profanity. Vivian knew she'd never live up to Hattie's exacting standards even before she left Texas.

True, it's probably not the best thing in life to cause such a commotion within your social circle that you don't feel welcome in your own hometown for years, but there's always more to the story than the gossips let on.

From their point of view, Vivian fell in love with a rich New Yorker, dumped her husband, left him with their young daughter and fled to the Northeast. This is where the gossips would pause for dramatic effect and then say, "That poor little girl. Can you imagine coming from a mother like that?" The listener would shake her head no and say something like, "Just awful. A mother should never leave her children." Thus in one five-minute conversation a picture of Vivian as a cruel uncaring woman would be so deftly painted she could never undo it. Perhaps if she were living in Dallas, after years of giving to charities, working hard and enduring snubs, the cold judgment might break. But it was an iffy proposition and Vivian didn't like iffy. She also didn't like being snubbed. Plus, the gossips didn't have the whole story. She'd be sorely tempted to tell the whole truth to the first self-righteous society lady. What good would that do? She'd hurt dozens of people instead of just herself. Life gets so complicated when you add love, money and sex into the equation. Though if someone with a slight knowledge of her history read the red leather-bound family cookbook and looked at the entries from forty-six years ago, she could figure out what happened.

The life she had built for herself in New York was snub-free. If anything, the scandal made her more fascinating when she first arrived. It showed a kind of bohemian forward thinking that so clashed with her manners and carriage that people were entranced. They wanted to know more, and this is where Vivian's training in Dallas came in handy. A good Texas woman knows how to seem incredibly friendly without ever revealing anything about herself—the trick involves a certain kind of listening. It's keeping words to a minimum but talking back with your body language, eye contact and laughter. Whoever you are "listening to" feels so well attended she walks away thinking she had a fabulous conversation when it was really a monologue. Vivian was a master.

She rose up the social ranks quickly because of the mystery

surrounding her, her listening skills and the money her new husband possessed. Charlie Osterhaut was the only child of a manufacturing behemoth who was smart enough to sell the manufacturing before he died and tie all the money up in investments. He knew Charlie wasn't any good at working. Charlie, to his credit, did go to an office every day where he puttered around, ran ideas by his financial advisors and was generally told no, as well as the reasons why his ideas where on the wrong side of brilliant. He was a pain in the ass both at the office and at home.

He had inherited the desire to rule, but not the ability. So he ended up whining a lot. A trait that Vivian had grown to hate more and more with each passing day and year. He whined about the time they were having dinner, who they went out with, the color of the walls. Even when all that he had whined about was changed, he whined some more. The courtship had been quick and passionate, but Vivian knew within the first few months of being married that she would never have children with this man. The gene pool was too weak. She also knew that divorce wasn't an option. Divorce once, cause a sensation. Divorce twice, people think something is wrong with you.

So she went about setting up her life despite her husband. She collected friends she liked and who could tolerate Charlie. She made her charities and other hobbies things that kept her out of the house when he was home. She negotiated a tolerable sexual relationship. Fortunately he lacked the mythical drive of the behemoth as well. But he did require enthusiastic twice-weekly visitations and he did like to be the dominant one. Vivian acquiesced to those demands and did things she never imagined she'd do—a little role-playing and a couple positions she thought more appropriate for a dog. But every life has trade-offs, doesn't it?

It was such a relief when Charlie had a heart attack in his sleep. No, that sounds callous. It was a sad event. There were some things she had enjoyed about her husband. He was attractive. If you saw him in a picture you would think he was an Adonis. It was only when he spoke and moved that he lost eighty percent of his allure. Over the years his voice had become a disinterested whine. His movements were languid. His whole being conveyed the feeling that there was nothing you could do or say that would fascinate him. That was the problem. Everyone wants to feel vital and interesting. Charlie failed at both. She knew he did care about her. He gave her generous presents and he always seemed to want to be with her, but those were his only good points.

She couldn't shake the feeling that when he died her life could begin. She could date. She could move. She could eat whenever she wanted and whatever she wanted. She could see her daughter and granddaughter. She was an autonomous being. She hadn't ever been that really. This, finally, was her chance.

It sounded like Ansley needed some shaking up too. Her letter was apologetic, self-effacing in a bad way. It said, "I'm leaving Dallas with my tail between my legs." Completely wrong. Even if you are leaving a place with your tail between your legs, you act like it's the best decision you ever made. Acting can take you a long way in life. She'd have to teach Ansley that. How you weather a scandal dictates a lot about where you end up in life. That was probably not a lesson included in Hattie's cautionary tales.

Vivian took the letter she wrote to Ansley and the one to

the IRS out of the to-go pile, walked downstairs, slipped on her leather Capri sandals and Jackie O. sunglasses and walked out of the townhouse. She would personally mail both letters.

As she walked to the mailbox two blocks away she saw the telltale lavender and white flowers and smelled their delicate fragrance. The lilacs were already in bloom. They scented the whole street and made it feel like a home rather than a city. Her granddaughter would love New York, she thought. "Granddaughter"— the word made Vivian pause for a second before putting the letters into the post office box. Maybe she should've signed her note to Ansley "Grandmother." She let the letters drop into the box. It was better not to overthink the situation. Let it happen naturally, like the cupcake she created the other night.

• *Taste of Spring Zucchini Cupcakes* •

½ cup vegetable oil
2 eggs, room temperature
¼ cup buttermilk
1 cup grated zucchini
½ teaspoon lemon juice
1½ cups sugar
2 cups cake flour
1 teaspoon salt
1 teaspoon baking soda

½ teaspoon cinnamon
½ cup chopped walnuts
½ cup chocolate chips
Powdered sugar for dusting on cupcakes

To Make the Cupcakes:
1. Preheat oven to 350° F. Place twelve paper liners in a cupcake tin.
2. Mix oil, eggs, buttermilk, zucchini and lemon juice.
3. Combine dry ingredients in separate bowl.
4. Combine wet and dry ingredients. Stir until just combined.
5. Add nuts and chocolate chips.
6. Scoop batter into cupcake papers.
7. Bake for 24 minutes or until a toothpick inserted in a cupcake comes out clean.
8. Place cupcakes on a rack to cool.
9. Dust with powdered sugar.

Yield: 12 cupcakes

Chapter 5

As Ansley debarked her plane at LaGuardia she knew she had better figure out a new plan fast.

Whenever she stepped into a New York area airport the reality of it always struck her, but it was harder this time. There was no fantasy, no promise of great things at these airports. They were all low-ceiling messes with decrepit public bathrooms, cramped snack shacks, and if there was a coffee shop, it gave the impression of being one step away from being closed down due to health code violations.

"This is my life now," she said to herself as she walked bravely on through the airport corridor. "I have to set up some new goals."

She walked out of the terminal into the muggy air. New York was unusually warm this summer and smelled like a cocktail of stale beer and urine. Dallas was hot but at least it smelled nice. She waved to the car and driver with the sign that read "Ansley." Her grandmother was thoughtful. She had no idea what else one could say about her.

As they pulled up to Vivian's townhouse on 62nd Street, Ansley's misgivings about her decision all bubbled to the surface. She had never seen this woman. What would it be like to live with her? She shuddered—it couldn't be any worse than the last few weeks. She'd stayed at her parents' house while she waited for Vivian's reply, doing little but crying, watching TV, and talking to Patty, who had been an unexpected ally. Patty had stopped by almost every day, usually with a bag of hot, fresh McDonald's French fries that always cheered Ansley up and calmed her nerves. When a letter with a New York City postmark finally arrived, Ansley could barely contain her excitement. She booked a one-way flight that left in exactly two weeks and sent the information back to her grandmother. Now all she had to do was tell her parents. She hadn't mentioned a word about her plan—she knew Hattie was unlikely to take the news well. But today was the day.

An hour later, Hattie walked in the door from her nail appointment, and Ansley cautiously explained the situation and showed her Vivian's letter. It took mere seconds for Hattie to go from calm to incalculably angry. Hattie screamed every nasty word she had ever used against Vivian, and in general, in an unstoppable stream—"selfish, self-involved, cruel, unfeeling, materialistic, gold digger." All of Ansley's life one thing was always clear: Hattie hated her mother. The feeling came across in the stories Hattie told, the language she used and the fact that Ansley never met her. When Ansley was a twelve-year-old and they were on an adventure to the city and she asked about visiting Vivian, Hattie said simply, "Not in my lifetime."

Hattie forbade Ansley from going to New York. She threatened to never speak to Ansley again, to remove her from the will, to disinvite her to all family holidays and to cut her out of family photos. When she screamed the last part she picked up a photo of Ansley from high school graduation and threw it into the living room fireplace. The glass cracked in one loud snap and ripped the photo as it broke in two.

Hattie went on like an emotional tornado for a couple of days, punctuating her anger with more thrown items. Ansley tried her best to keep her calm. Her father nodded in agreement with everything Hattie said and when she left the room squeezed Ansley's shoulder and said, "Hang in there." This was always her father's way. He flitted in and out of the family like a congenial acquaintance. He provided the money to make the family go, gave soft-spoken advice and attended gatherings. That was all that was required of him.

When her mother quieted down Ansley reminded Hattie that her marriage propositions in Dallas were slim. "I have to start all over again, Momma. What choice do I have?"

"Marry a loser or go live with your grandmother who abandoned me when I was five—those are the choices?" her momma replied.

Every time Ansley spoke of her marriage possibilities she could tell she was burrowing deeper into her mother's psyche. By day three her mother responded with, "What about Atlanta? That's just a quick plane ride. Or Houston? That's even better."

"I need to do something bigger. I need for people to think I'm doing this for a reason besides shame," Ansley said as she shifted on the couch.

Hattie started to cry. She didn't want her daughter to ever

feel shame. Since the day she was born Hattie swore she would protect Ansley in ways her own mother never had. She wouldn't ever let her little girl feel unloved, afraid or alone. Her daughter would never go to bed wondering where her mother was or if she cared. She wouldn't ever have to worry about kids taunting her and saying her mother didn't love her. She'd never have to feel the shame of being tossed aside. Hattie had never anticipated Ansley would be left by a man and feel abandoned. She didn't have a plan to counteract those feelings in her daughter.

The fact that she couldn't make it better for Ansley had been driving her crazy for the past few weeks. All Hattie could think of to offer her daughter as a salve were spa dates and shopping. Ansley didn't bite on either option.

Hattie was at the end of her rope.

In Hattie's eyes, Ansley was the cream of the crop. She was five foot eight inches of pure beauty and grace, plus she was smart, well mannered and a natural blonde. Her face was heart-shaped. There was such a sweet curve from her earlobe to her chin that Hattie didn't know how any man could resist her. Then there were her eyes. They were a shade of dark blue Hattie had never seen on another person. They conveyed soulfulness even when talking about shopping. They were the shade of a blue sky before it turned into night. Her daughter, no matter what the circumstances were, should never have to feel abandoned.

On day five of Hattie's screaming fit, she stopped and said, "Screw it. Move to New York. You're too good for Parish or anyone else like him."

Hattie's hatred and anger toward her mother hadn't even slightly receded over the past couple days. But the realization that moving in with Vivian was the only thing that got Ansley off the couch in the past couple of weeks came into sharp and painful focus. Agreeing to let Ansley go was a huge sacrifice, but Hattie knew she had to make it.

Hattie gently caressed Ansley's hair. "We're gonna find something even better for you to be. When you come back to Dallas those sorority sisters of yours are going to be so jealous they'll be queasy."

Ansley hugged her mother tightly. She could smell Aqua di Parma on her mother's neck. It was her grandfather's old aftershave. For as long as she'd been alive it was the only scent her mother wore.

"Why did I have to fail so big? I would've taken a DWI or case of herpes over this," Ansley moaned into her mother's shoulder.

"You've always been an achiever," Hattie said, and they both laughed.

Throughout Ansley's childhood Hattie had found things to make her laugh even in the toughest of circumstances. Her mother was her closest friend. It was good to have her as an ally once again.

"Vivian is everything I said she was, but she's also smart. Look at how her life turned out. If anyone can help you, she's the woman. I know you have to go but I don't want to hear anything about it. I don't want to know about that woman," Hattie counseled as she put Ansley on the plane headed to New York and handed her the recipe book. Though the book was well past two hundred years old, it was in remarkably good shape. The true sign of its age was on the edges of the leather. The color had gone from red to paper bag brown. Inside, the pages were mostly food-free. Long ago the women of

Ansley's family had decided to treat the book like a relic and not touch it with food-covered hands.

Each entry was handwritten in black ink. So many different styles of penmanship were present—flowing cursive, blocky print, calligraphy. It seemed to Ansley like a collection of love letters from all her grandmothers.

"I can't take this," Ansley said, and tried to thrust it back into her mother's hands.

"No, you'll need it," Hattie said cryptically.

Ansley kept it in her hands most of the flight.

Now, as the car pulled up to Vivian's townhouse, she hugged the book to her chest. The house was made from carved white stone and was simple but elegant. Its width was no more than that of Ansley's parents' three-car garage. It stretched up four stories but it was small, Ansley thought.

She got out of the car and smelled the faint flowery lilac odor mixed with exhaust. The acrid smell of urine was missing, which must be one of the advantages of living in a wealthy neighborhood.

Ansley walked up the steps ahead of the driver and rang the bell. A maid, dressed in a tidy black shirtdress, answered the door.

"You must be Ansley. Vivian will be down in a moment," the maid said, and left Ansley standing in the entranceway clutching the cookbook. A staircase framed the center of the room. Delicate wooden chairs with pale blue and gold floral cushions stood against the walls. Ansley sat down in one to wait. Across from her was a tall wooden clock that had been whitewashed. It was a little beaten up, but it retained its elegance in shape and the carvings around the clock face. At the moment it said she had been sitting there for twenty minutes.

She had the strong urge to run out of the house and back to Dallas. The only things keeping her there were her lack of an engagement ring and the logistics of her luggage. The driver had unloaded her things, which were stacked neatly by the clock.

Finally, Vivian descended the stairs. Two men trailed behind her. One was the carbon copy version of the other, but older. Both were wearing three-piece navy blue suits in conservative cuts. They had that attractive short-haired muscular look of military officers but with an aristocratic air.

Vivian was tall like Ansley. She stood so straight it made her seem younger than her biological years. Her hair was white, curly and shoulder length. She had curves, beautiful Ava Gardner curves that she was obviously proud of. She wore a wrap top with flowing linen pants. Everything about her grandmother said both luscious and unattainable. Ansley stood and gently placed the book on the chair.

"This needs to be resolved. My question is why am I responsible for Charlie's mistakes even though he's dead?" Vivian asked the men as she smiled at Ansley. It was a very kind smile. Ansley returned it, grateful for the hospitality. She didn't know what she was expecting, but warmth wasn't high up on her list.

"You're going to have to play nice with the IRS, or, well . . ." The older man trailed off.

"Remember the Graftons. That lovely mansion in Connecticut, and now it's a school for wayward girls," the younger man said.

Lovely? Ansley thought. *What man says "lovely?"* The phrase stuck out as much as if he wore a hot pink tie with dancing flamingos on it.

Vivian nodded her head and introduced Ansley as her granddaughter to Arthur and Thad Wheeler, father and son financial advisors. Vivian explained they'd been in charge of her accounts for years, though Ansley sensed something had gone seriously wrong recently. Arthur was crisp and refined. Thad looked to be a few years older than Ansley and he had the air of authority about him that telegraphed a warning: *Don't talk to me unless you have something interesting to say.*

Arthur pulled Vivian a couple feet away from the group and signaled that he needed a couple of minutes.

"So you're a native New Yorker?" Ansley asked Thad. Her natural state defaulted to small talk. But by the expression on his face, she had not met the minimum criteria to speak to him.

"Yes, I am," he replied curtly, and looked back at Vivian and Arthur. It seemed like he was trying to lip-read.

"Can you recommend some good places to go?" Ansley asked.

"It depends on what you mean by 'good' and what you mean by 'go.' Really, I'd be of no help. I'm not one of the trendsetters of the city. I'm sure you'll meet them soon enough and they'll be an enormous help to you," Thad said as he surveyed Ansley's sequin-covered high heels and her tank top with jewels sewn into the neckline. Ansley was like a magpie when it came to clothes. The shinier they were, the more she liked them. She had indulged in quite a bit of shopping recently since most of her old clothes were a little too tight, thanks to all the McDonald's she'd eaten with Patty, and extra sparkle made her feel better about going up in size.

Thad stepped away from Ansley to get a better view of Vivian and Arthur. He stared at them with intensity, like his job was on the line.

Ansley absorbed the insult and the manner in which it was delivered. He spoke in a polite old-fashioned way that clearly said, *You and I aren't in the same league so don't even bother.* She couldn't remember ever being so thoroughly blown off by a man. She was stunned.

Her grandmother walked toward her and ushered Arthur and Thad out the door. "I'll be ready to go forward next week," she promised them both. Thad looked greatly relieved that Vivian was finally on board with whatever they were recommending she do.

"Lovely to meet you," Thad called as he left. There it was again. He sounded like a throwback to an Edith Wharton novel, New York high society circa 1918.

Once they left, her grandmother grabbed her hand and pulled her into the living room. She placed Ansley on the couch right beside her and asked the hovering maid for some tea and snacks.

"Thad was a bit curt," Ansley said.

"His father just put him in charge of my account so he has a lot to prove," Vivian said, and paused, lost in her own thoughts. "Oh, you don't measure up to the blue blood standards either. Thad comes from one of the families that came over on the *Mayflower* and they've only risen in prominence since their arrival. You're a newbie from the South. Don't worry, I went through that too when I came here. You can ignore those people. It takes them a few years to come around and there's nothing you can do to change that. The good news is they get over grudges, scandals and bad blood, unlike Texas women, and there are plenty of people to socialize with be-sides them."

"But I'm a debutante. I was top of my class at Baylor. I went to Hockaday, for God's sake," Ansley started to defend herself.

"Darling, it doesn't matter if you're the sweetest, most mannered girl around. What matters is your pedigree, and from their viewpoint you have none," Vivian said as she looked around for traces of her maid or any of her other staff. She patted Ansley on the hand. "We have a lot of catching up to do. Let's start with what happened with you and your boyfriend."

"Huh," Ansley choked.

Ansley was having a moment of supreme embarrassment. She thought she was holding herself together so well. She was going through all the appropriate steps to start a new life. She had written a letter to Vivian that didn't mention any trauma, and she hadn't intended to talk about Parish once she arrived. She had decided to erase the incident from her mind—new city, new life. It's moments like these, when someone is able to peel back a layer of yourself that you didn't want exposed, that you feel uncomfortably naked. Ansley felt like she was still the loser on the couch who hadn't showered in days.

"I didn't say anything about a boyfriend," Ansley stammered.

"I know," Vivian said, and waited.

Ansley cried. At first it was just a trickle as she began the story with when she had to give back the ring at the kegger, but it became a river of saline and ugly sniffing by the time she got to the blood clot cupcakes, her sorority sisters' erosion of support and her certainty Parish was already dating other women.

Vivian listened intently to her granddaughter. She patted her hand kindly, and when the crying went to stage one uncontrollable, she took Ansley in her arms and rocked her. It felt awkward, more like a polite stranger than family.

"Didn't anyone tell you you can't have one plan for life? You need to have exit strategies and safety nets. I'm angry you didn't have a better response for all those prissy girls on the spot," Vivian said.

Ansley looked at her, not expecting tough love.

"Momma didn't," Ansley whined, "and things turned out right for her."

"Your mother got lucky. She found a man she stayed in love with. One should never plan one's life around luck," Vivian said as she poured Ansley some iced tea and offered her a lemon cookie with a powdered sugar coating.

Ansley took a sip of the wonderfully sweetened iced tea and bit into the cookie. Vivian brushed Ansley's hair back from her face and continued, "Darling, there are worse tragedies in the world than being dumped. You can't wallow. Wallowing lets them win. You have to come up with your next thing that will make you so grateful you never settled down in Dallas at the ripe old age of twenty-two and popped out a couple of kids. You had an old-world view, now you need to expand."

"But, but—" Ansley sputtered.

"Having a great life is a painful process," Vivian said as she rubbed Ansley on the knee and stood up. "Come on, I'm gonna show you where you're staying and then I have to go. I have a dinner commitment. I'll give you eight weeks to find a job. If you don't, you can pack your bags and move back to Dallas."

"What?" Ansley stuttered.

Vivian walked out of the room. Ansley put down her tea, popped the rest of the cookie in her mouth and followed her grandmother up the stairs.

"Are you sure? I thought we were going to bond. A few weeks doesn't make up for the years I never saw you," Ansley said as they tackled the second flight of stairs. She was pulling out the guilt card and hoping it would work. It was her strongest manipulation tool.

"We have plenty of time," Vivian said as she trotted up. She didn't seem to mind the climb at all, while Ansley was getting winded. "Stairs keep you young and give you good calves."

"Are you saying there's no elevator?" Ansley huffed as they moved on to the third flight.

"I'm saying you're too young to need one," Vivian said as she reached the landing and waited patiently for Ansley to catch up. Ansley stood at the landing for a few moments to catch her breath. Those extra pounds she'd put on had impacted her ability to climb the stairs. As she stood there she noticed how light and airy the floor was. It felt like a country house. The wide oak plank floors were bare except for small woven silk Oriental rugs scattered about sparingly. The walls were all a moonstone white. They shined with an iridescent quality. Vivian led Ansley into a bedroom with windows that looked down on 62nd Street. The bed was piled with white and blue check linens and brown and white check pillows, as well as a white silk duvet. The furniture in the room was painted but didn't all match. The bed was an off-white with a solid curved headboard. The dresser was a pale blue with delicate porcelain pulls. The chest had hints of red, green and blue, all fading and chipped. This was the kind of furniture that looked casual, but cost a great deal of money, Ansley could tell. The room's general lived-in feel did encourage comfort though. The nightstand clearly wouldn't object to a water glass without a coaster and the dresser was perfectly okay with a load of lipstick and blush strewn across it.

"Perfect," Ansley said as she placed the recipe book on the dresser and sat on the bed.

"Good, we'll talk later," Vivian said as she traced her fingers on top of the book. Ansley had to stop herself from jumping up and taking the book from under her grandmother's fingertips.

"Are you serious about the job? I'm getting over a bad breakup. I should have time to recoup, to heal and to build a relationship with you," Ansley said, and looked at her grandmother pleadingly.

Vivian lifted her fingers, leaned against the door frame and pressed her lips together. She looked like she was softening to Ansley, like she was going to change her mind. She knocked on the door absentmindedly and smiled so tenderly at her, Ansley wished Vivian had been around when she was a little girl. That smile could've stopped her crying over scrapes from bicycle accidents and bee stings.

"If you sat here and did nothing for the summer, you'd obsess, sink into depression and make a lot of hang-up calls. If I backed down from the first thing I requested you do, you'd take that as a sign that you didn't have to listen to me. You're my granddaughter. I might not know you well personally but I know you well by blood. You need a good kick in the pants. Get a job or you're out," Vivian said, and fixed Ansley with a look that said she wasn't messing around. Vivian turned swiftly and left.

On second thought, maybe it was better Vivian wasn't around when Ansley was growing up. Ansley lay back on her bed and thought, *My grandmother is sort of a bitch*. She didn't have a lot of expectations for her grandmother, but the one thing she hadn't expected was that she'd be so much like Hattie. When push came to shove both of these women dug their heels in and pushed back even harder.

Ansley felt a profound ache inside. She didn't think she had ever been this alone. She knew no one in the city. She felt small and meaningless.

She dialed her mother's number. Hattie answered on the first ring.

"Thank God. Did you get there all right? How'd you get to her house? Are you okay?" It was like Ansley was a twelve-year-old taking her first solo trip.

"I'm fine, Momma. Vivian sent a car. She lives in a townhouse in the Upper East Side. It's sort of small, cozy," Ansley said as she stretched out on the bed. She debated whether or not she should tell her about Vivian's declaration about employment.

She did and in quick succession also told Hattie about Thad's treatment of her and Vivian's dinner date, thus leaving Ansley all alone.

"She's sort of awful," Ansley said, feeling guilty about talking ill of her grandmother in the woman's own house.

"She's known for that," Hattie said. "But I think she's right about the job. You have to do something with yourself."

"What am I going to do? Get a job in a coffee shop?" Ansley asked. It was ridiculous. Had things gone according to plan, she'd be too busy planning her wedding and enjoying lunch dates with sorority sisters to get a "job." Jobs were the superfluous and glamorous things you got once your children were grown. They normally involved some sort of design.

"You're going to have to find a new way in the world. You're gonna have to learn to support yourself. You might want to think about going back to school next year," Hattie said with a note of sadness in her voice.

"School for what? What am I going to get a degree in? Law?" Ansley's voice trailed off. Law school could be a good way to meet a man.

"Law school could be a good way to meet a man," Hattie echoed Ansley's thoughts. "It's new territory in New York. You have to swim with the natives."

"The natives don't want to swim with me," Ansley said, thinking of Thad.

"It was one native of a very particular class of people. Honestly, I don't know what they're so proud of with the *Mayflower* connection. Doesn't that mean that they were more hated in England than the rest of us if they left first?" Hattie asked.

This is why she'd called her mother. Hattie always put the right spin on situations.

"I love you, Momma," Ansley said, about to hang up.

"Just one more thing, baby. If Vivian mentions your grandfather, call me and tell me exactly what she says," Hattie said with more seriousness than Ansley had ever heard in her voice.

"Why?"

"It's important to me. I love you, baby," Hattie said, and hung up.

Ansley had intended to unpack after the phone call but it had exhausted her. All the thought processes and plans she'd have to alter to live in this city were overwhelming. Added to that she had a strong sense of unease about why her mother wanted to know about what Vivian said about her grandfather. What had Vivian done to Ansley's grandfather? She knew Vivian had left him, but had she done more than that?

The papa she knew was a mild-mannered man. He drank himself into a quiet stupor that made him more like a piece of furniture than a person. His personality was watered down to pleasantries and requests for drinks: "Darling, would you be so kind as to bring your papa a scotch?"

She saw in old pictures that he was attractive. He had a chiseled jaw and bronzed skin. Still, it was hard to picture vibrant Vivian with him. Maybe the marriage had been "arranged." Christian parents in the social set that Ansley knew her grandparents had swum in were, and still are, all about not-so-gently pushing their children into an appropriate match. After all, marriage is designed to bring fruit (i.e., children) and that fruit should be bred with consideration. Or maybe they were young, dumb and in love. They were married six years. Ansley had heard the span between eighteen and twenty-four years old can wreak seismic shifts to one's personality. She was undergoing one at the moment.

None of this explained why her mother wanted Ansley to report back to her Vivian's words about Papa. According to everything Hattie told her growing up, Vivian's departure from Dallas, motherhood and marriage was pretty straightforward. "She loved that man and her freedom more than family and decorum," Hattie had said often over the years. Why would her mother want to know anything else? All these things to think about and do made her limbs feel numb.

She needed to clear her mind. She took a deep breath and started to calculate how to turn a banana bread recipe of hers into a cupcake. Making up new recipes always calmed her. She kept her good inventions in a small leather-bound book, a tribute to "the book." Of the family book's two hundred pages only two were still blank. Ansley hoped to fill both of them and start a new book for succeeding generations.

Ansley was carefully calibrating how much flour she would take away from the original recipe for her cupcake recipe when she fell soundly asleep.

• *Moving Blues Banana Caramel Cupcakes* •

½ cup (or 1 stick) unsalted butter, room temperature
2 room-temperature eggs, separated (will use the yolks in the frosting)
3 tablespoons whole milk
½ cup mashed ripe bananas
½ cup plus 2 tablespoons sugar
1 cup flour
1 teaspoon baking powder
2 tablespoons potato starch
½ teaspoon finely ground salt, either sea or iodized
5 pieces of soft caramels

To Make the Cupcakes:
1. Preheat the oven to 350° F. Place 10 cupcake papers in pan.

2. Cream the butter and ½ cup sugar in an electric mixer until fluffy, about 3 to 5 minutes.
3. Add bananas, baking powder, potato starch and salt, and beat until smooth.
4. Fold in the flour with a rubber spatula.
5. Add the milk and mix until combined.
6. Beat the egg whites in an electric mixer until soft peaks form. Do not overmix. It's better if the peaks are slightly soft than too stiff. This takes about three minutes on high speed in an electric mixer. Gradually add the 2 tablespoons of sugar.
7. Fold the egg-white mixture into the batter until combined.
8. Scoop into lined cupcake pans. Fill each cake three-fourths of the way to the top.
9. Cut 5 caramels in half and submerge one piece each in a cupcake.
10. Bake 25 minutes, or until a toothpick inserted in the middle of a cupcake comes out clean.
11. Cool for 5 minutes and then move to baking racks.

Yield: 10 cupcakes

Caramel Frosting

6 soft caramels
¼ cup milk
¼ cup banana
¼ teaspoon finely ground salt, either sea or iodized

2 egg yolks, room temperature
½ cup powdered sugar
1 cup (or 2 sticks) unsalted butter, room temperature

To Make the Frosting:
1. Place caramels, milk, banana and salt in a saucepan over medium heat. Remove from heat when the caramels are melted.
2. In separate bowl beat egg yolks and powdered sugar with an electric mixer until thick, about 3 minutes.
3. Slowly add the yolk mixture to slightly cooled caramel mixture. I suggest placing the caramel mixture in a cool saucepan to aid in dropping its temperature. If the caramel is too hot, it will cook the egg. But we don't want to completely cool it because the mixture is about to be heated on the stove again.
4. Place the combined mixture over medium-low heat for 1 minute, stirring constantly. Transfer to a bowl and refrigerate until cool.
5. Beat 2 sticks of unsalted butter, room temperature, at high speed until light and fluffy, about 3 to 5 minutes.
6. With mixer on low speed, slowly add cooled caramel mixture.
7. Once caramel is added, beat at high speed until frosting is fluffy.

Chapter 6

The repeated knocks on the door startled Ansley. They were staccato bursts of noise that invaded her head at an hour that she was sure she should still be asleep.

"Meet you in the kitchen in ten minutes," Vivian called behind the door.

Ansley peered at her clock. It was 7 A.M. All summer she had been getting up closer to 10 A.M. She couldn't remember the last time she had been awake at this hour. As she walked down to the kitchen she smelled the acrid, warm scent of fresh coffee. Vivian was pulling corn muffins out of the oven.

"They smell great," Ansley said, obviously surprised that her grandmother still knew how to use the oven. She sat down at a stool next to the marble countertop.

"I have a few tricks up my sleeve," Vivian said as she handed her a muffin and a butter dish.

Ansley broke the muffin in two and slathered butter on it. She hadn't lost the ten pounds she gained since the breakup, but she wasn't in a rush to lose weight. To her surprise, she liked eating things like corn muffins with butter on them a little too much.

Ansley surveyed the kitchen. It was the most beautiful work space she'd ever seen. Copper pots hung along the beadboard walls, tinkling in the light like candles. Large expanses of soapstone surfaces and a marble-covered island said, "Bake on me." Two sets of double ovens as well as professional-quality gas burners let Ansley know this kitchen was used for serious entertaining. She couldn't wait to open up one of the several pantry doors to see what kind of ingredients inside waited to be beaten into a cupcake. From her stool she could see fresh mint and lavender standing upright in glasses of water, almost like they were bouquets.

"Ansley, what's your plan for the day?" Vivian asked.

"I don't know. I thought I'd unpack, start to get familiar with the city, hang out with you," Ansley said as she bit into the muffin. It was good, better than good. It was moist with traces of honey and real kernels of corn mixed in. This recipe could be a contender for the book.

"I have a full day of meetings. I could meet you for dinner at 8. You may cook," Vivian said and then gave Ansley a smile. "Dear, you have to get going on your life. Start looking for a job. Start doing something. Forward motion is the only thing that makes people happy."

"Right," Ansley said as her cell phone began to ring. She carried it with her everywhere in hopes that Parish would come to his senses and insist she move back to Dallas within the hour. She took the phone out of her robe pocket. It was her mother. She answered it. "Momma, can I call you back? Love you too."

Vivian watched Ansley and listened to the conversation with the intensity of a parent checking out her daughter's new boyfriend. She didn't say anything. Ansley broke the silence. "Hattie's doing well. She's planning the fund-raiser for the opera this year so she's knee-deep in appetizers today. She's finalizing the menu."

Vivian walked over to the coffeepot and poured herself a second cup, "Don't call your mother 'Hattie.' It's disrespectful." She looked at her watch. "Oh, I have got to go."

Vivian bustled out of the room to get ready for a nine o'clock meeting. Ansley bet her grandmother's days were as filled as her mother's calendar. Even though Hattie didn't work, she managed to put in a full eight hours each weekday, serving on committees, going to lunches with other "society" women and doing the work she's assigned from committee meetings. Most people don't realize the number of hours one has to put in to generate a couple million dollars in annual donations for a charity. There's a lot of schmoozing and then there's the organizing of parties that make people want to give to the cause so they can go to the parties.

Vivian left Ansley holding a half-empty coffee cup and the tail end of a muffin. Ansley finished her meal and headed up to her room.

She called her momma back.

"Why on earth would you be calling me so early? You can't wait to talk to your mother again, can you?" Ansley teased.

"Vivian can rot in a locked subway car, for all I care. I have some bad news and I wanted you to hear it from me," Hattie said. "Parish is engaged."

"What?" Ansley screamed.

"To Patty. They're announcing it tonight," Hattie said.

"What? I can't believe it," Ansley said as she sunk into the bed.

"He's low. It's good things didn't work out with him, because he is a snake of a man," Hattie said.

"I don't understand. Patty is my friend," Ansley said in shock.

"You sound good, calm," Hattie said.

"That's because I'm hoping to pass into a coma for a few days. I think I'm close to it," Ansley said as she laid back on her bed and stared at the silver chandelier.

It took most of her concentration to breathe. She felt as if she were spinning down a long flight of stairs and knew the landing wasn't going to be pretty.

"He still loves you. I know it," Hattie said.

"Did he ever love me?" Ansley said as she started to choke. For seconds she couldn't breathe as her whole body built up to let out a long loud sob that gave way to an uncontrollable cry.

Her mother stayed on the phone with her as she moaned like a speared walrus. The sound was deep, guttural. It came from the bottom of her stomach and wouldn't be silenced. She had told herself that she would get back together with Parish. She had convinced herself things would work out, but his engagement to Patty was a hard fact to reckon with.

Patty had been so kind to her in the weeks after the breakup. She was so patient while Ansley droned on and on about Parish. Ansley replayed some of the conversations in her head, remembering the questions Patty asked—they all centered around Parish's likes and dislikes. Patty had used Ansley to find the way to Parish's heart, all the while telling Ansley to forget about him. Worse than the manipulation, Ansley was now positive Patty had enjoyed seeing her so depressed.

"What am I going to do?" Ansley wailed.

"You're doing it," Hattie said. "You're going to show these sons of bitches that you have something better in store."

Her mother's speech crackled with determination. The tone softened Ansley's crying. She sat up in bed. She was going to make Parish regret trading her in for Patty.

Ansley hung up the phone and lay back down on the bed, letting her body make an indent in the down comforter like it was a layer of snow and she was in the middle of making an angel. Her mother's words played over and over again. Her grandmother's admonishments about finding a job echoed in her mind. She would've liked to do both, but even showering seemed like a monumental task, up there with painting the whole exterior of the Empire State Building in one day.

She didn't move for two hours. She didn't sleep. She didn't even think all that much. In her mind she kept asking, *Why me?* over and over again. What had she done that was so horrible as to deserve this?

She always meant to adopt a needy family at Christmastime but never did it. She lied. She gossiped about enemies, strangers and friends. She called other girls fat if they retained a few ounces of water after they ate dairy—but not to their faces, of course. She scorned balding men and women with cellulite. She thought they had brought those maladies on themselves because they slipped in their personal hygiene. Ansley thought she'd never slip. She had a fake nice thing to say to everyone's face and a mean thing to say behind their backs. What kind of friend had she been?

Ansley forced herself up. She needed to accomplish something today so she could feel even slightly good about herself. She unpacked. She'd pull a piece of clothing out of her bag, sit down on her bed with it, stroke it and then maybe twenty minutes later put it away.

Ansley took the recipe book from the top of her dresser and slid it under the bed. She wanted to keep it safe, even from her grandmother.

She was made aware of her ridiculous appearance and the fact she hadn't eaten all day when the maid, Olga, came up to her room, lightly tapped on the opened door and asked if she'd like anything from the store.

"What? Oh, right, she said I should make dinner. I don't know. What does she like?" Ansley asked, embarrassed that she had no idea about who her grandmother was, including what type of food she preferred.

"Nothing with pork or asparagus," Olga said.

"What about roast chicken? A nice lemon and rosemary chicken with fingerling potatoes and tomato salad? Or maybe an avocado and grapefruit salad," Ansley said.

"She's on Lipitor," Olga said.

"What does that mean?"

"No grapefruit. It interferes with the drug. She has incredibly high cholesterol," Olga said, suppressing exasperation.

Ansley was annoyed. She had just met her grandmother, so how would she know what kind of medication she was on. That was the point, though, wasn't it—what kind of person meets her grandmother for the first time at the age of twenty-two? She was about to tell Olga that she worked for her grandmother and she should remember her place, which could easily be in the unemployment office. Instead of making a comeback she gave Olga a list of ingredients and shut her bedroom door.

Ansley wanted to be a better person. She didn't know exactly how to do it. All she could do was make tiny changes like not bitching out Olga and hope they would eventually add up and turn her into a good friend, wife and daughter.

Olga was a key ally to have too. She didn't want to find scorch marks on her clothes. So far Ansley had met four members of Vivian's staff—Olga, the house manager; Tati and Dru, the cleaning ladies; and Dan, a chef who cooked when Vivian had guests—he also made a few appetizers every week to have on hand. The rest of the time Vivian liked to do her own cooking or, now, have Ansley do it.

Ansley hopped in the shower, dressed and took out one of her favorite aprons. She spent the rest of the day slowly unpacking, headed downstairs at five, when she was sure the ingredients she requested would be there and the staff would be gone. The kitchen was blissfully quiet and sunny. She tied on her apron and cut up tomatoes. What would she be doing if she were in Dallas right now? Getting ready for dinner with Parish or a group of friends.

Now she was scared of even taking a step out of the townhouse. So, developing a whole new social set seemed impossible. She felt so badly burned by her experience in Dallas that she couldn't imagine she'd ever trust again. Her broken engagement and Patty's treachery put into sharp focus the fact that not that many of your so-called friends stick around when your life implodes. That realization left Ansley wondering why it was worth the time to cultivate friendships if they evaporated so easily—all that work, all that time spent creating experiences with people, and it was gone within hours.

Ansley prepped the chicken and potatoes, but they didn't need to go into the oven for another hour. She had time to kill and a heartache to relieve. She walked over to the pantry, whose contents she had been itching to look at since this morning, and opened two large doors. Inside there were shelves of ingredients that made her dizzy—Callebaut extra-bitter 70 percent cocoa baker's chocolate, Scharffen Berger 62 percent cocoa semi-sweet chocolate, a glass jar filled with Madagascar vanilla beans, agave nectar, light brown muscovado sugar and saffron. She took a step back and inhaled deeply. The scents of this cupboard—especially the cinnamon, vanilla, chocolate, orange—put her at ease. This was a baker's fantasy, a paradise of the finest and most difficult to obtain ingredients. If she wanted saffron in Dallas she'd have to buy it in thimbleful increments. Here it was in her grandmother's cabinet in a large glass jar, beckoning to be used in all its golden deliciousness.

Ansley studied the cupboard for minutes and then began to work. She pulled out light-as-air cake flour, potato starch, triple-milled baking powder and the muscovado sugar, and neatly arranged them in a line on the marble island. Potato starch is a baker's secret ingredient. Add two tablespoons to your batter and it will produce a soft, moist cake. Ansley was impressed her grandmother had it.

She opened the refrigerator in hopes of gaining more inspiration. She wasn't disappointed. On the shelves were ceramic bowls filled to the brim with blueberries and peaches. There were the herbs she had spied this morning, mint and lavender stood in glasses alongside basil and thyme. Someone in this house was a good cook, probably the part-time chef.

Ansley picked out two peaches. They were underripe and wouldn't ripen in the refrigerator. She grabbed a handful of mint as well, and placed both on the marble countertop. She searched for and found all the equipment she could hope for—mixing bowls, measuring cups and spoons with enough heft that they felt competent.

She took a paring knife, cut each peach in two and placed them cut-side down on a baking sheet in the oven. She'd let them roast until they browned and softened.

She sifted her dry ingredients and creamed the others. Then she mixed everything together. The peach with the golden brown sugar would taste like a Texas afternoon. To cut the sweetness, Ansley mixed finely shredded mint with the American buttercream frosting—not to be confused with the French or Italian buttercreams. Those frostings require a whole different level of expertise to master. Ansley hadn't attempted them yet, but she had a strong desire to try.

After destroying her first, second and third batch of American buttercream when she was little, Ansley had become an expert at reading the different shades of butter and their meanings, as well as the different temperatures. For instance, Ansley had learned the hard way that one should never ever use ice-cold butter unless one was making scones or some sort of pastry. Then, cold butter was essential. Otherwise it was a total disaster that would make cakes leaden and frosting lumpy. The color was equally important. Butter had to reach a pale yellow, almost white, hue to be of any true use in batters and frostings. That pale yellow indicated that it had been beaten enough to easily release its delicious fats and flavor and that bubbles of air had been created, which added lightness to batter. The inexperienced baker always makes the mistake of turning off the mixer too soon. Butter, unlike flour, can't be overwhipped. That's the beauty of it. Butter needs the abuse.

"Tastes like home," Ansley said as she sampled a spoonful of batter, slid the cupcakes into the oven and immediately started searching for another cupcake she could make that would remind her of the comfort she took for granted just last year. As she walked back over to the pantry she picked up the phone and dialed Parish's number. She had resisted last night and the last few weeks she had left in Dallas, but now she was too heartbroken to stop herself.

It rang and then went to voice mail. Ansley took a chance and entered in her birthday. He hadn't changed the code yet, maybe there was still a reason to hope. The voice mail began to play. There were a couple from frat brothers about the party that evening. His mother left a message about his laundry being ready to pick up at the house. Every week he brought his dirty clothes over and she washed, ironed and folded them. The last one was from Patty. Her voice was breathy. She sounded like she was in the middle of sex. She said she missed "your tongue in my mouth and other places—we'll have to take a bathroom break tonight."

Gross, Ansley thought, and hung up the phone. They were going to have oral sex or something like it in the bathroom during their engagement party. Patty wasn't only mean, she was tacky too. Could Parish actually like that?

Ansley dialed Patty's number next. After the first ring it went to voice mail. Ansley thought about leaving a message but hung up instead. There weren't words to describe what Patty had done. She had never liked Patty. But Patty had invested hours upon hours into sitting with Ansley on her darkest days. Technically, that qualified Patty as Ansley's best friend in the world. Over the month of June, Ansley had begun to see Patty's positive attributes. She was a good listener. She knew exactly what Ansley's needs were and catered to them, bringing McDonald's every day, which now that Ansley looked at her hips, probably wasn't such a kind gesture. She made Ansley laugh. Ansley realized that all that attention and kindness had been an act. Patty was after Parish the whole time.

Ansley was beyond wallowing. She was destroyed and angry. There's a decorum, a method for sorority sisters to date the ex-boyfriends of other sorority sisters. Because there's a limited pool of eligible boyfriends in her social circle, dating castoffs was allowed but there was a required six-month no-dating period between girls of the same sorority. This rule was followed religiously because when it wasn't, fights and emotions between girls were known to get physical. Maybe Patty didn't care about the rules? She never was a team player. Ansley cursed herself for being the one to get Patty into the sorority. If she had gone with the other girls' first impulse—to flatly reject her—Ansley bet she'd be in Dallas this very moment, engaged to Parish instead of Patty.

Ansley put the chicken and potatoes in the oven to roast and placed the ingredients for more cupcakes on the counter. She needed to keep her hands from dialing any more numbers. She started baking.

When Vivian walked into the kitchen she saw that every countertop had been claimed by Ansley in the name of baking—there were mixing bowls, ingredients, cooling racks, frosting bags everywhere she looked. Ansley could tell by her expression that she was surprised.

"Don't worry. I'll clean it all up," Ansley said as she pulled the roast chicken and potatoes out of the oven.

"What are you doing?" Vivian asked, still absorbing the damage.

"I'm making cupcakes. I've done a peach one and a tea cake. I'm working on a couple more. I did make dinner: roast chicken with tomato salad," Ansley said, "and I set the table, so we can eat whenever you're ready."

Vivian walked over to the wine refrigerator, pulled out a bottle and poured herself a glass. She moved over to the cooling racks Ansley was hovering over and examined the frosting. Ansley was in the middle of creating an intricate shell design on one of the peach cupcakes.

"Impressive," Vivian said as she walked over to the table with her glass and the wine bottle. "Wine?"

"Yes, thank you," Ansley said, as she hurried over to the table.

"So what did you accomplish today?" Vivian asked Ansley as she handed her a glass.

"I created a couple kinds of cupcakes," Ansley said and braced herself for a lecture on how she should spend her time.

"They're beautiful," Vivian said, picked up a peach one and took a bite. "This is good."

"Yeah," Ansley said tentatively.

"Really good. Though I'd grill the peaches next time. It'll add more—"

"Layers of flavor," Ansley cut her off. "That's a good idea."

"The peak is great," Vivian said as she looked at the high domes of the cupcakes.

"I preheat at four hundred," Ansley said.

"Higher temperature, better reaction from the baking powder. Smart," Vivian said.

"I've been baking since I was three. Guess it's in the genes. I learned a lot from the book," Ansley said.

"Trying to make it into the book?" Vivian asked. Ansley felt uneasy when Vivian talked about the book. In her mind, the book had disowned Vivian when she left the family.

"Yep, I've come close but haven't made it in yet," Ansley said as she sat down with Vivian and dug into the chicken.

"I made it in a few times. My first time was—" Vivian said.

"Butterscotch cookies," Ansley interrupted. "Momma makes them every Christmas. One of the few butter cookies that don't need frosting to make them good."

"I still bake a lot," Vivian said.

"Really? The corn muffins were great. Momma always said you weren't much of a baker, more of a cook. She said the butterscotch cookies were surprising," Ansley said.

Vivian laughed in a forced way, "I guess your mother has forgotten about all the cakes I made for her tea parties and birthdays."

"Five. You were there for five of her birthdays," Ansley said.

"So, what's your plan?" Vivian asked, ignoring Ansley's comment.

"Plan?"

"To get a job. You have to get out there," Vivian said.

"Yeah, I'm working on that," Ansley stammered as Vivian finished eating her chicken.

"This isn't a class you're taking, this is your life. What do you want it to be?" Vivian asked.

"Married in Dallas," Ansley answered, hoping somehow Vivian could make that happen.

"I've been where you are. You can't go back, no matter how

much you want to," Vivian said sympathetically. "Don't waste years of your life hoping."

Vivian got up and took both her and Ansley's plates to the sink. She walked back over to Ansley and kissed her head. Ansley grabbed her grandmother's arm. They held the position for a few moments.

"I have to get some things together for the IRS. I'm going up to my office. Let's say dinner eight o'clock tomorrow night," Vivian said.

"What are you doing tomorrow?" Ansley asked.

"I have to work on the fund-raiser for the Central Park Zoo. We need to build a new habitat for the polar bears, so this gala has to be amazing. Then I have to try to make some sense of Charlie's request in his will that I set up a charitable foundation in his name," Vivian said.

"He didn't tell you what charities?"

"He wanted the biggest bang for his buck. Whatever charities would display his name the most prominently would get the money, so I am in the process of interviewing several charities; I do that at Charlie's office. Better to keep home separate," Vivian said, and left.

Well, if cooking dinner every night for her grandmother was the price Ansley paid for staying with her, it wasn't that bad of a deal. Ansley didn't want to go to her room, so she opened her grandmother's pantry again and let her mind wander.

Hours later she could hear drunken voices carry down the street and saw by the microwave clock that it was 5 A.M. She took a step back and looked at all she'd created. Every counter of the massive kitchen was filled with cupcakes. There were sweet-tea cakes with ginger frosting, coconut rice pudding, and deep-fried Snickers cupcakes. A tequila, raspberry and lime pastry took up the kitchen table. The black-bottom cupcakes were still cooling on a rack outside the kitchen door.

The smell of melted chocolate, warm milk and frying oil made Ansley so content she felt as if she could finally sleep. She trudged upstairs to her bed and fell into it without bothering to pull back the sheets.

She slept in the same position for hours, waking up when an ambulance siren wailed and wailed on the street. She staggered to her window and saw the ambulance stuck in traffic on the tiny lane. She collapsed in her bed and groaned. Ansley tried to go back to sleep but couldn't block out the ambulance. She wasn't used to sleeping in the middle of horns honking and sirens blaring. She got back up and shuffled down to the kitchen. Her grandmother was already there. She was putting her coffee cup in the sink and walking out the door.

"I knocked but you didn't answer," Vivian said.

"I was up real late. Oh, my God. It looks like a bakery exploded," Ansley said as she shuffled over to the coffeepot.

"Feel better?"

"A little. I'm going to have to do a lot more baking to feel human again."

"I loved the coconut ones. The frosting on all of them is a work of art," Vivian said as she gave Ansley an awkward peck on the cheek and left.

As Ansley drank her coffee she walked around the baked goods, smelling the difference of each variety. The nutty spiciness of the peach cupcakes made her think of a peach cobbler served with homemade vanilla ice cream on a screened-in porch of a lake house. The fried sweetness of the Snickers cake evoked the Texas State Fair, where one walked around with a

giant turkey leg in one hand and a fried Twinkie in the other.
The sweet-tea cakes reminded her of almost every lunch she'd
eaten in Dallas. Sweet tea was like water there. Each cake was
lovely. Ansley had painstakingly decorated the icing with lat-
tice and seashell designs.

They deserved to be eaten. They deserved to be loved. But
how? Ansley couldn't plow through all of these no matter
how depressed she was. But she couldn't throw them away.
They were too pretty to be put in the trash, never tasted.

Ansley walked back upstairs, determined to shower and
dress today, inching toward normalcy. After blow-drying her
hair and putting on her makeup, she looked at herself critically
in the mirror. She smiled, testing out her attractability. Other
people would find that smile pretty and approachable. She
wasn't wearing her misery on her body. She decided it was
time to get out there. It's time to do some test marketing to
determine if her cupcakes were as good as she thought they
were. The only way to know if she had a viable contender for
the book was to get it to the public—business school 101 basics. She'd try the cupcakes out on a few people and incorpo-
rate their suggestions and then have her grandmother—and
someday, her mother—taste them.

She put on a cotton summer dress and heels, ran downstairs and found a basket. She piled cupcakes into it and
placed a stack of napkins in one corner, then took a deep
breath and walked out the front door. People dressed in business suits walked briskly down the sidewalk, passing the people who were walking their dogs or pushing strollers. Sunlight
filtered through the trees. It was a soft warm light. Ansley
questioned whether she needed sunglasses. The air was warm

but not like Texas. Ansley thought she should invest in cotton sweaters. She could hear horns honking a few blocks away. She looked in both directions and had no idea where to go. She stood there as several people passed by her and diverted their eyes. Finally she got the courage to stop a woman about her age with a Yorkie. The woman was allowing the dog to poop freely under a tree on the sidewalk outside her grandmother's townhouse. She didn't appear to have anything to pick it up.

"Excuse me, is there a park near here?" Ansley asked the woman, who seemed like she would've been a sorority sister.

"Uh, yeah," the woman said. "Uh, Central Park, couple blocks that way." She walked past Ansley with a disdainful look as if Ansley had asked her for change and touched her with dirty fingers.

"Thanks," Ansley said, gathered her confidence and walked toward the park. As she walked she noticed that all the other women on the sidewalk had on ballet flats or flip-flops. Her shoes were beginning to peel some skin off her heel, but foot pain was something she learned to deal with in high school.

As Ansley approached the park she felt comforted by the large expanse of green. *People are always more friendly in natural settings*, she thought. She crossed the street and felt a little withered by the heat the asphalt reflected at her. Once she got to the park's entrance she made sure her posture was at its straightest and her smile was in place. As soon as she hit Central Park's shaded pathways she purposely made direct eye contact with everyone walking toward her, held forward her basket and said, "You look like you could use a cupcake."

Some people peered in and asked how much. When she told them they were free, the people quickly walked away.

Others didn't even give her that courtesy. They waved her off and kept walking. It's like they thought she was offering them dirty needles or something.

She kept rallying herself, but after two hours of constant rejection she needed a break. She sat down on one of the green benches that framed the path and put her basket beside her. She studied the cupcakes. They looked like they tasted good. What was the problem?

She watched the young and prosperous rush through the park, headed for meetings, lunches, shopping—things with other people. The men looked liked photocopies of Thad Wheeler, the snotty banker she met at her grandmother's house, all groomed and scrubbed. *How do I rebuild my life?* she thought and felt more defeated than she had yesterday. A man pushing a shopping cart filled with plastic and glass bottles was coming toward her. She watched his slow progress as he stopped at each trash can and methodically examined its contents, picking out other bottles and unspoiled bits of food. When he was a couple feet away from her she stood up and walked toward him.

"Cupcakes?" she offered, and held out the basket.

"What's the catch?" he asked, and eyed her with the same suspicion everyone else had.

"No catch. I made too many and can't eat them all myself." She smiled.

"What's in them?" he asked as he critically inspected her offerings.

"Madagascar vanilla bean, organic Earl Grey tea, crystallized ginger," she said about the sweet-tea cakes.

"I don't like ginger. It reminds me of eating soap," he said. "What's this one?" he asked, and pointed to the peach and mint cupcake.

"That's brown sugar, peach and mint. Tastes like Texas," she said proudly.

He grabbed it and scarfed it down. "Not bad," he said as he reached for a chocolate one.

Other homeless people noticed and wandered over. Ansley went through her spiel about each cupcake and soon the crowd were sampling all her flavors.

"Now, take some for later. I have some napkins to wrap them in," she encouraged, feeling relief that her basket was noticeably getting lighter.

It wasn't until the horse carrying a policeman was right next to them that any of them noticed him.

"Miss, do you have a permit for this?" the policeman asked in a gruff and confused voice.

"No," Ansley confessed.

"It's illegal to sell food in the city without a permit," he said, and whipped out his ticket book.

"But I'm not selling it," Ansley replied.

The policeman first looked mystified and then terrified. "Why would you give away food? What's in these? Are you poisoning these people?"

The homeless all stopped in mid-bite to look at Ansley. Ansley's face flashed confusion followed by amusement.

"Are you joking? I wouldn't poison anyone. That's what bad cooks do," Ansley said jovially.

The homeless still weren't convinced. Their mouths were frozen.

"Honest, there's no poison in those," she said, this time more assuringly. She even took a cupcake out of the basket and took a bite and smiled. "See, they're fine."

The homeless continued chewing and walked away from

her. They didn't grab any more cupcakes. She still had half a basket full of baked goods. The policeman was in the middle of writing up a ticket.

"Do you see what you did? You scared them off and I still have lots of cupcakes to give away," she whined.

"I'm going to need your name and contact information," he responded, impassive.

"Because?"

"If any of those people show up dead I'll know who to call," the policeman stated, and looked at her.

After she had given all her pertinent information, she didn't have the heart to try another baked goods giveaway. She placed the rest of the cupcakes in the trash, hoping that some of the homeless would eat them, and she headed back to the townhouse. As she crossed the street toward the house she felt a young woman walking almost step for step with her. She turned toward her and smiled. The woman was her age. She had straight black hair, skillfully applied makeup, a lovely fifties-inspired button-up cornflower-colored blouse and brown pencil skirt on. The best thing about her was she wore heels, elegant peep-toe heels.

"I saw what happened back there. I would've tried one," she said, and smiled at Ansley.

"Well, thanks. You're the only employed person today to say that. Everyone else thought I was a crazy poison-wielding opportunist," Ansley said.

"That's New York for you. Offer someone a good deal and she immediately becomes suspicious: 'What's your motive? What do you want?'" The woman said, "I'm Dot."

She held out her hand. Ansley shook it and introduced herself.

"Obviously not from New York," Dot said.

"Dallas. Does it show that much?" Ansley asked, worried that she'd never feel at home here.

"Only when you talk, make direct eye contact and smile at people," Dot said and laughed. Ansley laughed with her. She guessed she looked ridiculous to someone who was a native.

"Did you just move here?"

Ansley partially filled Dot in on why she was in New York City indefinitely without a plan, friends or a job—bad breakup sans the details. Dot told Ansley she'd gone to the requisite New York private schools, i.e., Spence, wasn't thinking marriage until her thirties and ran a party-planning business. She symbolized New York as Ansley thought of it. It was a whole different mind-set. What girl of legal age didn't at least contemplate what it would be like to be married?

"You know, I think you were thinking too small with the cupcakes. Instead of handing them out for free, why not get paid and why not have people come to you, start your own business?" Dot asked.

"Really?" Ansley asked, overwhelmed at the scale Dot was talking about. She had been very tentatively toying with the idea of approaching bakeries about carrying her cupcakes. Starting her own bakery hadn't been in her calculus.

They had stopped outside a vacant store on 64th Street. It was a quiet little space with big windows on the ground floor. It must have once been an Italian restaurant—inside was a black and white check floor and empty bottles of wine turned into candleholders.

"Look at this place. It would be perfect." Dot dusted off the window and peered deeper into the interior. "You could rip out the bar, put in some display cabinets. You might be able to use some of the tables for a café."

Ansley followed her gaze and pictured everything Dot said as she spoke. It would be a lovely thing to wake up to each morning. She'd have a purpose. She could talk to people. Her grandmother would be over the moon. Maybe it would impress Parish.

"We should have lunch tomorrow," Ansley offered.

They made plans to meet at a little café not far from where they stood. Dot waved good-bye to Ansley and walked in the opposite direction. Ansley just about skipped home. This was a good omen. She dialed her mother's number.

"Guess what, Momma? I made a friend," Ansley gushed into the phone.

"Bouncing back, baby, bouncing back," her mother hummed.

"I made a peach cupcake with praline topping last night," Ansley said.

"Sweetie, that's so creative. I don't think I've ever had the two together."

"Grandma loved it. Said it was the best thing she ever tasted."

"Are you calling her 'Grandma' now?" Hattie asked. There was an iciness in her tone.

"Well, yeah. I can't call her Vivian, especially not to her face. It'd be disrespectful," Ansley said. "You know, she's not all bad."

"That's what you think," Hattie said vaguely.

"Momma, why don't you visit and see for yourself," Ansley encouraged. She already missed her mother horribly. They used to talk several times a day and Hattie had let Ansley know in every way possible that she was the most important thing in her life. Whenever Ansley asked her mother to do something she dropped everything to get it done. The morning after Parish broke off their engagement she asked her mother to pick her up in Waco, where Baylor was located. She must've driven ninety the whole way because she was there in less than an hour. Hattie arranged to have Ansley's car delivered to Dallas and drove her daughter back without complaint. Ansley had never been apart from her mother for more than a few days, even when she was in college. In fact, her mother came to Waco so often the local coffee shop knew her order. Now Ansley was going through support system withdrawal.

"It's not a good time, darling. I have that fund-raiser," her mother rattled off.

"Is there ever going to be a good time, Momma?"

"Darling, I miss you. You know I want you close to me. Sweetie, this is a lot for me," Hattie said, "but I'm gonna try to visit."

"I think Vivian really wants to see you," Ansley said.

"I love you," Hattie said in lieu of a good-bye. She'd also sidestepped commenting on Vivian.

Ansley felt unsettled. For the first time, she realized her mother wouldn't always be in her life and it made her indescribably sad. Then she thought about her mother and grandmother and how they never got a chance to form the kind of bond Ansley and her mother had. She didn't know which was worse, eventually losing a mother you are best friends with or never knowing your mother.

Ansley walked down her grandmother's street to the townhouse and noticed the flower boxes in the windows for the first time. They were packed with a glorious assortment of dark purple and pale green cabbages and orange strawflowers. They looked beautiful against the white stone.

You have to take nature where you can get it, Ansley thought, and missed her mother and her garden more than ever.

Vivian opened the front door and walked outside. "I saw you from my study. Admiring the cabbages? They're a strange thing to have in a flower box, but they're so beautiful. Your grandfather once gave me a cabbage in a bouquet because he thought it was gorgeous. I laughed at him, but I can see his point now," Vivian said.

"You ever think about him?" Ansley asked.

"Absolutely," Vivian said, and walked back inside.

Ansley followed. She was about to ask her grandmother more about her grandfather, but Vivian shot upstairs and into her study. She closed the door firmly. Ansley was pretty sure that was the end of what Vivian intended to say on the matter. The question was, how to get her to say more.

• *Taste of Summer the Way It Used to Be— Peachy* •

⅓ cup vegetable oil
¾ cup whole milk, divided, room temperature
1 egg, room temperature
1 teaspoon vanilla extract
1 cup sugar

2 cups sifted cake flour

2 teaspoons baking powder

2 tablespoons potato starch

½ teaspoon finely ground salt, either sea or iodized

½ cup chopped pecans

6 peaches, skin removed, grilled or roasted, and diced or
  pureed

To Make the Cupcakes:

1. Preheat the oven to 375° F. Place 24 cupcake papers in
   the trays.
2. In a mixing bowl combine flour, sugar, baking powder,
   potato starch, salt and pecans. Mix with a whisk or sift
   together to ensure the dry ingredients are fully
   incorporated.
3. Add the vegetable oil, egg and half of the milk to the
   dry ingredients. Mix until combined.
4. Then add remaining milk, peaches and vanilla. Stir
   until thoroughly combined, about 1 minute.
5. Fill cupcake trays halfway with the batter.
6. Bake at 375 for 20 to 25 minutes, or until a toothpick
   inserted in the middle of a cupcake comes out clean.
7. Cool for 5 minutes and then place on baking racks.

Yield: 24 cupcakes

Praline Topping

¼ cup melted butter

¾ cup brown sugar

18 pecan halves

For the Frosting:

1. Combine melted butter and brown sugar. As soon as cupcakes come out of the oven, spoon mixture over them.
2. Place a pecan half in the center of each and promptly return them to the oven for 5 minutes.

Chapter 7

Vivian hadn't expected to feel this way. When Ansley had walked into her life she felt a pit of longing for all the years she'd missed. Being around Ansley was worse than being completely cut off from her daughter and granddaughter. Why had she left?

Well, she'd had to. There was no choice in the matter. But two years or five years or ten years later, why didn't she go back?

It would've been difficult. Asher could've gotten nasty. He never made up with her. He died five years ago and she'd had to hear about it from a friend. Hattie herself would've been distant, cold, angry, more and more angry as the years went on.

Every couple years Vivian thought about going. She even booked a ticket once, but her own mother told her not to come. She talked Vivian out of it every time by telling her how much Asher was drinking. Vivian had always known that Asher had the tendency to depend on a drink when times were tough. She suspected if pushed too far he could drink himself into oblivion. She didn't want him taking her daughter with him. He was Hattie's full-time parent—there was nothing she could do to change that and she certainly didn't want to make the circumstances worse, so she disappeared into the background, hoping her absence would make Asher stronger. It didn't. But at least he didn't get any weaker. He held on at a functioning alcoholic level for the rest of his life.

When Hattie was an adult Vivian could've approached her. Asher didn't need to be a factor at that point. But she couldn't. She chose to throw away her relationship with her daughter rather than allow Hattie to find out the truth about her. For Hattie to know how weak she had been was more damaging to her than to never talk to Hattie again. She could hate Vivian as long as she respected her.

She had rationalized the years away and now her granddaughter was a grown woman and what could be said about her own daughter? Hattie was solidly middle-aged. She didn't even know what she looked like. When Hattie called Ansley, Vivian had a terribly strong impulse to grab the phone. The only reason she resisted was because she had no idea what to say.

She didn't want to tell the whole truth or any of the truth. She didn't want to create an elaborate lie, but if she said nothing, she didn't think there was anything that would stop Hattie from hating her. Hattie needed to know what it was that made her mother abandon her. If she didn't have another reason to fill her head, she'd go on thinking that she wasn't enough for Vivian to stay. Nothing could be further from Vivian's heart.

Hattie was her world. For the five years she lived with her daughter, Vivian absorbed every moment—playing dolls, whipping up tea parties, brushing her teeth at night. She loved just listening to her daughter talk. Little girls keep up a constant monologue. It filled Vivian's heart with pleasure to listen to her daughter recount the blow-by-blow of a play date or try to figure out how she could convince Vivian that she should be allowed to have cake every day. Right before Vivian left Hattie for good she was calling everything tiny. Dimes were tiny money. The two-seater convertible was the tiny car. Her dollhouse was the tiny house.

It was such an adorable phase. Vivian wondered how long it lasted. That wasn't the kind of thing Asher told her after she left. He mainly let her know that Hattie was still breathing, and he liked to remind Vivian that he still despised her. One night she told him that circumstances had changed and she begged him to take her back.

There was silence on the phone. She could hear Asher's breathing quicken. Elation radiated out of her chest. He was going to say yes. She could feel it. She mapped out how the rest of the conversation would happen. They'd talk logistics— when she'd come back and how she'd move her stuff, whether it was better to ship it or hire movers. They would dance around the emotional stuff because it was too much to talk about on the phone and because it was obvious they still loved each other.

"I can be there tomorrow night," Vivian said, feeling truly happy.

Asher finally spoke. "No. I don't want you to come." There was no waver or hesitation.

"But I thought you'd be happy. We can be together again," Vivian sputtered. The image of sitting in the lounger on their back patio was fading.

"Together? What would people say if we were together? They'd laugh at me," Asher said.

"You can't let other people decide this," Vivian said.

"I'm not going to let you decide this either," Asher said, belligerent. He had been drinking. He could get very surly then. Vivian should've called during the day.

"Okay," Vivian said, "let's talk tomorrow."

"Don't call me tomorrow or the next day or ever. I'm never going to talk to you again," Asher said.

"You don't mean that," Vivian soothed.

"I do. Watch me," Asher said, and hung up.

Vivian called every day, several times a day, for a week. She would let the phone ring and ring and ring. She'd call and cradle the phone with her head and shoulder while she got dressed, ate lunch, answered mail. She held the phone like that so much that her neck involuntarily bent that way sometimes when she wasn't holding the phone. The ringing had to be driving Asher crazy. She imagined him getting so angry that eventually he'd pick up. He'd yell at her at first and then they'd have a real conversation and make up. But no matter how many times she called, he never answered.

Asher really didn't want her back. It started to sink in. A cold ball of anxiety and sadness sat in the pit of her stomach. It wouldn't move.

Vivian broke down. She went to bed and didn't get up for days. Charlie was understanding at first. On day five he was miffed. He insisted she get dressed and ready for dinner out. His life needed to go on. So Vivian's version of life needed to go on too and it did blindly for decades. She had put the thought of reconnecting with her daughter into the category of life after Charlie, since she knew there was no way Charlie would be on board with her spending the weeks on end in Dallas necessary to slowly coax Hattie into liking and trusting her again. Charlie didn't have the patience for that. He wanted—no, demanded—a wife who was available for all social and sexual occasions he required. Like it or not, that was the deal Vivian made when she married Charlie.

Now that her husband was dead she had time to touch base with Hattie, but did her daughter want to hear from her? Vivian was sure Hattie had filled the void she left with many surrogates: Vivian's own mother for one; all of her mother's closest friends and her mother-in-law. Hattie probably hadn't even needed her, Vivian thought.

Vivian held out hope that Ansley would ignite a relationship between Hattie and herself. If she could prove that she could help her granddaughter, her own daughter might soften toward her. Hattie might see that Vivian had worth as a person. It was a way in.

The question was how to mold Ansley. The girl was shattered glass. She was catatonic in bed one moment and the next baking until dawn. She seemed capable of dissolving into a puddle of tears without warning. Vivian didn't want to criticize the girl too much. There was a fine line between encouragement and dictatorship that she had to balance.

She needs structure, Vivian thought as she sat up in bed. It was 6 A.M. She didn't need an alarm clock anymore. This is the time she woke up each day without prompting. Every morning she would lie in bed for a few minutes and think about what she had to do that day. Since Ansley came, many of her

thoughts centered around her granddaughter. She had given
her the task of making dinner every night so Ansley would feel
some pride of place. It seemed to be working. Ansley put
thought and effort into the meals and it was a good time for
them to talk. She felt like she was slowly forming a relationship with her granddaughter. She was relieved that she liked
most of who the girl was. Ansley was smart, had a good, dry
wit and was determined. She was obviously focused on getting
one of her cupcake recipes into the book and she was going
after the goal with laserlike focus. Since Ansley had lived in
Vivian's house, she was sure the girl had gone through several
pounds of sugar and flour testing her creations.

What was the next step for Ansley? How could Vivian
push her into living her life in New York instead of simply bid-
ing her time? Ansley needed more anchors. Vivian could include her in more of her life, to make Ansley feel more vital,
more needed. She could also help provide Ansley with a social
network. Thad was an exemplary youth. Granted, the two of
them didn't get along at their first meeting, but if she threw
them together enough, Vivian was confident that an attraction
or at least a friendship would grow.

Vivian turned over and burrowed beneath her creamy cotton sheets. The problem of her own life buzzed in her head at
this time every morning too. Now that Charlie was gone she
could do whatever she wanted. It was exhilarating and fright-
ening at the same time.

It was true that Charlie was often a nuisance, but there
were some positive aspects just to having contact with another human being. She missed waking up beside him. She
wanted someone to be concerned if she looked tired or had a
cough in the morning. What if she fell? How long would it

take someone to realize she was on the floor? Hours? Days? When would the maid feel it appropriate to disturb her? Because that's who would find her—an employee, not family.

It would be nice to find someone she loved or at least liked a lot to spend time with. But she was seventy years old. She knew men her age didn't date seventy-year-olds. Just people-watching in the city told her that men her age either were very affectionate with their daughters or dated much younger.

The thought of those men with their young girlfriends killed the beads of hope that were forming in her brain. She knew it would be very unlikely for her to find the connection she wanted with a man. She desired to sleep in the same bed with someone she liked. She wanted sex. Was it impossible? There had to be a few men her age who wanted to date a woman who knew who Johnny Mathis was. She had to focus on finding that kind of man. He would be the type of man to appreciate a perfectly crusted filet mignon. He would take walks, maybe sail. He would never attempt yoga.

She surveyed herself in the mirror while she was brushing her teeth. Her hair was white but it was full. She wasn't skinny but she wasn't fat. She had a nice curvature to her. She was afraid to look at where her breasts fell without a bra. Her skin was wrinkled and there were bags around the eyes, but she did have the creases around her lips filled in regularly by her dermatologist. Her neck was in good condition. She had a smattering of age spots across her forehead and into her hairline. She knew she looked good for seventy, but that was of course the problem.

When was the last time a man came on to me? Vivian thought as she got dressed. It had to have been ten—no, twenty years ago. So for the last two decades men had been polite and respectful and nothing more. She hadn't noticed. She had been wound up in Charlie and trying to be respectful in a marriage that was a disaster. She put her blinders on to sexual overtures and was aged before she knew it.

She walked into her office and collected the mail from the tray. There was another letter from IRS agent #1432. She opened it first.

"Dear Mrs. Osterhaut, we are looking into a llama ranch your husband is reported to have owned. Do you have documentation? P.S. I prefer hydrangeas to lilacs."

This agent was getting belligerent. First of all, why would she and Charlie own llamas? Did they seem like the type of New York power couple who would own llamas? Was any New York power couple the type to own llamas?

Second of all, who could possibly prefer hydrangeas to lilacs? Hydrangea didn't possess the complex scent of lilacs. They didn't have any scent.

Well, at least he was reading the letters she was writing, including her P.S.

That was the only positive portion of the whole document. The rest enraged her. She stomped over to her desk, determined to write the meanest letter she could back to Agent #1432. She grabbed her pen and a piece of stationery.

She wrote, "Dear Agent #1432, you are ridiculous. You are obviously taking your anger at being a mid-level government employee out on me. I would prefer for all further contact to be between me and your supervisor, since you are obviously insane. Best, Vivian Osterhaut."

She neatly folded the letter and placed it in an envelope. She put it in her to-go stack and walked toward her unopened mail. She stopped halfway across the room. *I should double-check about that llama ranch*, she thought.

She pulled out every financial document she had and placed them all on the floor of her study. The effort took nearly two hours and covered most of the floor. The stacks of paper were organized by year. She had written a year in a thick black Sharpie on a plain piece of paper and placed one on top of each mound. She took 1990 and started going through it page by page. An inch into the papers she found an investment in Oklahoma that was a ranch. In fact it was a llama ranch.

"What the hell?" Vivian asked aloud, using language she hardly ever uttered.

A sinking feeling enveloped her. The IRS was right. Charlie had been up to something. Charlie, that passive-aggressive piece of proper Northeast upbringing, had been pissed about something or was trying to prove something. Vivian was sure none of his financial advisors knew about a llama ranch. Maybe Charlie was trying to prove he had business acumen and was making his own investments with the limited funds he was granted free rein over. His advisors let him use a couple million as he wanted.

Vivian eyed the remaining two inches of paper that represented 1990. With two million dollars Charlie could've bought a lot.

Vivian got up to retrieve the letter she had written to the IRS agent. She should tear it up and write something with a whole different tone. Now she knew she had to be nice because she had no idea what other financial blunders lurked out there. Charlie was stupid, she thought, and decided she needed a drink before she confronted the rest of the 1990 stack.

She headed downstairs and made a margarita. It was her comfort drink. She was taking the first sip, really enjoying how the salt mixed with the lime in her mouth, when Ansley walked into the kitchen. Ansley was in her bathrobe. Her hair was a rat's nest from fitful sleep. She had obviously just stumbled from her bed to the kitchen. Vivian was immaculate. Her oxford blue and white striped shirt was crisp. Her wide-leg tan trousers were perfectly fit.

"It's 8 A.M.," Ansley said.

"Not everywhere in the world," Vivian replied.

"Here in this kitchen it is," Ansley said, looking concerned.

"I need a little pick-me-up and then I'll be fine. I've been having issues with the IRS," Vivian confided.

Ansley got her own glass and filled it from the margarita pitcher.

"Reminds me of Dallas," Ansley said as she took a big gulp.

"What's your excuse?"

"Complete and total heartbreak coupled with having to reinvent my life," Ansley said.

"Speaking of which, I think you may be able to help me. I have to comb through a lot of financial documents and you can help me review," Vivian said as she finished her drink.

"How is that speaking of which?" Ansley asked.

"The more busy you are the better you'll feel," Vivian said.

"Okay," Ansley said hesitantly.

"Baby, you're my granddaughter and I really don't want to have to kick you out in eight weeks because you don't have a job. You need to get some motivation. Come with me to my office after dinner tonight and we'll review," Vivian said as she grabbed the pitcher and her glass and headed upstairs.

"I'm doing fine," Ansley called after Vivian. Her tone didn't convince either one of them she was okay.

• *Margarita, Hold the Salt* •

¼ cup lime juice
1½ teaspoons lime zest (1 lime)
1 cup soy milk (plain or vanilla)
¼ cup vegetable oil
2 teaspoons tequila
½ teaspoon vanilla extract
1 cup sugar
1⅓ cups all-purpose flour
¼ teaspoon baking soda
½ teaspoon baking powder
2 tablespoons potato starch
½ teaspoon finely ground salt, either sea or iodized
1 pint fresh raspberries

To Make the Cupcakes:
1. Preheat the oven to 350° F. Place 12 paper liners into cupcake trays.
2. In a large bowl, mix together lime juice, lime zest, soy milk, oil, tequila, vanilla, potato starch and sugar.
3. In a bowl, measure flour, baking soda, baking powder

and salt. Whisk or sift together to ensure they are thoroughly combined.

4. Add dry ingredients to lime mixture and stir until just combined.

5. Gently fold fresh raspberries into the batter with a rubber spatula.

6. Pour into paper liners. Fill three-quarters of the way to the top.

7. Bake for 20 to 24 minutes, or until a toothpick placed in the center of a cupcake comes out clean.

8. Let cool for 5 minutes and then place on baking racks.

Yield: 12 cupcakes

Tequila Lime Frosting

¼ cup salted butter, room temperature
1 tablespoon soy milk
3 tablespoons lime juice
1 tablespoon tequila
2 cups, plus more if needed, of powdered sugar

To Make the Frosting:

1. Beat together butter, milk, lime juice, tequila, and 2 cups of powdered sugar until smooth and creamy.

2. If the frosting is too thin, wait 5 minutes. It will thicken. If it's still too thin after 5 minutes, add more sugar very slowly. The frosting should be stiff, but spreadable. If the frosting becomes too thick, add more lime juice or milk.

3. Spread the frosting on cupcakes.

Chapter 8

French buttercream is possibly one of the most frustrating and painful things to make. It involves putting boiling hot sugar and corn syrup into egg yolks without cooking the yolks or crystallizing the sugar, which is near impossible. There is a sweet spot, a merging of the right temperature of eggs and liquid sugar with the right amount of sugar mixed into the yolks at the right speed. It's timing, and when it works you get a light-yellow foaming mixture that has more flavor than any American buttercream, because the egg yolk adds an extra layer of taste.

Ansley yelped in pain as boiling-hot liquid sugar painted itself across her wrist. Through the pain she managed to hold on to the pan as she poured the liquid into a bowl of egg yolks. The yolks weren't curdling, but the sugar was being thrown onto and sticking to the sides of the bowl. It was hardening in small beads as it cooled.

"Damn it," Ansley cursed as she rushed the pan to the sink

and doused it in hot water, "I'm never going to get this." This was Ansley's third attempt today. She was no further along in mastering the art of French buttercream, but she was short two dozen eggs and two pounds of butter. She couldn't quite explain why mastering a difficult frosting recipe was more important to her than finding a real job. She left the pan in the sink to soak, raced the family cookbook back to her room and rushed to lunch to meet Dot. The burn on her wrist was turning a bright red and itching.

Why do I have to master this recipe? Ansley silently asked herself as she walked to the restaurant. There are dozens of other frosting recipes out there. She couldn't come up with an answer except for the fact that she had to. Nothing with butter, sugar and eggs in it was going to conquer her. She had a long, rich heritage to live up to. Would her great-great-great-grandmother who emigrated from France give up on making the buttercream of her homeland? No. Neither would Ansley.

Ansley was still mentally dissecting what she had done wrong when she sat down to lunch with Dot. She didn't give the conversation her complete attention until Dot said, "I have to confess something to you."

It was shortly after they had been seated at a French bistro that opened all its windows to the street, so you felt as if you were outside but were nicely shaded and protected from the city's humidity due to the air conditioner working overtime. It was the kind of place that Dallas didn't have—wasn't capable of having—because Dallas didn't have pedestrian-friendly streets and the heat was too unbearable for five months of the year to leave the windows open even a crack.

"What?" Ansley asked as she lifted a croissant from the basket on the table. She patted her tiny tummy. She sort of liked it. Even though she used to mock girls with the exact same pooch, it made her feel sexy.

"I used to live in the South. In Atlanta," Dot said.

"I knew there was a reason I liked you," Ansley said.

"I loved it. Didn't want to move. I was thirteen when we left. I thought about going back for college but you can't go back. You can never go back," Dot said.

"Of course you can go back," Ansley insisted.

"Ansley, you can't really go back," Dot said with an emphasis on "you."

"Okay," Ansley said, not wanting to give anything away.

"I know something bad happened to you. Something humiliating." Dot said.

"How do you know?" was all Ansley could muster.

"Why else would you leave? I can tell that you love Dallas," Dot said.

"I can still go back," Ansley stammered.

"No, once you leave, people move on. Your friends will never see you the same way," Dot said. "I never thought I'd settle in New York—always thought I'd go back to the South after school—but here I am. I have to make the best of things."

"But Parish . . . I love him," Ansley stuttered.

"That's your old boyfriend? I bet he's moved on," Dot replied.

"She's not right for him. I am," Ansley said.

Ansley told Dot everything, including how Patty used her.

"I mean, she came to my house every day and listened to me talk about Parish for hours," Ansley said.

"So, she was being a good friend," Dot said, sounding somewhat confused.

"No, she was gathering information to use to get Parish," Ansley said.

"It doesn't matter. You're never going to get Parish back. You have to move on," Dot said, and speared a piece of steak on her salad and dropped it into her mouth. Dot watched Ansley sag as she cradled the café au lait the waiter had just put down on the table. There's a moment in most people's lives when they realize that there are limits. You are not going to get everything you want. You will not be famous. You will not be extraordinarily rich. You will not be the most beautiful. The realization is crushing for a moment. Maybe longer than a moment, depending on how invested you were in the idea of a grandiose future. For Ansley, it was worse. Instead of knowing she'd never be famous or disgustingly rich, she knew with a certainty that invaded every level of her being that she'd never get the life she'd thought she would have. This was it. There was no do-over. There was no second chance. This was her life, now and for the rest of her future. She had been thinking of New York as a temporary exile, but she was fooling herself. You can't go back to your old life, because your old life has moved on. Even if she went back to Dallas it would be changed. Parish would be with Patty. Her sorority sisters would ignore her because she had been so insufferable.

Ansley gulped half her coffee in one sip and hyperventilated. Without a plan for life, she was lost. Her identity wasn't what it had been for the past twenty-two years. The life plan that was etched into every diary she had since she was ten was gone. No society marriage in Dallas. No young motherhood. No sorority of sisters forever. What was she going to do with her life?

"I can make this work for now," Ansley said quietly, like it was her new mantra.

Sitting there, eating pomme frites and spinach salad with Dot made Ansley feel slightly better. At least she had a friend who understood where she was coming from.

"So are you dating? Tell me about him," Ansley said and seemed cheered by the possibility of gossip and more confiding.

"I'm not dating anyone. Haven't found the right guy yet," Dot sounded uncomfortable for the first time since Ansley had met her.

"Come on. There has to be someone you like," Ansley said encouragingly.

"Dating is completely different here than in the South. The men aren't interested in marriage or commitment. Those are the last things on their minds. They want sex and a girl with no expectations," Dot said.

"Huh, so how do you get married?" Ansley asked with earnest interest.

"Trickery. You have to make them think you're so uninterested that the only way they can see you is to get serious about you. You have to keep up that level of disregard and find new and creative ways to convey it all through the courtship, until they propose," Dot explained.

Ansley was silent. She seemed to be thinking about something embarrassing. She paused in a way that a girl in sorority mode usually doesn't. Sorority mode means gushing everything without hesitation or pause.

"What about sex?" Ansley asked.

"What about it?" Dot asked, and sipped her water.

Ansley took Dot's hand and said with teary eyes, "I've only had sex with one person and I thought I was going to marry him."

"Well, if you plan on dating, then you—" Dot started.

Ansley cut her off. "I may date but I can't under any circumstance have sex."

Ansley wasn't about to cat around. She was only going to have sex with someone who mattered.

"When you do date, tell the guy you can't have sex because you're not that interested in him, or you can even make it mysterious. Whatever you do, don't tell him you've only had sex with one person. He'll think you're a freak. Like a religious nut case."

"Okay . . ." Ansley said, obviously not completely understanding what the big deal was.

"In this city, most girls over the age of fifteen have had sex with several people. Those who haven't are considered backward, frigid or ugly. New York's religion is based on how entertaining or powerful you are, not how devoted to Jesus," Dot said.

All the things she had been led to believe that guys wanted—attention, flirtation, doting and purity—were the opposite of what guys desired here. Could she completely revamp her view of dating? It was amazing to her that there was such a difference between Dallas and New York.

Dallas prided itself on being cultured and cosmopolitan and she firmly believed it was. It had dozens of buildings designed by the most cutting-edge architects. It had the opera, theater, beautiful art. There were hospitals with up-to-the-minute technology. Every major designer had a store there. The fact that religion was more a focus in people's lives didn't downgrade its image as cultured, but it softened its sensibilities. Dallas was competitive and cut-throat but it had an old-fashioned side. One that still encouraged a man to marry his college sweetheart and to stay married to her. Sure, trophy wives—second, third and fourth wives—were accepted, but Dallas still cheered the women who stayed married for thirty or forty years.

"It's a lot more difficult here," Ansley said as she tore a piece off the peach tart they'd ordered. The pastry was light, flaky and loaded with butter. It melted in her mouth.

"No, I wouldn't say that. I'd say it's a lot more detached, more 'leave your emotions at the door until you have a good reason to be invested.' It's a skeptical, cynical place," Dot said as she took a bite of the pastry. "This is amazing. You should make these."

"I don't do pastry. All I want to do is cupcakes," Ansley said as she dug in for another bite. Ansley had fallen in love with cupcakes when she was a little girl. They reminded her of her childhood. They symbolized a rose-colored sense of innocence. They were also deceptively difficult to make well. It took a real baker to raise the cupcake to the level of art. There were temperature considerations of the ingredients and the oven. There was the trick of using a baking stone under the cupcake tray to make them rise better. There was the quality and freshness of ingredients to consider, which made a huge difference in how the cupcake baked.

"Yeah, but cupcakes and donuts are trendy. You don't want to fall out of fashion by owning a cupcake shop," Dot said.

They both were now indiscriminately pulling off pieces of pastry. There was only a small patch of it left on the plate they were sharing.

"Delicious cupcakes don't fall out of fashion. Delicious anything doesn't fall out of fashion. What stops being popular is something that doesn't taste good. Behold the rice cake," Ansley said. She fell silent as an attractive Wall Street type of man walked too close to their table, made direct eye contact and smiled.

When he was clear of listening distance, Ansley hissed, "What was that?"

"He wants to have sex," Dot said.

"How do you know he wasn't interested in anything else?" Ansley asked.

"Because I don't know him. Only date within your circle," Dot advised.

I don't have a circle, Ansley thought, a little demoralized. Though Dot was a start at a circle, and that wasn't bad after two days in New York. She decided to tell Dot about her negative encounter with Thad Wheeler, hoping for a social-code translation. Dot listened carefully and asked, "So, he knew you were Vivian's granddaughter when he acted that way?"

"Yep, was just introduced," Ansley affirmed.

"You do have an accent." Dot trailed off for a second and then lightly slapped Ansley's hand. "There's another thing you need to know about New Yorkers. They're horribly prejudiced against anyone with a Southern accent. They think Southerners are all dumb Bubbas. Crude and crass and nouveau riche."

"So five seconds after he met me he decided I was crude and crass," Ansley said, shocked at the appraisal. She had been taught to be polite in even the most difficult circumstances. It was a true sign of character if under duress you could maintain a smile and a friendly tone.

"No, the second after he heard you speak," Dot said. "Scratch that—the second he saw what you were wearing, and that impression was reinforced by what you sounded like. I know him through friends. He's like that."

"Wow," Ansley said.

"I know. That's the first thing I changed when I moved, got rid of 'y'all' and any trace of an accent, and then the clothes. Think black," Dot said as she pointed to Ansley's hot pink cotton cardigan with the rhinestone buttons, her gold lame shoes and bag.

"Got it," Ansley said as a mother with a nanny and two small boys in tow walked by. The scene was idyllic. The mother was young, thin and fashionable. The boys, with their white blond hair and updated sailor suits, looked like angels. The nanny appeared to have come straight from Paris.

"Don't you just wanna get married and have little babies?" Ansley cooed.

"Never say that out loud to anyone," Dot warned. "Everyone here pretends that's the last thing on their minds until they hit their upper thirties. Girls our age talk about career goals, ruling the world and clubbing."

"Okay," Ansley said as they walked out of the restaurant, "Brunch this weekend?"

"That'd be lovely," Dot said, and hugged Ansley good-bye.

Ansley watched Dot walk off with the quick purposeful stride of most New Yorkers. Everyone had someplace to be and they always were ten minutes late. That's what that stride said. Ansley sauntered to 64th Street to the empty storefront. She took out her mobile phone and called the number on the sign in front. She arranged for a showing that afternoon.

For the next few hours she had nothing to do so she walked slowly, enjoying the day, looking in windows and imagining owning her own little apartment somewhere nearby. Unfortunately her reverie kept getting interrupted by people bumping into her as they skittered past. Finally one man said, "Slow stays to the left," and when she moved over, it had the magical effect of her being left jostle-free.

She made it to her grandmother's house after an hour of meandering and sat down in the kitchen with a pen, pad and her laptop. Now was the time to put her business school training into action. She started listing all the costs that opening a bakery would involve, as well as how many months she would need in extra cash until she made a profit. She filled five legal-sized pages with calculations. A couple hours later, satisfied with her math, she placed a cupcake in a decorative box she found in her grandmother's gift closet and headed out.

When she reached the empty store the realtor was already waiting, jangling her keys impatiently. Ansley waved at her from a few feet away. The woman waved back and unlocked the door and stepped inside. Ansley followed a few seconds later.

"I'm Ansley," she said, and produced her hand. The realtor shook it in a perfunctory way. Ansley also handed her a pink polka-dotted box shaped like a house. Inside it was one tres leches cupcake. The white frosting was spread smooth and shined in the light while the candied orange peel on top glistened invitingly.

"Cute," the agent sneered as she took the cupcake out of the box. "So the rent here is pretty high because this is a prime location. The owner wants to lock the next tenant in for at least three years—quick turnover is bad for the block. We'd

need to see you have the assets to cover at least a year's rent,"
she said as Ansley walked around. The realtor took a bite of
the tres leche cupcake, followed quickly by another. She was
devouring it.

The ceiling was tin painted brown. The walls were all lined
with built-in shelves that looked like they had twenty coats of
paint layered on them. The black and white tile floor was actually black and white marble. The bar was solid wood, probably oak. Ansley walked into the kitchen. It was competently
industrial—all stainless steel and no-slip tile. It had large
commercial-grade ovens and even a wood-fired one. What
was truly impressive though were the quantity and scale of
windows. Fully two walls from where the appliances ended to
where the ceilings began were steel-framed windows. The
kind you see in elementary school cafeterias built in the
1950s. The windows let in so much light that the kitchen actually seemed to have some charm. The back windows looked
out on a small patch of grass no bigger than a Hummer SUV,
and the side windows revealed a pleasant faded mural of mer-
maids.

"What happened to the last tenant?" Ansley asked.

"His Italian food fell out of favor," the realtor said, picking
crumbs off her hands and putting them in her mouth.

"It was bad?" Ansley asked.

"It wasn't good," the realtor admitted. She was softening to
Ansley a little bit.

"What was here before?" Ansley asked.

"A bagel shop. It was a heavenly bagel shop. Was here for
years. In the mornings you could smell the fresh bagels—the
onion, the poppy seed. The owner retired and his kids didn't
want to take over. It was such a loss," the realtor said, getting

lost in her memory of a fine doughy bagel with fresh cream cheese melting.

"Did he do well?"

"Well enough to own an apartment nearby and one in Israel," she said, obviously still saddened by the loss of a quality bagel.

Ansley had a similar listening technique as her grandmother and she got the realtor talking for a half an hour about the store. She found out what it had been originally—a small club for gentlemen. The front part was the old library, hence the built-in bookshelves. She also found out the foot traffic on this block was particularly good, because it was a route to the subway, a busy street to hail a cab and, of course, Central Park. The realtor said she was amazed it hadn't been snatched up yet, but she had plenty of other appointments scheduled, so she bet by the end of the day papers would be signed with someone.

"I'll take it," Ansley said as she pulled out a statement showing she had $285,000 in investments—money from her father's parents that she'd thought would help fund her young married life.

"That's not enough," the realtor said.

"Why? Rent is $6,000 a month and this more than covers two years," Ansley said.

"Yes, but what about construction, start-up inventory, staffing and insurance," the realtor countered.

"I'll use less than $70,000 for all that," Ansley said.

The realtor laughed.

"I've already calculated it," Ansley explained.

"Let's hear it," the realtor said, obviously unconvinced.

"All right, costs before I open include: $30,000 for construction, $20,000 for new kitchen equipment, $4,000 for start-up inventory, $10,000 for furniture, $3,000 for pots, bowls, dishes and $300 for permits," Ansley rattled off. She felt more and more confident as she went. Thank God she took the entrepreneur class in school. The realtor was starting to take her seriously.

"That's a tight budget," the realtor said.

"I can work on a tight budget," Ansley said.

"What's your backup plan if you can't?"

"That's my problem to solve," Ansley said as she authoritatively placed her purse on the table as if she already owned the place.

"Your assets alone barely meet the criteria, but your product is good," the realtor said.

"Of course it is," Ansley said as her stomach churned. She was all fake bravado at the moment.

The realtor clapped her hands together excitedly. "Let's make this happen." She told Ansley she'd draft up an agreement and have it ready by tomorrow afternoon at the latest. The realtor said she still lived in the area and was very happy about a new bakery opening within walking distance.

"Bring another one of these tomorrow," the realtor said as they walked out of the building and locked up. She was still clutching the pink polka-dotted box Ansley had handed to her.

"Absolutely. Glad you liked it. It's a new recipe I'm trying out," Ansley said a little bashfully.

"Don't change a thing. It was fabulous," the realtor said, and hugged Ansley. A New Yorker hugged me, how strange, Ansley thought.

As they parted ways, the enormity of what she had just done hit Ansley. She had verbally committed to paying an incredibly high rent for three years for a business she had never done before in a city she didn't even know if she liked.

There were so many things that could go wrong with this plan, it'd be a miracle if just one or two things went right.

"Karmically, I'm due," Ansley reasoned as she tried to calm herself down on her walk back to her grandmother's house. Plus, Vivian did require her to get a job and this was a job. Though her grandmother had probably been thinking more along the lines of entry-level public relations or a small dessert-catering business.

She dialed her mother's number on the walk home.

"Momma, I just leased space for a bakery," Ansley gushed.

"What? Did Vivian put you up to this? That's so like her, she'd feed you to the lions if she thought it'd be amusing. That's what she did to your Granddad." Hattie launched into what Ansley knew would be a long angry tirade against her grandmother.

"No, she doesn't know anything about it. Please don't tell her. Wait, what am I saying? Like you would talk to her even if your hair were on fire," Ansley said.

"Darling, this is risky. What do you know about running a business? What do you know about baked goods besides cupcakes?"

"May I remind you that I was a business major at Baylor? And the beauty of this plan is that I'm only going to do cupcakes. It'll be a cupcakery," Ansley said.

"That sounds silly," her mother scolded. "How easy do you think it's going to be to lure customers to your store if you only sell one thing? What about all the people who don't like cupcakes? What about the donut people? The cookie people?"

"Momma, everyone likes cupcakes," Ansley said.

Her mother grew silent. It was true. Ansley hadn't, and she knew Hattie hadn't, ever heard anyone say they didn't like cupcakes. Cupcakes were universally held up as a symbol of all things good in childhood. When school districts in Dallas tried to ban parents from bringing cupcakes into the classroom, along with brownies and candies, the parents revolted. They lobbied the state legislature and the Safe Cupcake Amendment was passed, legally guaranteeing the safe passage of cupcakes in public schools across the state. In Dallas, and Ansley bet New York, the cupcake was more American than apple pie.

"Well, you may have a point there," Hattie conceded.

"And it's not like I'm making only one kind of cupcake. I have a dozen different recipes I've created," Ansley said.

Her mother started to cry. Ansley could hear the hiccuping gasps on the other end of the phone. Ansley started to get choked up too. She knew what her mother was thinking.

"I never thought you'd have to work for money," Hattie said, and sounded so forlorn, like she had somehow failed Ansley.

"It's okay, Momma. I'm real excited about my new life," Ansley said. "One more thing, when I tried to ask Grandma if she ever talked to Papa, she got real weird and wouldn't answer the question. What does that mean?"

"Well, she broke that man," Hattie said scornfully.

"So that's it. She doesn't want to talk about him because she left him?" Ansley asked.

"That's a lot," Hattie said, and told her daughter good-bye.

Ansley could sense there was more to the story than that. She just had no idea how to find out about the rest.

• Tres Leches Made Small •

6 eggs, room temperature, separated
1 cup heavy cream
½ cup whole milk
1 can sweetened condensed milk
1 can evaporated milk
¼ cup dark rum
½ cup sugar
1½ cups all-purpose flour
1 tablespoon baking powder

To Make the Cupcakes:
1. Preheat the oven to 350° F. Place 12 papers into cupcake pans.
2. Separate 6 eggs.
3. Beat the egg whites with an electric mixer until foamy and soft peaks form, about 3 minutes. Add sugar. Do not overbeat. It is better if the egg whites are on the softer side.
4. Add 6 egg yolks, one at a time.

5. Sift flour with baking powder and fold into the egg mixture in three parts, alternating with whole milk, using a rubber spatula. Begin and end with the flour mixture.

6. Pour batter into cupcake pans. Fill three-quarters of the way full. Bake for 30 to 35 minutes, until a toothpick inserted in the middle of a cupcake comes out clean.

7. As the cupcakes are baking, mix in a bowl the sweetened condensed milk, evaporated milk, heavy cream and rum.

8. Remove cupcakes from oven and pierce them several times with a skewer. While they are still hot, spoon the milk mixture over the cupcakes. Give the mixture time to soak into each cake and then repeat the process until all of the liquid is gone.

9. Allow the cupcakes to rest for 4 to 6 hours before you frost them.

Yield: 12 cupcakes

Whipped Frosting

1 cup whipping cream
½ to 1 cup powdered sugar
½ teaspoon vanilla extract

To Make the Frosting:

1. Pour the cream into a mixing bowl and beat with an electric mixer until the cream begins to thicken and

form peaks when the mixer blades are lifted out of it. This takes about 3 minutes.

2. Add the powdered sugar and vanilla. Mix and taste. If ½ cup powdered sugar isn't sweet enough for you, gradually add more to suit your palate.

3. Frost the cupcakes.

Chapter 9

Ansley treated her burgeoning bakery like a boyfriend. She spent hours sitting in the shell of the old Italian restaurant trying to figure it out. She had to know what it wanted to become before she touched it. She scrubbed the checkerboard floor on her hands and knees. Years of grime, disintegrated gum, and ground-in cigarette butts slowly came off, revealing creamy white and grayish black marble. It felt cool and clean to touch. Ansley spent one afternoon just lying on it.

On her back with her knees bent she studied the brown-painted tin ceiling and the white bookshelves. She turned on her side and examined the bar with its thick scarred wood and its brass footrest. Her natural instinct was to tear everything out and start over again. That's what she'd do in Dallas, but here she wanted to preserve. She decided she would peel the layers of paint off the ceiling and the shelves, keep the bar as a counter to sell behind and for customers to sit at. She'd get furniture more typically found in a posh library. She could imagine customers relaxing and eating cupcakes. She wanted to make them feel unrushed for this small slice of their day.

She decided to start with scraping the paint. She walked twenty blocks in her heels to a hardware store and asked a salesman how one scraped paint from wood. The man behind the counter had the decency to only smirk silently as he explained the process and filled a bag with the items she would need. She bought paint thinner, metal scrapers, rubber gloves and steel wool.

When she got to the bakery she laid out newspaper on her newly clean floor as the man had instructed and in her heels, skinny jeans and beaded tank top applied the paint thinner to the shelves.

The bookshelves ran the length and width of one whole wall. Thirty feet by ten feet was three hundred square feet of scraping.

After two hours she had scraped about one foot of wood. Her shoulders ached. Her tank top was stained and sweaty. Her jeans were destroyed. She had even taken off her heels.

There were at least five layers of paint, each one more stubborn to get off than the next. She'd never get this done. She called Dot.

"Hey, I need to hire a remodeler. Do you know of a good one?" Ansley asked.

"A remodeler?"

"You know construction. You said your dad is big into remodeling." Ansley said. "I leased the Italian restaurant."

"What?" Dot's voice was excited and concerned.

"It's crazy, but I have to do something crazy right now or I'll go insane. So I need a construction guy."

"You're really that crazy?"

"Beyond it."

Dot gave Ansley the name of one of her dad's best contacts. This was a man who stuck to budget and showed up to work, every day, on time—a myth of a construction worker. Normally, Dot said, she wouldn't even consider giving the name out, because once he got popular, her dad would never be able to hire him again, but Ansley sounded desperate.

Ansley called him and arranged for the crew to start work in a week.

"I haven't even seen your place," the guy said.

"I know. I have to get this going. Come tomorrow. Give me a price, think cheap, and let's get going," Ansley said, relieved to hire someone to do the dirty work.

She hobbled the six blocks back to Vivian's house. Her feet were on fire. It was a lot more difficult to walk around New York City in heels than it looked. Pounding the balls of your feet into unyielding and never-ending cement was punishing. On top of that, the heat rose from the cement during the summer and burrowed directly into your feet; it was pure torture. It took all the power of her pride not to take off her shoes and walk barefoot home.

"Dirty, dirty, dirty," she chanted to herself as she stared at the sidewalk.

A furniture store was the only thing that distracted her from her pain. In the window she could see the club chairs she envisioned in her bakery. She ran inside and slid into a deliriously comfortable black silk velvet chair. Her body felt supported but caressed. This was the kind of chair her customers deserved. She found the tag at the arm of the chair and flipped it over to look at the price; $5,000 for one chair. Ansley hopped up, offended by the piece of furniture and the fact that she could never own it.

She raced back to Vivian's house with the balls of her feet burning more and more with every step. As soon as she walked through the front door of her grandmother's house she threw her shoes, angry at them for betraying her.

It was six o'clock. Ansley had to wash up and prepare dinner. She was so tired that all she wanted to do was order pizza and curl up to some bad TV with a big glass of wine in hand.

"God, that's what I'm going to do," Ansley said as she called Dot, got the name of a great pizza place and ordered in.

"Hey, do you know of a cheap place to get furniture?" Ansley asked before Dot could hang up.

"The street," Dot said.

"Oh, where is that?" Ansley asked, poised to take down the address of some out-of-the-way but hip furniture store.

"No, I mean the street. On garbage day we'll have to pick through what people throw out and we'll have to do it early. There's lots of competition," Dot said.

"Gross. What about a thrift shop or something?"

"Thrift shops are a bargain in other places but not here. I'm serious about the street. Just about everyone I know has scored good furniture from the sidewalk in New York. It's nothing to be ashamed of. What do you need to get?"

Ansley explained that she had to furnish the inside of her bakery for $10,000 or less, and her desire to make the bakery look like a private club.

"All right, I'm going to help you rent a truck, and for the next couple of days we'll go out at 5 A.M. to troll for furniture in neighborhoods with trash pickup that day," Dot said.

"Really?" Ansley said, already disgusted by the smell of rotting food she knew they'd be surrounded by.

"See you tomorrow, bright and early," Dot said.

Ansley showered, put on sweats that had black sequins stitched on the side and slipped on another jeweled tank top. She applied stay-at-home makeup—tinted moisturizer, blush and liquid eyeliner—and headed to the kitchen to raid the wine rack.

When her grandmother arrived, Ansley was a wineglass into pleasantly numbing reality television.

Vivian didn't look amused.

"Where's dinner?"

"Pizza, really good pizza. I waited to eat till you got here," Ansley said, and gestured to the pizza box on the coffee table.

"This won't do," Vivian said as she marched over to the box, took out a slice and bit into it.

"What? Doesn't every New Yorker like a good pizza?" Ansley asked.

"I'm not allowing you to live here for free in exchange for you dialing a restaurant," Vivian said. "You will cook unless otherwise instructed."

"Okay, I apologize," Ansley said.

Vivian took a bite and closed her eyes in pleasure. It was one of those perfect marriages of crispy and soft, with the right amount of sauce. Ansley grabbed a piece and nibbled.

"It's great. Where did you get this?" Vivian asked, astounded by the quality.

"John's."

"In SoHo?"

"Yeah."

"They don't deliver," Vivian said as she examined the top of the box.

"They do if you call the number I have," Ansley said, and thanked God she had met Dot.

"Where did you get the number?" Vivian asked.

Over pizza and wine Ansley told Vivian everything she knew about Dot. She was in friend-crush phase and everything about Dot was wonderful.

"So this girl befriended you on the street?" Vivian asked suspiciously.

"Yes, isn't that crazy?"

"I'd be careful," Vivian said.

"Why?" Ansley asked, offended on Dot's behalf.

"Because something about this doesn't sound right," Vivian said.

"All right." Ansley yawned, trying to ignore her grandmother as politely as she could.

"Are you tired?" Vivian asked.

"Oh, God, I'm exhausted," Ansley confessed, and quickly shut up. She had decided not to tell her grandmother what she was up to with the bakery until its opening day. Ansley shifted her position on the couch so that her heel was digging into her hamstring, causing her twinges of pain—she wouldn't fall asleep now.

"Are you eating properly?"

"Yes. You see me eat more than my weight every day," Ansley said, now much more perky.

"Are you clubbing?" Vivian asked.

"Sure, I'm going out with all my friends late at night. I slip out of the house once you fall asleep," Ansley joked.

Vivian was puzzled.

"Being dumped makes you hungry and tired," Ansley said as she took another bite of pizza. Ansley was bursting to tell her grandmother what she was up to. She wanted to see pride wash over her face, but at this point she wasn't sure if her grandmother would think she was ambitious or stupid. The bakery needed to be up and running before Vivian saw it— that way her grandmother could only be impressed.

"I know. I baked a lot right before I left Dallas," Vivian said. "Put a few recipes in the book that last week."

"A few?" Ansley asked, shocked that her grandmother put more than one recipe in the book in the span of a decade. Then she remembered her grandmother had contributed ten recipes to the book. She could name them all and how often she'd eaten them, but she had never noticed that a few of them had been put in the book in a week's time. Ansley didn't think any other ancestor of hers had ever done that. She would have to go back to look. How did the process work with a few? Did you get your tasters together and make all of them? If her grandmother put them in right before she left Dallas, would she really have had the time to get approval from two family members? Ansley couldn't believe her grandmother would put recipes in the book on her own; that was the most outrageous thing she had ever heard.

"Heartache and upheaval makes you very creative," Vivian said.

"I know," Ansley said as she flashed to all the cupcakes she had popped out of the oven the past few weeks. Strange that her grandmother said "heartbreak" since Vivian was the one who left Papa. What would she be heartbroken about? And why hadn't Ansley noticed that several recipes were added in a short time span? She felt like she had memorized most of the book. She knew just about every recipe in there. In fact, she had made most of them.

Now Ansley wondered if the bad things she had heard about her grandmother were true. What had really happened to make her leave Dallas?

"Time to sort the finances. Ready?" Vivian said as she rose, grabbed another piece of pizza and walked toward her study.

Vivian had told Ansley she was going to enlist her help with sorting financial documents. She had held her breath when Vivian neglected to follow up. Maybe, she thought, Vivian forgot. Of course she hadn't. Vivian didn't forget anything.

Ansley marched upstairs behind her grandmother. When they entered the study Ansley was startled by the sheer amount of paperwork spread across the floor and every other available flat surface.

"Dusting in here would be a challenge," Ansley said.

"No one is allowed in here but you, me and Thad," Vivian said.

"What's Thad going to do?"

"He's helping with the documents. He's very good and has taken over for his father where my accounts are concerned."

"He's very pompous."

"Why don't you start over there with 1996. I need you to look at every page, catalog it on this form and then file it into the accordion folder marked '1996,'" Vivian said.

"Okay, but this is going to take forever."

"Do you have a better way to discreetly figure out how much financial shenanigans my late husband dipped his fingers into?"

"No," Ansley answered, chastened. She sat down on the floor and started reading. Four times in the next hour Ansley caught herself nodding off while reading. She was so tired all she wanted to do was push the papers aside and stretch out on the floor. The only thing stopping her was the fact that her grandmother would kill her. She kept stealing glances at Vivian, looking for signs of fatigue. The woman was annoyingly spunky.

At 11 P.M. Vivian finally announced they should call it a night. Ansley hopped up from the floor and practically bolted from the room.

"We'll start up again after dinner tomorrow," Vivian said.

"Are you kidding? If we only work on this for three or four hours a day it will take years to get done," Ansley said as she stood in the doorway, waiting to be released.

"You have a point. I'll enlist Thad to help you during the day. I'll give you a small stipend for your trouble," Vivian said.

"I can't do that," Ansley said.

"Why not?" Vivian asked.

"I have to find a job," Ansley blurted out. She was trying her hardest not to tell her grandmother about the bakery. Every time she said something about her day, she had to make sure it had nothing to do with the bakery. She was constantly censoring herself.

"Well, I'll suspend the eight-week time frame while you're working for me." Vivian said.

"No, I can't do that. I need to find a job," Ansley insisted.

"I need you to work on this," Vivian pleaded. Ansley looked at her grandmother surrounded by mountains of paper and knew she had to help. Hopefully Thad and she could do all of this very quickly.

"Well, of course I will. I just feel it's important that I continue to look for a job. I'll do both," Ansley said.

Her grandmother looked so relieved. Ansley would have to
figure out a way to get the bakery up and running and also act
like an unofficial tax auditor. She had to do this.

After her grandmother hugged her tightly and said good
night, Ansley went up to her bedroom. She was going to lie
down on the bed, fully clothed, with unbrushed teeth, and fall
asleep, but she remembered her grandmother's comment
about the recipes. She took the recipe book out of the closet.
She sat down on the bed and paged through it. There were
recipes for gravies and sauces dating back more than two hundred years. Most still held up to today's culinary standards.
Ansley had made the flax cake that was recorded by her first
relative to live in the United States. It was moist, sweet, nutty.
Maybe she could convert that to a healthy cupcake.

She flipped the pages until she got to her grandmother's
feathery handwriting. She turned three pages and then saw two
recipes that were entered on the same day, March 10, 1964. The
first one was for hot potato salad with pickle juice. It sounded
good, and it was. Ansley had eaten it at most of the family bar-
becues of her childhood. The second was for a twelve-layer cake
with a chocolate syrup poured on top. Hattie had made this for
Ansley's father's birthday two years ago. It was dramatic, like a
stack of pancakes a kid would dream up. Vivian must have been
cooking up a storm. She had created two completely different
things on the same day. The question was why?

Ansley knew that her family cooked when they were
happy and when they were angry. When they were irretriev-
ably depressed they usually ate, as Ansley had for the month

of June. She was pretty sure Vivian wasn't in the throes of joy on March 10, 1964. That was five days before she left her husband and her daughter, Hattie, for good. What was happening in her life? How could Vivian have gotten approval for these dishes before she left? Ansley wondered as she put the cookbook down and got ready to go to bed.

There were several other recipes in her grandmother's writing, but Ansley was too tired now to analyze them. And she had to wake up early and go trolling for furniture on the sidewalk.

• Going Nuts for Coconut •

¾ pound (or 3 sticks) unsalted butter, room temperature

2 cups sugar

5 eggs, room temperature

1½ teaspoons pure vanilla extract

1 teaspoon pure coconut extract

3 cups flour

1 teaspoon baking powder

½ teaspoon baking soda

2 tablespoons potato starch

½ teaspoon finely ground salt, either sea or iodized

1 cup coconut milk

14 ounces sweetened, shredded coconut

To Make the Cupcakes:

1. Preheat the oven to 325° F. Place 24 paper liners in cupcake trays.
2. Cream the butter and sugar together with an electric mixer until fluffy, about 3 to 5 minutes.
3. Add eggs, one at a time, and beat another two minutes.
4. Add vanilla and coconut extracts.
5. Whisk flour, potato starch, baking powder, baking soda and salt together.
6. Alternating the flour mixture and coconut milk, add them to the batter. Start and end with the flour mixture.
7. Fold in the coconut.
8. Pour batter into paper liners. Fill three-quarters of the way to the top.
9. Bake for 25 to 35 minutes, or until a toothpick inserted in the middle of a cupcake comes out clean.
10. Cool for 5 minutes and then place on a baking rack.

Yield: 24 cupcakes

American Buttercream

¾ pound (or 3 sticks) unsalted butter, room temperature
1 pound cream cheese at room temperature
1 teaspoon pure vanilla extract
½ teaspoon pure coconut extract
1½ pounds confectioners' sugar, sifted

To Make the Frosting:

1. Cream butter, cream cheese and extracts together with an electric mixer until fluffy, about 3 to 5 minutes.
2. Add the sugar and mix until smooth.
3. Frost the cupcakes.

Chapter 10

Ansley's baking had surprised her. So Vivian encouraged it. Ansley was even better than she'd thought. She had baking in her genes. Every woman in Vivian's family had that natural ability, which was coupled with years of practice. When Vivian was growing up she couldn't remember a day her mother didn't make biscuits. That kind of experience invades your pores. Your fingertips are as accurate as toothpicks when testing if a cake is ready. You can smell if a batter has enough sugar.

Real baking took more than the ability to follow a recipe, though that did help. Their success lay in their instinctual knowledge of flour, baking powder, sugar and salt. They were natural alchemists, able to turn the most basic ingredients into creations that people always wanted more of.

Vivian still baked several times a week, but she hadn't expected Ansley to carry on the family tradition. She thought Ansley would be like so many of the young women she met these days, unable to boil an egg and uninterested in learning how. The girl was her mother's charge, though, and all those years growing up in Hattie's kitchen had rubbed off on her. Even as a five-year-old girl, Hattie helped in the kitchen while Vivian baked. At such a young age her daughter was already a more accomplished baker than many grown-up women. Vivian was sure that Hattie had continued to develop her skills and passion for cooking as she grew.

The flavors Ansley put together were complex, unexpected. Vivian had hoped these small accomplishments in the kitchen would build up Ansley's ego enough for her to seek employment. In her spare time, if she had the gumption, Ansley could work on baking as a sideline. She had mentioned trying to take her cupcakes to local cafés and bakeries to sell, but Vivian didn't realistically see how baking a few dozen cupcakes in a home kitchen was going to help Ansley succeed in a meaningful way. There are times that a child has to find her own way, Vivian thought, and this was one of those times.

Ansley had gone to bed as soon as Vivian released her from looking at tax documents. Vivian had noticed her granddaughter nodding off a few times. The first time she saw her snoozing in the study, Vivian was tempted to send Ansley to bed but she didn't want to be too easy on her, so she made Ansley stick it out an hour. Then Vivian went down to the kitchen to bake. Baking always soothed her worries and she was able to solve her problems the quickest when she was in the kitchen. She guessed her subconscious was problem solving while her conscious brain was busy measuring and mixing.

Vivian took an orange out of the refrigerator and zested it. She was careful not to grate any of the white pith that is the layer under the orange color of the fruit's skin. The pith is bitter and ruins anything it touches. The outermost layer of the skin, the bright orange part, is a different story. That millimeter-thin cover holds citrus oil, which is more citrusy than the juice of the orange itself. Vivian could always tell an experienced baker from an inexperienced one by whether or not she kept a stock of fresh oranges, lemons and limes in the fridge. If there was a bottle of lime juice in the door Vivian didn't put much stock in the woman's culinary skills.

Vivian didn't stop zesting until she had a small mound of feather-light orange shavings in a bowl. Then she took the orange, which was now white on the outside, and threw it onto the cutting board. She beat it again and again on the board, throwing it hard like a baseball, until it felt as soft as a beanbag in her hands. When you beat an orange or lemon before you squeeze it, you double the amount of juice you get. It's like you're roughing the fruit up so it will comply, and it does. Vivian cut the orange in two and gently squeezed. A steady stream of liquid ran into an empty bowl.

She took a sip of the juice as she debated what to make. The answer came to her in a flash. The orange reminded her of the chocolate-covered orange peels she'd eaten in Paris. The bitter and sweet orange rind with the rich chocolate made her slow down her chewing and focus on the food. It was a complex combination. It was the kind of sweet Vivian would only eat one or two of and be satisfied for the whole day. That was a rare event. She started to put together a chocolate cake batter as she thought of how she'd make the orange frosting.

Chocolate-covered orange peels reminded her of Asher, her first husband. They went to Paris for their honeymoon and found the confectionery by chance. It was a block from the Luxembourg Gardens and they had wandered that way accidentally. Every time she'd gone back since, she made a pilgrimage to it. It reminded her of being young, in love and stupid enough to believe that both things last forever.

If only she hadn't let her own youth get in her way, she would probably still be in Dallas, happily married. Epic mistakes like she made are the result of too much idle time and the arrogance of thinking there will always be something better around the corner.

Vivian had met Charlie at the Adolphus Hotel bar. She had started going there one night a week when her daughter began kindergarten and in ways not tangible enough to put into words just didn't need her as much.

Thursday nights were Asher's poker night. Vivian hired a sitter, told her husband she was having a ladies' night since he was having a guys' evening. After he left she headed for the bar. She'd sip a cocktail or two by herself and then head home. She told herself she needed a couple minutes alone, that's why she was sneaking over to the bar. But one night she was there and there was no reason to go home. Hattie was sleeping over at her grandmother's house and her husband was out of town. In walked Charlie Osterhaut. He was in a cream linen suit and a pale blue shirt with a matching handkerchief tucked neatly into his jacket. His top button was undone, revealing a tan and muscular neck. His thick hair was dark brown, long on top and short on the sides and back. It flopped into his eyes, giving him a boyish look. He was a little tipsy, not slurring but liquored up enough to approach Vivian with no inhibitions in his way.

He swaggered over and leaned on the empty chair across from her. Vivian was also eating dinner at the bar. He smiled and slowly said, "I like a lady who's not afraid to eat."

"Or drink," Vivian said, and raised her glass to him. She had

drank just enough to feel saucy and flirt with the edge of pro-
priety. She invited him to sit down but only if he ordered
dessert. He ordered the baked Alaska.

"I prefer chocolate," Vivian said and gave him a sideways
smile. She was immediately attracted to his brashness. He sat
down next to her and acted like they'd known each other for
years. There was an instant familiarity that felt wrong but so
powerful.

"Who said it was for you?" Charlie asked when the dessert
was placed on the bar and he dug in.

"A gentleman would offer a bite," Vivian said.

"A gentleman would protect a lady from herself and her
vices," he said as he took another bite. In two bites he had already eaten half the dessert. He looked at her and smiled.
There was a friendliness to his face that drew her to him all
the more.

Vivian cracked a half smile mixed with a sneer, flagged
down the waiter and ordered a piece of chocolate cake. Charlie interrupted her. "Instead of a piece, please bring the whole
cake."

"I thought you had to protect me," Vivian said.

"Either protect or indulge. Women need both," Charlie
said.

The banter continued to ignite an attraction. As they both
dug into the cake and two more bottles of wine they became
more and more flirtatious. What would people say if they saw
them? Vivian pulled herself away from the bar for a moment,
determined to go home, but she couldn't. It was too irre-
sistible. She had to see what happened next. In her life for the
past few years she knew everything that would occur. There
were no surprises. Now that she had an unknown quantity

right in front of her, Charlie Osterhaut, she couldn't turn away.

When the restaurant was closing, Vivian was manic inside. She had no idea what she would do or what her options were. She waited for Charlie's actions. He got up from the table, went behind her chair, pulled it out and held her hand to help her up. Once she was standing he didn't let go of the hand. Was she okay with this? She was, she thought. He walked out of the bar, slightly leading her toward the elevators. They talked about the *Mona Lisa*. It had just arrived in the United States for the first time. Vivian desperately wanted to go to the National Gallery to see it. It was beautiful. Smaller than he thought it would be, but the most beautiful painting he had seen, Charlie said. He sounded intelligent.

They got into the elevator and rode up to the sixteenth floor. They walked to his door in silence. He only let go of her hand to put the key in the lock. Vivian kept thinking, *Am I really doing this?* She knew she could back out at any time, and that knowledge was what kept propelling her forward. That and her curiosity about how these things happen. *This is how a one-night stand develops*, she silently said to herself, never having realized how by chance these encounters really were. They must be less frequent than I thought, she said to herself, because finding two willing parties with the free time and the right amount of alcohol in them would be difficult.

Charlie opened the door. Vivian walked in. Things would never be the same.

Vivian started whipping butter for an American buttercream frosting with orange juice, grated peel and orange extract in it.

The triple layering of orange in a baked good was the only way one could really taste the orange. Otherwise it tasted like baby aspirin.

In a way it was good that Ansley had her heart broken early, before things got messy with a marriage and children. Parish wasn't the one for her granddaughter; she knew that without having to meet the boy. Ansley needed a man who was more than a set piece of the Dallas landscape. She needed someone who challenged her and she needed her own life. Even in their short time together Vivian could see Ansley was a lot like her, and Vivian knew with detailed clarity what hadn't worked in her own past.

Vivian was sure that she could guide Ansley through this phase. She could teach her granddaughter how to be proud of being able to take care of herself, just like Vivian had learned to do all those years ago, when she was suddenly thrust into a life in New York City with Charlie. At first she despised the city. It was too loud. It smelled too strong. It didn't have Dallas's subtlety. But over the years, she had adjusted. She grew to appreciate aspects of it. She loved the food and the constant variety. The clothes were always sophisticated and two steps ahead of the rest of the country. The people weren't friendly like in Dallas, but they were nice in their own way. She could strike up a conversation with an investment banker as easily as a construction worker while standing on a street corner waiting to cross the street. She became enthralled with how quickly the city changed. In many ways Dallas was always the same old town. She adored the ability to get lost in New York, no matter who you were. The chance to be anonymous.

Ansley would see the city the way she did soon enough. Vivian was sure of it because she understood that they were very much alike. They shared similar senses of humor, taste in food and a desire for privacy about their failures. How Ansley's face crumpled on the first day in New York when Vivian outed her about being dumped by Parish . . . the girl didn't want anyone to know she was hurting, was still in intense pain. She had planned to pretend she was fine until she was fine. Vivian knew exactly how she felt.

Vivian also knew her odds of drawing her daughter into the city increased the longer her granddaughter stayed. She could tell the two were close, best friends really. When she heard Ansley talk to Hattie on the phone she heard the intimacy in Ansley's tone and saw how relaxed her body became. It was the relationship Vivian had hoped to have with Hattie when she was first born. It was the traditional Dallas family arrangement. The mother and daughter were so tight they saw each other daily throughout their lives. Daughter and father were usually bound through the mother and in a more reserved way.

Vivian imagined Hattie coming in the fall. She didn't think her daughter could stay away longer than that. It would be the perfect time. New York was its most beautiful in autumn. She wondered if Hattie would stay in her house or insist on a hotel. It would be rude to stay in a hotel and Hattie was all about manners. But Hattie did have a palpable and well-founded hatred for her mother, so she might let that override decorum.

When Hattie came, Vivian would have to say something about why she left Dallas. It was the only way to forge a new bond with her daughter. Vivian had run the scenario of telling the truth in her head over and over again. She changed the way she told it, where she told it, who she told it to first. Nothing changed the outcome. Hattie would hate her even more. She had to keep working on the delivery, because she knew she had to tell it. She just hoped her daughter wouldn't hate her.

It made Vivian very antsy that Ansley had the book. She didn't think her granddaughter had enough information to connect the dots to figure out why Vivian had left her family but she might, especially if Ansley ever looked at any of Vivian's old correspondence or diaries, which were in the same office as the financial papers. Vivian desperately wanted to tear a couple of the recipes she created out of the book. She knew Ansley had it hidden in her room under her bed. She saw Ansley carry it in when she came to New York. Vivian searched for it once when Ansley was out. She had gone back a few times to look at it. She flipped to the five recipes she created in as many days. She was on the verge of ripping them out but she couldn't do it. She couldn't deface more than two hundred years of family history because she was embarrassed by her actions. That would make her even worse than she already was. After she lovingly perused the book, looking over old favorite dishes and reading what Hattie had added, she gently placed the book back under Ansley's bed, unscathed.

What will happen will happen, Vivian thought, and prayed Ansley wasn't overly curious. But she knew that a high level of inquisitiveness was sown into their shared DNA.

Vivian frosted the cake and put a pile of dishes in the sink for the staff to deal with tomorrow. She wondered what Ansley thought of her life, with staff and a large house and all the accoutrements Ansley had hoped for in a few years if she had married Parish. She had to teach her granddaughter that being wealthy wasn't only a stream of charity parties and shopping lunches. It was tedious and boring things, like taxes, tracking assets and meticulously charting the health and whereabouts of one's wealth. If you didn't do or understand one of these facets you were on your way to losing it all. Being wealthy wasn't easy and required constant vigilance.

Money was love, lust, revenge. Charlie Osterhaut understood the revenge part of that equation very well. As the weeks after his death unspooled, Vivian discovered more and more of what Charlie had done to repay her for any and all disappointment he felt in their marriage. Unfortunately, the illegal tax shelters and bad investments wound their way through the IRS's maze as well as Vivian's. Since she was the living part of the couple, she'd be held accountable for all of Charlie's shady doings.

Vivian had broken her own cardinal rule of life. She had not been vigilant. She'd always figured that it was Charlie's money. He had a host of investment professionals who advised him what to do with it and enough restrictions on what he was allowed to do put in place by his father that all should have been safe. But never underestimate the wiliness of a prideful rich man who has been neutered in the power department. All this financial chaos would be so much easier to sort out if she knew how long he had been doing it.

Vivian had been working with IRS Agent #1432 ever since the first phone-book-sized packet from the IRS arrived on her doorstep. She saw the crack in his professional composure when she mentioned the lilacs blooming in New York and decided to open it up further when she realized that Charlie probably had broken several tax laws. Vivian used her vast knowledge of plants as a conversational aphrodisiac with Agent #1432. In her next letter, she wrote about the design of her townhouse garden—xeriscaped with ornamental grasses and other plants that might be considered weeds by some.

"The whole thing caused such an uproar when I did it a few years ago. Some nicknamed it 'the fallow field' or 'the dump.' This year everyone is doing it," Vivian wrote.

When she opened up his response yesterday she could practically hear his heart racing. His handwriting was rushed as he wrote about his own garden, "I have always been a supporter of ornamental grasses. They're so beautiful in fall. I planted Oriental bittersweet in my yard two years ago and have not been disappointed. Though some think it's a nuisance plant, like kudzu, the bright orange berries add such a welcome pop of color and the birds do flock."

Vivian immediately wrote back about her squash garden, which had just produced a huge crop. "Gourds are as beautiful as flowers in their own way. I plan to put a heaping pile of them in my window boxes in a couple weeks. They are fall in plant form."

She knew their passionate discussions about plants would eventually fill up more on the page than news about the Osterhaut case. She was depending on this sort of distraction to give her time to sort out what Charlie had been up to. She knew she could draw out more and more information from Agent #1432. She was as good a letter writer as she was a listener.

She walked noisily up the stairs to her room, changed into her pajamas and sunk into bed. She caught herself imagining what Agent #1432 looked like. *He's tall, skinny but muscular, with tanned weathered skin,* she thought. She imagined a more patrician-looking Clint Eastwood and then realized the actor was married to a woman at least twenty years his junior. At the oldest, Agent #1432 could only be sixty-four. She couldn't imagine a person staying past sixty-five, the age he would receive full retirement benefits.

Still, she fantasized about gardening with Agent #1432. He came up behind her, put his hand on her wrist and guided her arm over to a plant that needed pruning. She could almost feel the heat of his hand on her wrist and the power of his body pressing into her back. She turned around and they kissed right there. It was the kind of kiss she used to have with her first husband. It was open and passionate and made her stop thinking about everything else until she opened her eyes and realized nothing more was coming. It was a fantasy that couldn't properly resolve itself.

Without Charlie, Vivian hadn't had sex for months and she missed it. She wanted to feel someone close to her again. She needed to feel desired. Vivian curled up under her sheets with her fantasies of Agent #1432 swirling around her mind. It was deliciously frustrating.

• Bittersweet Paris •

5 tablespoons butter
1 cup coffee
1 cup buttermilk
2 eggs, room temperature
1½ cups sugar

1 cup cake flour
½ cup cocoa powder
1 teaspoon finely ground salt, either sea or iodized
1 teaspoon baking powder
1½ teaspoons baking soda
2 teaspoons vanilla extract

To Make the Cupcakes:
1. Preheat oven to 350° F.
2. Melt the butter in the coffee. Then whisk the buttermilk in. Set aside.
3. Put the eggs and sugar in another bowl and mix on low speed.
4. Gradually add one at a time—flour, salt, cocoa powder, baking powder and baking soda. Mix until just combined.
5. Add the vanilla and the coffee mixture. Mix until combined.
6. Pour batter into paper liners. Fill almost to the top.
7. Bake 15 to 20 minutes, or until an inserted toothpick comes out clean.
8. Cool 5 minutes and then move to a baking rack.

Yield: 12 to 15 cupcakes

Orange Frosting

½ cup (or 1 stick) unsalted butter, room temperature
1 egg yolk, room temperature
1 teaspoon vanilla extract
1¼ cups sifted powdered sugar

1 tablespoon orange juice
the zest of one orange

To Make the Frosting:

1. Cream the butter with an electric mixer until fluffy, about 3 to 5 minutes.
2. Add egg yolk and vanilla. Beat 4 minutes.
3. Add orange juice and zest. Beat one minute.
4. Add sugar and beat until smooth.
5. Frost cooled cupcakes.

Chapter 11

True to her word, Dot was at Ansley's at 5 A.M. in a pickup truck. Ansley paid for it, but Dot told her who to call and picked up the truck. Dot was dressed in jeans, a T-shirt and sneakers. Ansley was in her pink Juicy Couture sweat suit with sequins running down the sides and designer "sneakers," made by Prada.

When Ansley got into the pickup Dot handed her a cup of coffee and started driving.

"Where are we going?"

"Across the park. It's trash day over there and there's a private school that I heard is doing some remodeling, so we might get lucky," Dot said.

Once they crossed the park Ansley could see a couple of other pickups, with empty beds and passengers leaning out of open windows, slowly driving the streets.

"Other people do this?" Ansley asked, a bit horrified.

"Of course, in New York very little is actually trashed. This city has been into recycling before it was cool," Dot said, and suddenly pulled over and jumped out. Ansley followed her tentatively.

Dot raced over to what looked like a pile of kindling. There were broken pieces of tables and chairs piled into a mini-mountain on the sidewalk. Dot was already frantically pulling broken bits out of the pile by the time Ansley got to the scene.

"Don't just stand there. Help," Dot said as she pulled the metal base of a desk out of the pile and dropped it behind her.

"With what?"

"See in the middle, there are a couple of chairs," Dot said.

"No," Ansley said as Dot handed her a piece of wet stinking wood. It smelled like several dogs had peed on it. Ansley dropped that piece of wood and pulled out other bits of furniture. She was doing this all halfheartedly, until she saw the club chair in the center. It looked close to the one she lusted after in the store. She started throwing pieces of furniture out of the way. Another pickup had pulled up behind theirs. A large woman with frizzy orangish red hair got out and raced over to the pile. She also was frantically pulling at things.

"Hurry up, Ansley. That woman isn't here to help us," Dot said.

"She'll try to take my chair?"

"You bet," Dot said.

"That's just wrong," Ansley said as she redoubled her efforts. She pulled a large oak table leg out of the pile. She squeezed her way into the middle of the pile and laid across the three club chairs in the center.

"They're mine," she called to the burly woman.

"Oh, yeah, we'll see about that," the woman said as she threw the back of a slated wooden chair out of her way. She looked like a bull headed for the red flag. Ansley didn't want this woman any closer. She could do Ansley serious physical damage.

Ansley coughed. The woman looked up with a slightly terrified expression. Ansley then spit on the chairs. The woman dropped a fake brass lamp.

"Why'd you do that?" Dot asked with a disgusted undertone.

"I'm marking my territory. I'll pee on them next," Ansley said as she stared at the other woman.

The woman's nostrils flared as she stared back. She sized Ansley up. Ansley undid the knot on her drawstring and started to pull down her pants.

"All right, no need to get gross," the woman said, and backed up.

Ansley waited until the woman pulled away and then she and Dot loaded their score—three club chairs with ripped seats, and one maple kitchen table—into the pickup.

Ansley felt giddy. She hopped into the pickup and slurped satisfyingly on her coffee.

"You really would have peed?"

"I wasn't about to let that cow get my chairs," Ansley said and realized that her baby pink sweat suit was gray and had lost most of its sequins. "You have no idea what these go for at retail."

Dot and Ansley did a sweep of the rest of the neighborhood and came away with a wire lamp shaped liked the Eiffel Tower and a reproduction Danish modern coffee table. They carted their finds over to the bakery, where Ansley was due to meet Dot's friend Jervis. Jervis was a pastry chef, who agreed to do a complete review of Ansley's kitchen. He'd tell her what she would need to make it a viable bakery.

As Dot and Ansley unloaded the last chair, Ansley asked her, "Dot, why are you being so nice? You barely know me."

"You need the help," she said, and turned away.

Ansley surveyed their finds. The chairs and tables had solid bones but they needed work. They also needed a way to unify them. She'd have to pay to get everything reupholstered and refinished in the same fabric and stain. She'd also have to find a lot more stuff. The chairs barely made a dent in the emptiness of the room.

Jervis walked in the bakery's front door like he was the first customer. He said a quick hello to Ansley and then started examining the place. He walked over to the patch of bookcase that Ansley had stripped, surveyed the wood, kicked at the floor and jumped on the bar.

"Solid. You're paying $10,000 a month?" he asked.

"Six," Ansley said with a sly smile.

"That's a good deal," Jervis said as his five-foot-eight frame pushed open the swinging door with more force than necessary and glided into the kitchen, "Oh, this is going to take some work."

Ansley's heart sunk. She'd been hoping for, "This is perfect the way it is." Her budget would do a lot better without the strain of paying thousands of dollars for new kitchen equipment.

He gave her the rundown on what she would need—two industrial stand mixers; huge three-foot-tall plastic containers, Tupperware on steroids, to store her dry ingredients; several cupcake pans with room for fifty or a hundred cupcakes each and at least two Hobart ovens.

"Make sure they're Hobarts. It doesn't matter if they have a convection setting. Convection is for shit for cupcakes," Jervis said as he made a disgusted face at her ovens.

"Really, I thought convection was great for every baked good," Ansley said, confused.

"Ever notice when you cook a cupcake with convection that the outside is dry and the inside isn't totally set?" Jervis asked.

At that moment Ansley swore she could see a halo ring his dark curly hair. His knowledge of her own cooking trauma was too good; he had to have some divine inside track.

"Yes," Ansley answered, a little unnerved. "How did you know?"

"Liquid content and volume," Jervis said. "Cupcake batter has a lot of liquid and a small volume. The convection all-around heat is too intense. It cooks it too quickly from the outside in. Much better for bread. Are you doing bread?"

"No," Ansley said, sounding more sure than she was. How did she know if doing only cupcakes was going to work? She might have to expand her product line just to make a living.

"Then these are for shit for you," Jervis said, pointing to the convection ovens lining one wall. "Sell them and buy Hobarts. They're the best oven and they do both convection and regular."

"Hobarts?"

"Hobarts are the king of baking. They cook high-sugar-and-liquid-content batter to perfection. Have you looked on Craigslist?"

"No. What would I be looking for?" Ansley asked. She only thought of Craigslist as an online dating service and she felt herself to be above it.

"Bakeries going out of business sell their equipment on it. Cheapest place to get what you need. Be careful though.

Some nutcases screw with their stuff before they sell it. They're pieces of shit," he said.

"How will I know?"

"Test everything before you buy," Jervis said.

"So I take ingredients to make cupcakes with me?" Ansley asked skeptically.

Jervis shrugged at her. The shrug said it was obvious, but Ansley knew she couldn't do that. She wasn't at that level of New Yorker yet.

"Well, thanks so much for your help. Can I get you anything? Coffee, tea, cupcake?" Ansley asked.

"Why don't we go out to dinner?" Jervis said.

"Because I don't do that," Ansley said awkwardly.

"Eat?"

"Look, I'll be up-front with you. The way you're looking at me indicates that you think that you have laid the ground-work to get some sort of payment for your advice. I assume you figure if you pay for a nice dinner on top of this or wow me with your own cooking that I'll have sex with you. I won't. I never have sex," Ansley said in one long breath.

"Oh, you've sworn it off," Jervis said.

"No, I intend to have sex with two people in my life. I had sex with my ex-fiancé. The next person I have sex with will be my husband," Ansley said.

"Get out of here," Jervis said, obviously not believing her.

"I grew up very religious in Texas. Just moved to New York. My kind doesn't have sex until they're married," Ansley said.

"Oh," Jervis said, backing toward the door.

"Yep, think red state," Ansley said as Jervis opened the door and fled without another word.

"Well, that was easier than I expected," Ansley said to herself as she turned to look at the wall with the bookshelves. Her small patch of peeled paint looked so pitiful. The workers would be here in minutes. She had to wait to let them in and then dash back over to her grandmother's house. She was due to meet Thad in a few minutes. They were beginning their work together today.

The workers didn't arrive until 9:30. She gave them a tour and bolted by 9:45. She was already fifteen minutes late to meet Thad.

Ansley walked quickly back to her grandmother's house. She phoned Dot as she hustled down the street.

"So, Jervis," Ansley began when Dot picked up.

"He hit on you," Dot said. "I thought he might. What did you say?"

"I told him the truth."

"What did you say?" Dot sputtered in shock.

"He'd have to marry me to have sex with me. He left without my prompting," Ansley said as she started to curse her footwear. Her designer sneakers actually had an inch of high heel hidden in them, baby heels, and her feet were killing her.

"Just don't do that with someone you're interested in. How's the furniture look?"

"I have to get so much more and the stuff we got needs a lot of work."

"It'll be fine. We'll find more stuff and I know a cheap re-upholster," Dot said.

Ansley hung up. She was hobbling the last block to the townhouse, repeating "Dirty, dirty, dirty," to herself to short-circuit the temptation to take off her shoes, when she saw Thad looking at his watch and bouncing up and down on his heels. He was standing on the first step to Vivian's townhouse, looking like a rejected prom date.

"Hi, I'm sorry I'm late. I haven't figured out how long it takes me to walk a few blocks yet," Ansley said apologetically.

All he said to Ansley in reply was, "Do you have them?"

He was so brusque that Ansley physically took a step back. "The papers?"

"Yes," Thad said in an exasperated tone.

"I thought we were supposed to go over them together?"

"I think it would work better if you gave me a year. I'll take it to my office to look at, then bring it back," Thad said as he motioned with his hand for Ansley to hurry up and unlock the door.

"Is that what Vivian wants?"

"I'm sure Vivian will be fine with it," he said.

Ansley walked through the door with Thad close at her heels. She turned around and knocked into him. "Wait here and I'll get them."

She motioned for Thad to have a seat in the entryway. Ansley walked upstairs to Vivian's office. She grabbed an etiquette book of Vivian's, sat down at her grandmother's desk and read a chapter about table settings. After ten minutes, she started to feel guilty about keeping Thad waiting. Wasn't this what the old Ansley would do? No, she said to herself, the old Ansley would've left the house through the back door and made Thad wait all day. A few minutes of discomfort for Thad were more than merited. In this situation he was the one being intolerable, and even the kindest woman wouldn't reward bad behavior. There had to be consequences to general surliness.

Ansley looked around for something else to read. There were two dictionaries on the desk and no other books in sight in the room. Ansley opened a couple of the desk drawers, hoping to find a hidden romance or thriller, but instead found Vivian's diary. It looked like her grandmother had written in it every day. Ansley flipped to the date she came to live with Vivian. Her grandmother wrote, "Ansley is here. She's a lovely, beautiful girl. She has my hair. She will need quite a bit of work."

Quite a bit of work? What did that mean? A makeover? Ansley flipped to the front of the book; it was dated January 1. Vivian must get a new book every year. Ansley carefully put the diary back in the drawer, feeling guilty for reading it like it was the novel she had been hoping to find.

Twenty minutes after she had gone to her grandmother's study she went back down with the papers, which she had crumpled and shuffled while she was upstairs.

"You know, I think there are more in the kitchen," Ansley said, and led the way toward it. Thad followed because Ansley hadn't given him the stack of papers she was holding. There were none in the kitchen, but she wasn't done torturing him.

"I know I put those papers somewhere," she said. Early this morning she had been in the middle of experimenting with a s'more cupcake. She walked over to her test area, the messiest part of the kitchen, and pretended to look for the papers under all the baking detritus. She could sense by the way his body tensed behind her that he was horrified that she could've left her grandmother's papers here. She heard him shuffling impatiently and when he sighed for the second time in annoyance she picked up a whisk that was thick with white chocolate from her baking experiment this morning and spun around. The force of the spin acted like a centrifuge and shot chocolate directly at him. He winced as some of the white liquid hit his face, right below his left pupil, and the rest spread across his suit jacket. Ansley smiled to herself and copied his earlier sigh of annoyance.

"I'm so sorry. A little cold water will take that right off," Ansley said, and headed for the sink. He grabbed her hand firmly but not forcefully and said the papers were all he needed.

"Well, here you go, then." Ansley said, and handed him the stack. "Now, what sort of trouble is my grandmother in?"

"I think it wouldn't be appropriate to discuss," Thad said as he double-checked what Ansley gave him.

"Inappropriate, or I won't understand," Ansley said.

"I can't speak to your mental capacity in financial matters," Thad replied curtly.

Ansley smiled and said, "It seems to me she or her husband let themselves be led down the primrose path of estate tax shelters and didn't bother to keep up with the IRS's feelings on the matter. I mean, one only has to look at the complete implosion of Jenkins and Gilchrist to see how things can shake out."

Ansley was referring to a white-shoe Texas law firm that closed its doors after the IRS went after it for giving legal opinions endorsing sketchy tax shelters. This wasn't something most people would allude to. It showed a level of knowledge that was impressive, and Ansley knew it.

Thad slightly smiled back as he walked toward the front door. Ansley followed.

"If your grandmother wanted you to know, I'm sure she'd tell you. Thank you," he said, and smiled condescendingly at her as he opened the door and walked out.

Ansley shut the door hard. She had a few hours before she

had to start cooking dinner. She practically ran up to her room, dying to know what else Vivian had put in the family cook-book.

She pulled the book out from under the bed and placed it on her lap as she sat down with pillows propping up her back. She flipped to the potato salad entry. It was an unusual one be-cause it had no mayonnaise—just yogurt, and a hint of pickle juice to provide moisture. Both she and her mother hated mayonnaise, and it seemed like her grandmother did too. It tasted like fat and runny eggs to her. Just awful. On the page after the potato salad, Vivian had recorded one of Ansley's fa-vorite desserts ever. The twelve-layer cake, with its microlay-ers, was a masterpiece. It looked like it was taken directly out of the pages of *Alice in Wonderland*.

Ansley flipped the page. The next entry was for French toast soufflé, a decadent, beautiful breakfast. There was the perfect combination of fat, salt and sugar in this recipe. When Ansley was in the midst of her teenage growth spurt she could easily eat half a pan of it and feel no guilt or food hangover. The recipe was added the day after the potato salad and cake recipes. Her grandmother must've been furious. Some bad things must've been happening right before she left for New York. Strange, because Hattie made it sound like Vivian's leav-ing was all very spur of the moment. Vivian after all only packed one light suitcase and didn't bother to ever send for the rest of her things. It was like she effortlessly and without a second thought walked out of her life in Dallas. These entries in the book seemed to say otherwise.

So far the one thing stuck out to Ansley: the unifying theme to the recipes Vivian had entered was that they were Ansley's favorite things to eat when she had a hangover. They were surefire cures for nausea. The salty and sweet always calmed her stomach.

Ansley heard a shuffling outside her door and then a knock. She hastily put the book back under her bed and then opened the door. It was Olga.

"Hi, Olga," Ansley said, "Good to see you."

"Vivian called to say she'd be early and she's hungry," Olga said. Everything Olga did was direct, using the minimum amount of words or movements.

"Thanks," Ansley called as she raced downstairs past Olga, who slowly walked down.

She took a trout out of the fridge, wrapped it with some vegetables and red potatoes in parchment paper and threw them in the oven. The whole thing would cook in its own juices and create a meal in the matter of twenty minutes. This was always Ansley's go-to meal when she had to throw something together.

Her grandmother arrived a few minutes after Ansley pulled the fish out of the oven.

"It smells good," Vivian said as she sat down at the table. Ansley brought the fish and vegetables over and served.

"Good day?" Ansley asked.

"Not especially. I went down to Thad's office and went through all the financial papers they had collected over the years on Charlie and me. Charlie didn't disclose quite a bit to them," Vivian said. She looked very tired. "What about you?"

"Well, Momma told me that Parish and Patty have set a date; November 15. They could just use my blueprint, if they wanted—it'd be easy. I heard she's wearing my old engagement ring," Ansley said.

"That's too tacky," Vivian said.

"It was a beautiful ring. It was Parish's grandmother's," Ansley sighed.

Her mother also told her about the ring and how disgustingly handsy the couple was in public, reportedly making out in their booth at P. F. Chang's. She had tried to block it from her brain.

"That man wasn't right for you. If he can so easily switch, that's a sign that he won't make it the distance. I give him a couple years with this Patty girl at most," Vivian said.

"Thanks," Ansley said, and felt a bit better. Maybe moving to New York and breaking up with Parish was truly the way her life was supposed to go. No, she thought, it wasn't, but she had to make the best of it, and the bakery was a start.

"I know it's tempting to fall into a comfortable life with the first man you have a crush on in Dallas, but those things don't usually work out well. People change too much. They shouldn't get married young," Vivian said.

Ansley was listening intently. There was an edge to Vivian's voice. She wasn't just giving advice. She was talking from personal experience. Maybe she had grown bored of Ansley's grandfather? But that didn't explain how any woman could leave her daughter too. Ansley had never heard of a mother outgrowing her children.

• *Green with Envy Cupcakes* •

1 cup (or two sticks) of unsalted butter, room
   temperature
2 eggs, room temperature
2 large yolks
1 cup heavy cream
2 cups sugar
3 cups all-purpose flour
2 teaspoons baking powder
⅛ teaspoon salt
2 tablespoons ground or powdered green tea

To Make the Cupcakes:
1. Preheat to 325° F. Place 24 paper liners into cupcake
   trays.
2. Cream butter and sugar with an electric mixer until
   fluffy, about 3 to 5 minutes.
3. Add eggs and yolks, one at a time, beat until well
   incorporated, about 2 minutes.
4. Whisk flour, baking powder and salt together.
5. Add to wet ingredients. Mix to combine.
6. Mix green tea with the cream. Mix until soft peaks
   form, fold into batter.
7. Pour into cupcake tins and fill three-quarters of the
   way to the top.

8. Bake 22 to 25 minutes, or until a toothpick inserted in the middle of a cupcake comes out clean.
9. Cool for 5 minutes and then transfer to a baking rack.

Yield: 24 cupcakes

Ginger Frosting

1 8-ounce package cream cheese, room temperature
6 tablespoons (or ¾ stick) unsalted butter, room temperature
2 cups powdered sugar
2 teaspoons finely grated peeled fresh ginger
1 teaspoon ground ginger
¼ cup very finely chopped crystallized ginger

To Make the Frosting:
1. Cream butter and cream cheese together with an electric mixer until fluffy, about 3 to 5 minutes.
2. Add sugar and beat until smooth.
3. Fold in the powdered and crystallized ginger.
4. Frost cooled cupcakes.
5. Sprinkle fresh ginger on frosting.

Chapter 12

After another early-morning raid of sidewalk furniture Ansley took a cab down to the Lower East Side. She was visiting a failed bakery to buy what was left of its equipment. When the cab pulled up to the empty storefront she gave the cabbie an extra twenty and begged him to stay.

A man with greasy hair and unintentionally baggy jeans greeted her at the door. She walked into the shell of the bakery. All that was left was dirt on the floor and a pile of equipment pushed into the center of the room. The scene gave Ansley an all-too-real sense that failure was an option for her too. She walked around the pile and spotted the stand mixer she had been looking for.

"What happened to the bakery?" Ansley asked as she examined the mixer.

"Bad cookies. Not enough butter," the man said.

"How do you know that?" Ansley asked.

"I made them," the man said. "I'm better at cooking than baking."

"Huh, that reminds me, I need some ovens. What do you have back there?"

"Mainly convection, top of the line," the man said.

Ansley smiled sadly because she now knew the man's second problem—the seduction of convection technology to cook high-sugar products did him in. She walked into the kitchen and saw a small double-rack Hobart sitting abandoned and unloved in the corner.

"I'll take that one," Ansley said.

"Really?"

"I'll have someone pick it up tomorrow," Ansley said as she paid for the mixer and oven and made a quick departure. The smell of failure was soul-crushing, but the prices on the used stuff were so much better than the new she couldn't pass up the deal.

Ansley lugged the mixer, which was at least fifty pounds, into the waiting taxi. She probably could've left it for the movers to pick up the next day but she didn't want to chance losing it, so she lugged it with her. She teetered, on two-inch heels, with the shifting weight of the equipment. The blades of the mixer caught on the fake white pearls of her tank top, pulling one long strand free from her chest. The beads fell in one big drop as she arched her back and, using momentum, hoisted the mixer into the taxi.

She collapsed next to the mixer and was barely able to shut the door. She rode with the door handle digging into one hip and the black rubber pads on the bottom of the mixer into the other for seventy blocks. By the time the cab dropped her off at the bakery she was battered and bruised. She pulled the mixer out of the cab without any help from the driver. He didn't even look at Ansley as she wrenched the metal stand from the seat to the sidewalk.

"Thanks," she said as the cab drove away.

It took her half an hour to move the mixer three feet from the curb to the bakery door. In the trip from the Lower East to the Upper East Side she had lost her strength. She had no idea how she had moved it from the other bakery this morning. Maybe it was adrenaline? Whatever it was, she had lost it now.

Dozens of men passed by her. Not one stopped to help. As she was about to open the door and realized that it swung out and the mixer was blocking its swing, a construction worker took pity on her. He lifted the mixer over his shoulder like it was a feather-stuffed pillow, opened the door and asked her where she wanted it. She had never been so grateful to see a sweaty man with a Bronx accent in her life. From now on she was hiring movers.

"Thank you," she said, and offered to pay the man.

"No, no. Your dad should've taught you to do this. It's not your fault," he said.

"I'm a girl," Ansley replied.

"Any of my sisters could move this thing, no problem," he said as he left.

As she set up her used mixer Ansley began to mentally collapse. All her fears about life after Dallas and opening a business collided inside her brain. She wasn't trained for this kind of life.

She was brought up to live like a spoiled hothouse flower. Her mind wandered back to countless incidents in which she had someone else do her heavy lifting. At the sorority she delegated to the other girls. She had them make trips to the drugstore for her, made them lists of things that needed to be done for the parties and expected them to do them. She even had another girl wrap Parish's Christmas present last year and pick out the card. What had she been doing while everyone around her was working?

No wonder Parish could replace her with Patty so easily. She didn't bring herself to the relationship. She brought staff.

Ansley pushed the mixer against a pole in the middle of the kitchen and plugged it in. She turned it on. It spun to life. Okay. One mixer down. She turned it off and threw a plastic sheet over it to protect it from the renovations, which should be completed soon. When the last coat of paint was dry she'd move all her supplies here and start baking. She knew she wasn't supposed to cook in the bakery until the board of health certified it, but she reasoned she wasn't going to sell the baked goods she was making in the few days, so it was okay. It was getting hard to explain to Vivian the need to make so many cupcakes.

Ansley headed back to her grandmother's house to experiment. Luckily Vivian would be out for the next few hours so she wouldn't have to answer any questions about why she was making two hundred cupcakes.

Ansley walked into the kitchen and got out her ingredients and notes for coconut cupcakes. She was experimenting and she would either give or throw away the fruits of her baking trials.

Ansley was having a hard time adjusting her homespun cupcake recipes for mass consumption. She couldn't get the ratio of flour to butter right when she quadrupled the recipe. Depending on the day, the batter would be too dry or too wet. Ansley tried a half cup less flour one day and it worked beautifully. The next it was a disaster. She had purchased an old-school black and white composition notebook and was keeping meticulous notes on the tweaks she performed on the batter, the results and, more recently, the weather—temperature and percentage of humidity.

Ansley stood in the kitchen with her eyes closed and one foot in the air because it made her think better. Closing her eyes shut out distractions. Balancing on one foot made her focus. She had let the coconut cupcakes cool and had just taken her first bite of one. She held the cake in her mouth, appraising it. It felt brittle, crumbly. The cupcakes were too dry.

Ansley dutifully recorded the results in her notebook. She absentmindedly tapped the pen against her head, racking her brain for the reason they weren't moist and spongy like they usually were.

She hung up her apron and kept going over the variables in her head as she walked swiftly toward the store. She needed to restock a few ingredients before Vivian knew they were missing. She was so wrapped up in revising recipes and buying supplies that it was only in the checkout line that she realized she was supposed to meet Thad fifteen minutes ago. When Vivian had found out that Thad had taken documents with him, she went straight to the phone and told Thad that he would bring the documents back tomorrow, never take another piece of paper from her office and work a minimum of three hours a day at her house until the papers were all cataloged.

From what Ansley could decipher from Vivian's end of the conversation, Thad was embarrassed and cowed into doing exactly as Vivian asked. "Understood," Vivian said, "Yes, we all make mistakes. The important thing is we don't do them again."

Ansley's feet burned as she walked toward Vivian's house. Since she had been in New York she had scraped off the outer layer of skin around her heels and ankles. They were permanently red and raw. The balls of her feet felt like they had tiny marbles sewn into the muscle, because they were constantly in some form of muscle spasm.

"Dirty, dirty, dirty," Ansley chanted to herself again as she stared at the sidewalk. She would not take off her shoes. She was crossing the street when a sharp pain pierced the arch of her foot and immediately made it twist in on itself. It was the most horrible foot cramp Ansley had ever experienced. She took off her shoes and walked barefoot the rest of the way to Vivian's, and it felt good. For the first time in days she could enjoy being outside walking. It made it so much easier to face Thad. He was standing on the steps of the townhouse. His face was so tense he looked only a few seconds away from punching something.

"Hi, Thad. Sorry I'm late. Shoe emergency," she said, and waved the shoes.

"Are you ever on time?" he asked as he stepped aside, allowing Ansley to unlock the door and enter.

"You know, the maid could let you in," Ansley said.

"I do know that, but you could let me in if you were on time," he said. "You're filthy. What do you do in the mornings?"

The bottoms of Ansley's feet were black. The sides were a dark gray.

"Breakfast. I love the diners." Ansley said as she walked up the stairs toward her grandmother's office.

"You need to wash before you go in there," Thad said, and pointed Ansley to a bathroom.

"Of course, don't want to track on the carpet," Ansley said, and slunk off. Thad was his normal charming self. It was going to be a long afternoon.

By the time Ansley had cleaned up, Thad had established himself in the center of the documents. He handed Ansley a stack. "Look through these and catalog them," he said without looking up.

Ansley took the stack over to the love seat and started the long process of review. Two hours later she brought the papers back to Thad. He took them from her hands wordlessly and reviewed them. As he looked at them he occasionally clucked his tongue inside his mouth. She wanted to ask him what the problem was, but she sensed this would give him satisfaction so she resisted. A full ten minutes later he looked up at her and handed the stack back.

"Do it again," he said.

"What do you mean 'do it again'?" Ansley asked, outrage creeping into her voice.

"You didn't follow the color-coded system I've devised. Red for anything out of the ordinary, green for real estate concerns, etc. Refer to the top page. Your markers are over there." He pointed to the spindly table by the door.

"You saw me sit down without markers two hours ago. You could've said something," Ansley said.

"You could've read the instructions. I tacked them to the door," Thad countered.

Ansley put the papers on the floor, placed her hands on the arms of the chair Thad was sitting in and kissed him. Not a peck. Not a friendly European buss. She placed her lips fully on his and with all the emotion she had suppressed for weeks she kissed him. Thad's lips kissed back and then he pushed her away.

"What do you think you're doing?" Thad asked as he wiped off his mouth.

"Kissing you," Ansley replied with a pleased smile. It felt good to take charge of one area of her life.

"Why?"

"You looked like you needed it," Ansley replied as she picked the papers off the floor and went to get the markers.

"Don't ever, ever do that again," Thad warned, and Ansley could tell he meant it. She could read his face and it said he didn't like her one bit. There was no hidden passion lurking below the surface and yet Ansley was thrilled.

She walked back over to him, leaned down and kissed him again.

He pushed her away. "What are you doing?" he practically yelled.

"I'm not sure," Ansley said as she walked over to the love seat. He pushed the office chair as far from her as possible. He looked scared. As she watched him pat down his hair and wipe off his face she giggled. For the first time in weeks she felt giddy. She had done something so completely out of her comfort zone that it shook her out of her depression. Thad gave her a nasty look and then turned back around and hunched over the desk. All Ansley could do is laugh.

I can't possibly like him, Ansley thought. *He's horrible!*

"I tried your latest creation. I could really taste the chili. You're talented," Vivian said to Ansley after dinner.

"Thanks," Ansley said, and felt bashful but pleased. Late in the afternoon she had stopped making the coconut cupcakes out of frustration and turned to chocolate. She started experimenting with how to add some heat to a regular chocolate cupcake, making it a Mex-Tex cupcake. "You don't think the chili is overpowering?"

"No, it's just the perfect combination. Normally I'd add coffee to chocolate to amp the flavor but the chili does that beautifully. Reminds me of Javier's—that interior Mexican restaurant in Dallas. If I were you I'd use a simple chocolate ganache frosting—or, ohh, I love the Texas boiled-chocolate frostings with butter and vanilla. Those are my favorites. The book has the best recipe for one."

"I know. I've made it a lot. You created it, didn't you?" Ansley asked. She hadn't had time yet to go back into the book and examine all the recipes her grandmother had contributed.

"I did," Vivian replied, "Did your mother make it much?"

"For almost every birthday. It was my favorite."

"Oh, she must've hated that," Vivian said.

"She'd always say, 'Damn, that woman's awful, but she's a good cook,'" Ansley said. "She used to tell me these stories about you."

"Fairy tales where I was the witch?" Vivian asked.

"How did you know?"

"Because she couldn't use the similar word," Vivian said.

"You were a towering witch with a cloud of hair and a mole on your chin," Ansley said.

"I got that removed."

"And you lured children in with kindness and cookies and cut their hearts out."

"Well, I can see that your mother has some issues with me," Vivian said.

"You could say that," Ansley said.

Vivian cut into the beef tenderloin Ansley had cooked for

dinner and dropped the subject. Hattie had decades of justified resentment and anger built up. Vivian would have to perform a miracle with Ansley to get Hattie to lower her wall by even a brick. Vivian studied Ansley while she ate. There was something different about her granddaughter tonight. She seemed more relaxed and self-assured. Maybe working with Thad was improving her spirits.

"We found more stuff today. A couple shell corporations and maybe a bank account in the Caymans," Ansley said, filling the void.

"What years?"

"In 1990."

"All in 1990?"

"Yeah, it was a thick stack. It took us our whole time to go through it," Ansley said as she took a sip of wine.

If Charlie had found out what Vivian had done, she knew he would've exacted revenge, and what better way to do it than from beyond the grave. The question was what he knew and when he knew it. The financial documents would tell Vivian everything she needed to know. But there were still hundreds of pages that had to be culled.

As Vivian was thinking about her mistakes, Ansley was thinking about her own. Ansley kept reviewing how she'd kissed Thad. She rewound both incidents and played them in slow motion. What had she been thinking? She wasn't attracted to that pompous blue-blooded sissy man. Something else must be driving this, she thought. Maybe all that anger for Parish had landed on Thad. She noticed that she felt ninety percent better when she thought of Parish since she kissed Thad. For that reason alone, she couldn't wait to see Thad again.

"IRS Agent #1432 has a bug up his butt," Vivian said as she finished her last bite of steak.

"What happened?"

"He's asked for every bit of paperwork I've ever had. I even have to show canceled checks," Vivian said, "Who keeps canceled checks?"

"I do," Ansley confessed.

Vivian gave her a look of death. "At least he can spell and has good penmanship."

"How do you know that?" Ansley asked.

"I only respond to the written word in these matters. Telephone conversations can be mistaken too easily and I would never email about money," Vivian said.

"That's old-fashioned," Ansley said, a bit taken aback. As she had gotten to know her grandmother, one word she wouldn't use to describe her was "old-fashioned." Her grandmother was sophisticated, classic, steely, aloof and secretive.

"I'm old-fashioned when it comes to finances. I want everything done properly. None of this fast-and-loose stuff. It gets you in trouble. You do know that I could be charged with a felony for tax evasion," Vivian said, and smiled. Ansley did know that there was probably more than one felony Vivian could be charged with.

"This is serious," Ansley said.

"It is," Vivian said, and picked up a cupcake. "Do you think talking about underwear is flirtation?"

"With me?" Ansley asked, confused by the subject change.

Vivian blushed and then she told Ansley about how her correspondences with IRS agent #1432 had become friendly. Sometimes the letters were sent so regularly they overlapped. With each new correspondence one thing became apparent:

Vivian and Agent #1432 had much more in common than she ever had with Charlie.

"Did your late husband spend more than $100,000 a year on clothing?" Agent #1432 questioned Vivian.

"Yes, he bought mink underwear," Vivian replied in another letter.

"He's better dressed than Jackie Onassis," Agent #1432 wrote back, referring to the quote that Jackie O. gave when asked if she spent $40,000 a year on clothing, "Heavens no, I'd have to wear mink underwear."

Vivian wore the confused look on her face that every woman does when being thrust into the world of men again after years on hiatus. She was nervous, excited and self-conscious. Before now Ansley never thought she'd be able to help or advise her grandmother. But under the circumstances, her age and social condition made her an expert.

"Yep, that's flirting," Ansley said. "The question is, why are you flirting with an IRS agent who could put you in jail?"

"It pays to be nice," Vivian said as she finished a cupcake. "Mmm, s'more. Has Thad tried these yet? I know he used to love these as a boy. His father has a picture of him in his office covered in marshmallow and chocolate."

"In a manner of speaking," Ansley said, and flashed back to the moment when she covered his suit in white chocolate.

• S'more Cupcakes •

1 cup (or 2 sticks) unsalted butter, room
   temperature
4 eggs, room temperature
1 cup heavy cream
1 vanilla bean (scrape out and use the black seeds)
2 cups sugar
2¾ cups all-purpose flour
2 teaspoons baking powder
½ teaspoon finely ground salt, either sea or iodized
1¾ cups semi-sweet chocolate chips

To Make the Cupcakes:
1. Preheat oven to 350° F. Place 18 paper liners into
   cupcake trays.
2. Cream butter and sugar with an electric mixer until
   fluffy, about 3 to 5 minutes.
3. Add eggs and beat another two minutes.
4. Cut the vanilla bean into two and scrape out the
   brown innards. Add the mixture. Beat for 1 minute.
5. Whisk flour, baking powder, salt, and chocolate chips
   together in a separate bowl.
6. Add to the batter. Stop when the batter is completely
   blended.
7. Whip heavy cream in a cold bowl until soft peaks form,
   fold into batter.

8. Pour into paper liners. Fill three-quarters of the way to the top.
9. Bake 20 to 25 minutes, or until a toothpick inserted into the middle of a cupcake comes out clean.
10. Cool for 5 minutes and then place on baking racks.

Yield: 18 cupcakes

Marshmallow Icing

1 cup (or 2 sticks) unsalted butter, room temperature
5 ounces Crisco
2 cups marshmallows
2 teaspoons vanilla
10 graham crackers

To Make the Frosting:
1. Cream butter and Crisco together.
2. Melt marshmallows in microwave. Microwave 30 seconds, then stir. Repeat until thoroughly melted.
3. Whip melted marshmallows in blender or with electric mixer. Whip them until they are fluffy, about 2 minutes.
4. Add vanilla. Mix until combined.
5. Add butter mixture and beat until fluffy, about 2 minutes.
6. Frost cooled cupcakes.
7. Crush graham crackers and sprinkle on top.

Chapter 13

Vivian tried to remember the early days with Charlie. They were intense—passionate, urgent and loving. The first week they were in New York they didn't leave his classic six apartment. A chef brought and prepared food. Charlie made tea and coffee. He insisted Vivian not move a muscle. He said she needed to let all the stress of leaving Dallas melt off of her. They had sex several times a day. Often they didn't bother to get dressed.

The next week they shopped for and purchased their townhouse—the same one Vivian still lived in. Then gradually they went out together to purchase furniture, explore the city and meet another couple for dinner or lunch. They were always holding hands in those days. Vivian was in awe of Charlie. His knowledge of the city's history and social structure was vast. He was so self-assured in every circumstance and location. He wasn't bashful when he introduced Vivian as his wife, though technically they weren't married yet. It seemed like, to him, it was the most natural thing in the world to meet a woman a handful of times and propose marriage to her. His confidence allowed her to relax. She floated along as he cut through the waters of daily life. He planned their itineraries. She asked what she needed to wear. As long as she had him with her she was fine.

Those were the days when they were both, in their own ways, truly happy. That lasted three months and two weeks.

After that Vivian couldn't stand the life she had walked into. She wanted to go home to Dallas and Asher and Hattie. But no one, especially not Charlie or Asher, would let that happen.

She had to decide how she was going to survive. She imagined years of being with Charlie, and not just Charlie but a whole family. She had quickly discovered the things about Charlie that she had loved and trusted when she was emotionally damaged—like his insistence on taking charge of their calendar—were the same things she disliked after she recovered.

She visualized trying to parent with Charlie. It would be more like Vivian would be walking behind him undoing everything he did. He would teach the children that they were entitled and better than others because of the fact that they were born rich. He would teach them to take shortcuts. He would show them that in every room they walked into they could and should treat others like servants. He would provide the perfect example of what confidence and a lack of empathy can create—a snob. He would mold them into little shits, like Vivian was sure he was when he was a boy.

The first and most important promise she made to herself was that she would never have Charlie's children. Having his children would tie her to him in too intimate a way. It would give them a bond that she didn't want to have with this weak, self-centered man.

She promptly made an appointment at a discreet hospital in New Jersey under a different name and had her tubes tied. She told Charlie nothing. She thought he suspected nothing as well. They "tried" for years to have a child, because Charlie really wanted one. Of course it didn't work. Luckily this was before the era of fertility testing and IVF. After a few years Charlie had to reconcile himself that it wasn't going to happen. He seemed to take it well. When he accepted that it was just the two of them it made Vivian even more dear to him.

He was more tender toward her. He started bringing her tea in bed every morning. He would silently slide it onto her nightstand and leave the room to allow Vivian to continue to sleep. He thought she was a late sleeper. She never was. She woke up at 6 A.M. like clockwork, but she loved the ability to lay quietly with her thoughts, sipping her tea.

Vivian didn't know how or when he found out the truth. But it seemed clear that the moment he discovered that Vivian purposely made herself sterile was the moment that Charlie set his plan of financial fraud in motion. A plan that he was sure would only be uncovered after his death, leaving Vivian the sole heir to the mess. Vivian was awed at how he could plot the delivery of so much pain for years while serving her tea every morning. She was certain that this financial mess was meant to get back at her instead of proving to his long-dead father that he was a savvy investor, because she remembered him repeatedly laughing at the folly of buying llama ranches. Llama ranches became the punch line to anything he talked about that was financial idiocy.

So far it seemed that 1990 was a very active year for financial fraud for her husband. That meant, according to Vivian's logic, that he had probably started a few years earlier. He most likely began with a few minor scams and worked his way into full-blown tax fraud.

Vivian racked her brain for major life events in the years leading up to 1990 that would've tipped Charlie off to her tubes being tied. She had been in the hospital twice—once for a broken wrist, the second time for a hysterectomy. The surgeon would've known that her tubes were tied. It seemed strange that he would bring it up to her husband though. Except the surgeon was a friend of theirs who knew of their fertility issues, so it was a possibility that he might have. Though it wouldn't have changed anything. Both of them were at the point in their lives where having babies was no longer an option. Still, men are men, and the surgeon might have thought that Charlie would like to know that his manhood wasn't to blame for their childless state.

She had the hysterectomy in 1986. She'd have to have Ansley and Thad comb through that year.

In the meantime, Vivian was still doing her best to charm Agent #1432.

He had asked her for investment documents tracking back the last ten years. She wrote him back telling him he should have them already. He should pull up the past ten years of tax returns. She was stalling. She wanted to find out the extent of the fraud before she presented all her documents to him. Then she could figure out how best to negotiate a deal.

Agent #1432 told her she was being a smart-ass. Vivian wrote a note in reply asking about his view on heirloom tomatoes.

In Agent #1432's next letter to Vivian Osterhaut he addressed what he thought was the most pertinent matter first, "Heirlooms are the best. There is no question. They're what my grandfather grew. They are summer on a fork." Next most important, he still hadn't received a list of her holdings from 1997. "Could you have your financial people send it? FedEx would be helpful. I am distressed by the number of discrepancies we are discovering."

Vivian ignored the request for documents. Instead she sent a packet of rare heirloom tomato seeds, not a bribe, a distraction, she told herself as she pulled out a piece of her stationery, wrote "All the best, Vivian," and folded the seeds inside the paper. She walked to the mailbox and personally posted the letter.

She didn't detect a trace of whining in any of Agent #1432's correspondence. She liked that more than she cared to admit. She couldn't reconcile that the last forty-six years had been the unmitigated disaster they were. It was like she threw away this life with the thought that things would be better in the next. What if there was no next life? She had squandered an amazing amount of time.

The next letter she received from Agent #1432 was both welcome and an annoyance. He suggested proceeding with an audit at the end of August. He said that way everyone would be happy at the end of the proceedings. She had immediately responded and asked who he meant by "everybody." She knew for a fact she wouldn't be happy with an audit by any stretch of the imagination. He had written back saying that she "seemed like a woman who liked certainty and quick resolution to nagging problems," and this was the quickest way to achieve her goals. He had gone on to say that he would personally handle the audit and would start it in New York at the end of August. That gave her exactly two weeks to prepare.

Vivian began to panic. She dreaded remembering all her years with Charlie. How could she have spent more than forty years—more time than with any other person—with someone you're lukewarm about? And how could Charlie have been such a scornful idiot as to play fast and loose with millions of dollars and place them in a shady tax shelter? She didn't mind inheriting a few million less, as long as things were legitimate. Charlie never saw it that way. He was always trying to find the shortcuts in life and he always thought vengeance was an appropriate reaction to any situation that annoyed him. It was like he thought his privileged birth meant normal rules didn't apply to him. In most circumstances he was right. Look how he convinced Vivian to marry him. Unfortunately the IRS was a different matter. They didn't have secrets and needs that required tending. Or did they?

"What did I say in those letters to make him request an audit?" Vivian wondered as she shot up from her desk. She needed to get Thad and Ansley over here right away. They were going to have to work night and day to comb through the rest of the documents in the next two weeks.

Vivian called Ansley on her cell phone. Ansley picked up out of breath.

"Hello," she wheezed.

"What are you doing?" Vivian asked, mystified as to what Ansley could be up to.

"Hailing a cab," Ansley lied. She was trying to dump large bags of flour into gigantic Tupperware containers. She had never realized how little upper-body strength she possessed.

"Well, it's not an athletic sport. Just raise your hand and a cab will stop," Vivian said.

"I'm trying," Ansley said as she leaned against a counter and tried to catch her breath.

"I really am going to need a lot of time from you in the next couple of weeks. The IRS is coming to do a full audit and I need to get all my papers in order before they arrive so I know what kind of deal I can make. Hopefully I won't be in handcuffs when they're done." Vivian said.

This was the worst possible time for Vivian to ask for more help. Ansley was trying to open the bakery in early September, when many New Yorkers returned to Manhattan. She wanted to be open the first day that mothers were walking their children to school. That's when they'd be the most happy and willing to try something new—before they got into a routine.

"Okay," Ansley said. She'd have to find a way to do both. She might not sleep for the next few days but she'd get everything done.

Vivian breathed deeply and slowly and then said gratefully, "Thank you."

• Black Bottom Heartache •

1½ cups all-purpose flour
1 cup firmly packed light brown sugar
5 tablespoons natural unsweetened cocoa powder (not
   Dutch-processed)

1 teaspoon baking soda
¼ teaspoon salt
1 cup water
⅓ cup vegetable oil
1 tablespoon white or cider vinegar
1 teaspoon vanilla extract

To Make the Cupcakes:
1. Preheat oven to 350° F. Place 12 paper liners in cupcake trays.
2. Whisk together flour, brown sugar, cocoa powder, baking soda and salt.
3. In separate bowl mix water, oil, vinegar and vanilla.
4. Make a well in the center of the dry ingredients and stir in the wet ingredients. Mix until smooth.
5. Pour batter into paper liners. Fill three-quarters of the way to the top.
6. Spoon a few tablespoons of the filling into the center of each cake. The cupcakes will now be at the top of the paper.
7. Bake for 25 minutes, or until a toothpick inserted in the center comes out clean.
8. Cool for 5 minutes and then place on a baking rack.

Yield: 12 cupcakes

Filling

8 ounces cream cheese at room temperature
⅓ cup granulated sugar
1 egg, room temperature

**2 ounces bittersweet or semi-sweet chocolate, coarsely
chopped**

To Make the Filling:
1. Cream sugar, cream cheese and egg with an electric
   mixer until light and fluffy, about 3 to 5 minutes.
2. Fold in the chopped chocolate with a rubber spatula.

Chapter 14

When Ansley hung up with Vivian she sank to the floor and cried. Working for a living was harder than she ever imagined. Trying to put this bakery together had exhausted her savings, made muscles she didn't know she had ache and taxed every polite bone she had in her body. Dealing with all the people necessary to make a bakery ready to pass the health department inspection as well as get her city business license, fire department permit, building permit and sign permit was maddening. Construction was stressful. Trolling for furniture was gross.

Ansley spent several early mornings picking through cast-offs. The effort had destroyed several of her Juicy Couture tracksuits, but it had paid off. She had amassed a bakery full of furniture. She sent it off to Dot's upholsterer and refinisher with strict instructions—aged silver leather for the chairs (easy to clean) and ebony finish for all wood, and everything had to cost under $10,000. Not that hard since the upholsterer gave her Dot's deal, which was $700 a chair and $300 per table.

The construction, which was eating up another $30,000, was proceeding on schedule. Dot's man had scraped and refinished all the wood and was in the middle of installing the bakery cabinets. They were huge and made of plywood. Ansley wished she had found some affordable vintage ones to go with the rest of the décor but everything she had seen was way out of her budget.

There was a list of more than a hundred things that had to be done before the health inspector's visit in two days. Little specific nettling things had to be fixed, like the water temperature in the dishwasher. It had to be 150 degrees or above, and it was nowhere close. She got a water heater booster that her plumber was supposed to install in addition to calculating the hardness of her water so she'd know what kind of rinse aids she needed. But the plumber was in and inexplicably out of the bakery several times that morning without making the water as hot as it should be.

When he came back into the bakery shortly after Ansley had talked to Vivian, she buttonholed him, "What are you doing?"

"Well, I, uh, I, uh, left some tools back at my place and I had to get them. I should fix this in two days," he said.

"Get out!" Ansley yelled.

"What? I'm not done," he said.

"Yes you are," she said, and grabbed his elbow, escorting him out.

"You have to pay me for my time, lady," he said.

"No I don't," Ansley screamed. "I'm just a woman trying to make a go of things and you're taking advantage of me."

Ansley started sobbing. The plumber was uncomfortable but still wasn't moving. Ansley cried harder and included loud wails. The plumber edged out the door. Ansley bent down into a squat position and bowed her head; by the time she looked up the plumber was gone. No matter what she had to do, men were going to treat her like a lady, Ansley thought.

She called Vivian to ask for a reference for a plumber. She lied and told her Dot's apartment was flooding because of a busted pipe. She needed a good one. She usually used Dot. Dot was basically like the dream version of the yellow pages, a concierge and best friend. She had a number for every service imaginable and each person had been fully vetted. Everyone had been fabulous except for the plumber Dot recommended.

The plumber Vivian had recommended walked into the bakery two hours later and let out a low whistle when he stepped into the kitchen. "We have some work to do."

In addition to the water temperature, the drains had to be snaked. The old plumber had cut the stopper holders too short, so the sinks wouldn't properly close. They would constantly leak water. The customer toilets weren't secured, so they wobbled, and the way they were piped, they would eventually erupt water like a geyser.

"What? Why would he do that?" Ansley asked.

"I'm not him. Bad day," the new plumber said diplomatically.

"Could he have done this on purpose?" Ansley asked.

"Yeah," the plumber answered.

"But it could've been a bad day?" Ansley asked.

"Yeah, I know a guy who screwed up every toilet he installed for two months 'cause he was going through a divorce.

I know because I fixed just about every job he did," the plumber said.

"How long do you think it will take?" Ansley asked, cursing herself as soon as the words came out of her mouth. She should've assured him the work wasn't that much and tried to lock him in on a price.

It was funny, everyone else Dot recommended had been wonderful. But she guessed it was proof that no one was perfect—even Dot.

"Day and a half, everything done. Two thousand," the plumber said.

The figure almost made Ansley choke, but she knew it could've been worse. She could've paid that money for half-done work. She wrote a check while mentally grieving over her dwindling checking account.

Ansley patted him on the back and rushed to make some coconut cupcakes. She needed to get this batch done and then hightail it back to her grandmother's house. She had told Vivian she was in Brooklyn applying for a job and that she wouldn't be able to get back until early afternoon. Vivian sounded annoyed but believed her.

Ansley was dying to try a new tweak that could solve her problem with quadrupling recipes. Late last night she had consulted the family cookbook and there were a couple of recipes in the book for large parties and massive cakes. She read through the ingredients, two pounds of butter, twelve eggs, one pound of flour. She stopped. Why was flour being measured by weight?

She skipped to the bottom of the page, where there was a note written in light black ink: "flour compresses in large volumes, needs to be weighed rather than measured, for consistency." That was it. If she figured out the right weight of flour needed, she'd have perfect cupcakes every time. All that was left to do was make several batches of two hundred or so cupcakes per batch to figure out what the right weight was. She was disturbed she hadn't thought of it before. Surely she was capable of coming up with such a simple answer on her own.

It didn't matter—the book had come through once again. It had never let her down. It always provided the perfect recipes, answers to baking problems and now insight into her grandmother.

Ansley fell asleep studying the French toast soufflé recipe that her grandmother contributed. She kept thinking about how good it tasted when she was hungover. Ansley wondered if that was an intended result or purely coincidental. It was a very good possibility that all the stress of preparing to leave her family drove Vivian to drink, or maybe she was leaving because Asher was already well on his way to being an alcoholic. Maybe this was a dish Vivian wound up making Ansley's grandfather all too often. She could imagine Vivian putting it in the book just before she departed as a symbol of why she could no longer stay married.

She needed to know more about what Vivian was thinking before she left Dallas. If only she could talk to a friend of Vivian's from that period. The friend probably wouldn't tell her anything. The women from that era did not divulge secrets to the women of her era. It was some old-lady code: *Never let the granddaughters know all the trouble we got into and then we can lecture them without feeling hypocritical.*

There had to be another way. Ansley thought back to the diary of Vivian's she read that chronicled Ansley's arrival in

New York. There had to be a diary from the Dallas period. The question was, where would it be stored?

Ansley had accidentally read her grandmother's diary from this year when she was in the study. Knowing her grandmother, the rest of her diaries were neatly stored away there too. She'd have to explore late tonight.

Ansley got out her composition notebook, meticulously recorded what weight of flour, eggs, butter, buttermilk and oil she was using and whipped up a batch of two hundred cupcakes as quickly as she could.

Ansley arrived at Vivian's around 1 P.M. and spent the next ten hours cloistered with Vivian and Thad in the study. They drank endless pots of coffee, ordered out for food and only left the room for bathroom breaks. It was the most tedious thing Ansley had ever done. It was worse than statistics class. At least that was only three hours at a stretch. They couldn't listen to music, watch television or even talk much, because it took all of one's concentration to read such boring material and pay attention. Several times Ansley caught her mind wandering and knew she hadn't read the last five pages that she flipped. She had to go back and look at them all again. Vivian and Thad had the same problem.

"I don't understand how people get caught doing financial fraud. These documents are so boring, who would bother to look at them and figure out what was really going on," Ansley said as she got up and stretched out her back.

"Some people live for this stuff," Vivian said, and thought of her IRS agent. She could barely admit to herself that a large part of her was looking forward to meeting him.

At 11 P.M. Vivian said they should call it a night. Vivian went to her bedroom and Ansley walked to hers . . . she

waited twenty minutes and then stole down to her grandmother's study. She quietly opened up cabinets and looked
inside. The first couple she looked into contained boxes of
stationery and pens, neatly organized and obviously bought in
bulk to appease Vivian's specific tastes. The third cabinet had
slim cloth-bound books neatly placed next to one another.
These were the diaries. Ansley was conflicted. The books held
her grandmother's most private and intimate thoughts. They
weren't meant for public consumption. Ansley silently closed
the cabinet door without disturbing anything.

She respected her grandmother and that meant she needed
to respect her privacy, except that she desperately needed to
find out what happened all those years ago. If she knew what
made her grandmother leave her mother, maybe she could
help bridge the gap between them. She wanted to give them
what she had with Hattie. They needed that.

Ansley remembered seeing her mother crying and her father comforting her every March, the anniversary of when
Vivian left. Her father would say gently, "You weren't the reason she left. You know that?" Hattie nodded yes, she understood, but she continued to cry sometimes late into the night.
Ansley knew because she would get up and check on her
mother. She would be sitting on the living room couch with
crumpled tissues all around her, watching whatever was on
TV. Even though Ansley was close with Hattie, at those times
she was scared to approach her. Her mother didn't seem like
her mother then. Hattie was like a lost child, waiting for a
mother who was never going to come.

Ansley hesitantly opened up the cabinet again and took
one of the cloth volumes out and opened it. It was Vivian's
diary from 1972. Ansley flipped through a couple pages. Viv-

ian wrote about dinner parties, recipes she was trying out and Charlie, who was annoying her. Ansley closed the book and put it back in its place. She didn't want to know the intimate details of Vivian's marriage. Ansley counted backwards eight books, figuring that should get her to 1964, the year Vivian left. She grabbed the book, heard a noise and quickly fled to her room. When she got there she could hear the trash truck on the street. Then she heard a door close on the floor below hers. Vivian was up. She hoped the truck had woken her grandmother, not her. She opened the book; "1964" was written on the front page. Ansley started reading. Maybe now she could figure out what made her grandmother leave Dallas. But she fell asleep somewhere in February and woke up a couple hours later, knowing she had to run over to the bakery. She left the diary safely tucked between the mattress and box spring of her bed.

At the bakery, Ansley put on her pink apron and white ribbon headband—her baking uniform. Thankfully the construction in the kitchen was mostly done. They were working on the front of the bakery now. Plumbing would be fixed in a couple of days, but she didn't care about the water. All she needed to bake was a working oven and ingredients.

She stuffed the two hundred cupcakes she made yesterday into the trash. They were hard as hockey pucks, a clear sign that she'd added too much flour. Ansley took out her black and white composition notebook and began a new page, entitled "Coconut Cupcakes Measured by Weight." She started by weighing the flour, measuring out four pounds of flour instead of the four and a half she'd used yesterday and charted it in her book. Then she started weighing all the other ingredients. After she popped that batter in the oven, she began another batch with three and three-quarters pounds of flour. Of course, flour wasn't the sole ingredient she'd have to tinker with in relation to weight. She needed to weigh her eggs and oil as well, to make sure they were in correct proportion to the flour. Just changing one recipe from a homemade one to an industrial-sized one was going to take hours of work. The only bright spot was once she figured out the mechanics of it, changing the others would be a lot easier.

She pulled the first two trays out of the oven. One had the four pounds of flour batter in it and the other had less. She touched the cupcakes to test springiness. She took one from each pan and tasted them. She watched how crumbly each was and recorded all the observations in her composition notebook. Then she let the cupcakes sit. She would test them again tomorrow to see what had changed. It was crucial that cupcakes taste better the next day than they did the first. Baked goods should age well for a couple days. If they don't, you've either overcooked them, used too much flour or over-beat the batter. When in doubt, err on the side of an under-done baked good, with less flour and fewer minutes in the mixer.

Ansley was so intent on her experiment that she lost track of time. When she pulled the last batch of cupcakes out of the oven, she realized she was already twenty minutes late to meet Thad at Vivian's house and it was going to take her an-other twenty minutes to walk there.

"Crap," she said as she wedged her feet into the sneakers Dot had bestowed upon her with the warning, "Only use these in extreme emergencies or when moving furniture. It's a slippery slope otherwise. Six months from now I don't want to see you walking around in too tight jeans, sneakers and a baby tee, okay?"

Ansley had scoffed at her, "It's sweet, but I'll never wear these."

Now she was jogging toward her grandmother's on Park Avenue during the morning rush hour, for all the world to see. She hated to admit it, but her feet felt great. *I can't look that bad in these*, she thought as she turned onto her grandmother's street.

She could see Thad pacing the front steps. His face wore his usual grimace.

"How can I help you today?" Ansley asked as she brushed past him and unlocked the door.

"Being on time would help. What is different about you? You seem shorter," he said.

Ansley slumped a little, but she wasn't about to let Thad see that he got to her.

"Let the document review begin," Ansley said as she headed upstairs to her grandmother's office.

"I have something better for you to do. We're short on time. Vivian gave me a list with specific dates. Track these," Thad said, and handed Ansley a piece of paper.

The list was maddeningly vague in one sense and all too specific in another: "Investment documentation for September 1, 1986 to October 28, 1987."

It took her the better part of the day to get everything in order. Ansley kept having to go back to Thad for clarification. As soon as she started to ask him a question he raised his index finger toward her in a signal for her to be quiet and wait her turn. She was left standing before him like a pupil waiting for a teacher's permission to go to the bathroom. Worst of all, it took all the power of her manners not to look pathetic doing it. Whenever she headed toward a chair to have a seat, Thad would say, "Wait, wait," and then keep her standing in front of him for several more minutes as he ignored her.

When he would finish reading whatever small-print document he was reviewing he would look up at her silently. She would ask her question. He would nod his head as if to say, "You're an idiot for not understanding what's on the list," and would answer her in a similar tone. Ansley was getting more and more ruffled. This was punishment for the kisses she had planted on him.

Ansley wasn't in the mood to be trifled with by yet another man. She wanted to yell at Thad, throw documents at him or, better yet, shred documents that he needed. In front of him. Instead she got nicer and more solicitous as the morning wore on. She knew she'd kiss him again before the day was through.

"Thad, you look absolutely exhausted. You've been working like a dog on those papers. Can I get you something? Coffee? Tea?" Ansley asked as she handed him the last stack of papers he had requested. The two of them had been working for hours straight. It was after five and Ansley knew that both of their stomachs were growling.

"I'm starving. You could whip something up in your grandmother's kitchen, couldn't you? You're so good with food," Thad said in a new condescending tone that clearly telegraphed his lack of respect for people who were "good" in the kitchen. It was obviously a frivolous pursuit, in his mind. She had no doubt what kind of cook his mother was—horrible.

Instead, Ansley smiled like Thad had bestowed one of the biggest compliments she had ever been given and headed to

the kitchen. She wanted to serve this man an omelet full of ha-
banero peppers or wasabi paste. She wanted him to choke as
his throat burned. She had to get ahold of herself.

"Bring the papers. You work and I'll cook," Ansley said before she walked down the hallway.

She heard Thad sigh in annoyance.

"If I'm going to cook for you, then you're going to keep me
company," Ansley called behind her.

She took out ingredients for rouladen, one of the five entries her grandmother had put into the book just before she
left: simple German food that wasn't really known outside of
Texas. Ansley took slices of top round beef and pounded them
until they were very thin. Then she placed a stuffing made up
of pickles, onions, bacon and mustard on one end and rolled
the beef into cigars. She seared the beef in a skillet and then
poured beef stock into the pan and let it simmer on a low temperature for an hour, making the meat very tender. The aroma
filled the kitchen. Thad kept looking at the stove expectantly.

"That smells good," he said.

"It'll be done in a half an hour. In time for Vivian's normal
dinner," Ansley said, reading the look of hunger on his face. He
dove back into the paperwork.

"Find out anything new while I was chopping?" Ansley
asked.

"Underreported gains from some investments. Two businesses whose sole purpose seems to have been to lose money.
I don't understand how he could be so foolish. I know Charlie
wasn't the wisest financier, but he knew the basics," Thad said
in a rare moment of candor.

"Did you ever think maybe he did this on purpose?" Ansley
asked, going on an instinct she had.

"No. Why would someone do that?" Thad said, becoming his usual haughty self.

"How well did he and Vivian get along?"

"No one can know the inner workings of a marriage, but I would say he was devoted to her. It's preposterous, what you're suggesting," Thad said. "It's just like you to try to make respectable people's lives into a soap opera."

Ansley leaned over and kissed him. She caught him off guard and for a second he responded before pushing her away.

"Why do you do that?" he spit out, so flustered that his whole face turned bright red.

"Again, you looked like you needed it," Ansley said, immediately satisfied, even happy.

Thad was about to unleash a tirade against her—she could feel it—but Vivian walked in the room. Thad quickly changed his expression and point of attention.

Thad broke the news to Vivian. "There was a lot of activity in 1989. I guess that's why the stack was so big,"

"What do you think the IRS will do?" Vivian asked, visibly nervous about the possibility of jail time.

"You're the spouse. As long as we can show that you had no knowledge of Charlie's actions, I believe we're only looking at a fine," Thad said, almost as relieved as Vivian. He definitely had a soft spot for her grandmother, Ansley thought.

"That smells divine. What are you cooking?" Vivian asked as Ansley prepared the plates with mashed potatoes and beef.

"Rouladen," Ansley answered, and watched her grandmother wince.

Thad cleared the papers from the kitchen table and they all sat down to eat together. Ansley watched Thad dig into his food, devouring half of his plate in a few seconds. Vivian picked at hers.

"You don't like rouladen?" Ansley asked.

"I used to love it," Vivian said, "but I've lost the taste for it."

Vivian pushed away the plate and was trying not to gag.

"This is your recipe." Ansley said.

Vivian rushed away from the table and toward the kitchen sink. She heaved. Nothing came out. She quickly regained her composure with a few deep breaths.

"What's wrong?" Ansley asked as she ran over to her grandmother.

"The smell. I can't handle the smell," Vivian said, and rushed into the other room.

Thad wordlessly watched the scene unfold. When Vivian left, he chuckled. "You know how to clear a room, don't you?"

"I had no idea," Ansley said, shaking her head.

"Your cooking normally have that effect?" Thad asked.

"You liked it."

"I did, but I have a poor sense of smell," Thad said.

Ansley circled him, evaluating the perfect time to plant a kiss on him. This time Thad sensed what she was doing.

"No, stay there," Thad said as he moved away from her. Ansley followed him. Thad walked backward out of the room, only turning when he felt there was a large enough gap between them that he could make a run for it.

He shut the front door seconds later. She'd have another chance at him tomorrow.

Wow, I do know how to clear a room, Ansley thought as she sat back down to dinner.

• Taking a Bite Out of Frustration
Spice Cupcakes •

1 egg, room temperature
½ cup (or 1 stick) unsalted butter, room temperature
1 cup sour milk*
1 cup brown sugar
2 cups flour
1 teaspoon baking soda
½ teaspoon salt
2 tablespoons potato starch
1 teaspoon cinnamon
1 teaspoon nutmeg
½ teaspoon cloves
1 cup raisins
½ cup nuts, pieces or chopped
2 cups chocolate chips, semi-sweet
* *To make sour milk, add 1 tablespoon lemon juice or distilled white vinegar to milk and let sit for 15 minutes.*

To Make the Cupcakes:
1. Preheat oven to 350° F. Place 18 paper liners into
   cupcake trays.
2. Cream butter and sugar together with an electric mixer
   until fluffy, about 3 to 5 minutes.
3. Add egg and beat another 2 minutes.
4. Add sour milk and beat until smooth.

5. Whisk flour, potato starch, baking soda, salt, cinnamon, nutmeg and cloves together.
6. Add flour mixture to batter. Mix until combined.
7. Fold raisins, nuts and chocolate chips into batter.
8. Pour batter into paper liners. Fill three-quarters of the way to the top.
9. Bake 15 to 20 minutes, or until a toothpick inserted in the middle comes out clean.
10. Cool for 5 minutes and then place on a baking rack.

Yield: 18 cupcakes

Sugar Glaze

2 cups powdered sugar
2 to 4 tablespoons orange juice
1 tablespoon butter, room temperature

To Make the Glaze:
1. Pour powdered sugar into a bowl.
2. Gradually add orange juice until the glaze reaches a pourable but not too thin consistency.
3. Cream butter into glaze.
4. Frost cooled cupcakes.

Chapter 15

It was only when she explained the interaction to Dot that she realized how strange it was. She was getting joy out of kissing a man who hated her and most definitely didn't want to be kissed.

"That's odd, isn't it?" Ansley asked about her increasing desire to kiss Thad.

"Do you like him?" Dot asked as she handed Ansley two pounds of sugar.

After Ansley and Vivian finished looking at documents around 11 P.M., Ansley had headed back to the bakery. There was still a lot to be done. The most pressing concern was converting all her recipes from homespun amounts to batters that could make two hundred cupcakes or more. Dot suggested she come along to keep Ansley company. Ansley didn't argue. It was just the thing she needed, a little girl talk.

"I must. I mean, he is well mannered, attractive, smart, not at all promiscuous that I can tell. He's like a Southern gentleman without the charm," Ansley said, turned the mixer off and added the sugar. She was perfecting her dark chocolate cupcake. "Would you brew a pot of coffee?"

Dot went over to the coffeemaker and started a batch. The secret to truly rich chocolate cupcakes, cakes or cookies, for that matter, is a little bit of coffee added to the batter. It plays up the acidity in the chocolate. Which makes perfect sense when you consider coffee and chocolate both come from beans heavy in caffeine that benefit tremendously from roasting to bring out their flavors.

"Can you be sexually attracted to someone you hate?" Ansley asked as she added twenty-four ounces of eggs to the batter. She cracked whole eggs and weighed them. Depending on the size of the eggs, sometimes she added twelve eggs, other times thirteen or fourteen.

"Oh, yeah. That can be the best kind of sex—sort of like angry sex. It's all about the base instincts," Dot said, obviously replaying some of her own experiences in her mind.

"I don't like him. I know I don't like him. Maybe I'm just sexually attracted to him. It felt so good to dominate him," Ansley admitted and felt immediately embarrassed. Despite her many years of dating, Ansley had never been the aggressor. She was a quiet manipulator behind the scenes and hadn't ever made the first move and kissed a boy.

"Yeah, that's sexual. Why don't you have a one-night thing with him and get it out of your system?" Dot asked.

"You know I don't do that," Ansley said as she went to the burner to stir the dark chocolate she was melting, and nodded to Dot, indicating that she should check the coffee.

"Why not? Say you get married to a New Yorker someday, which is highly plausible since you do live in New York now.

If he finds out you've only had sex with one guy, he's going to be plain creeped out," Dot said as she brought the pot of coffee over to Ansley.

"Doesn't matter. Can't do it," Ansley said. Dot looked annoyed at this response but didn't push it any further. Ansley mixed together the rest of the batter, placed the two-foot-high mixing bowl on the steel counter and handed Dot an ice cream scoop. Dot started scooping the batter into the pan.

Ansley walked over to the other side of the table and started cracking and separating egg yolks and whites by hand. She was going to try to make a French buttercream again.

"There are a lot of yolks in this stuff," Dot said.

"That's what gives it its flavor. The fat and protein in the yolks adds depth," Ansley explained as she put them in a blender and whipped them.

"No frosting yet," Ansley said as the two girls she'd recently hired walked in. They must've come directly from a party. Both were wearing eyeliner so thick, a comparison to a raccoon wouldn't be out of line.

"Slow. You're gonna need to learn how to crack eggs a lot faster than that if you want to be in the game," Larissa said as she walked over to the sink, washed her hands with the same thoroughness as a surgeon, came over to Ansley and cracked ten eggs in less than ten seconds.

"She'll learn, or she'll pay you to do it," Rachel said as she grabbed cleaning supplies and headed up front. "We figured we would clean up the mess the refinisher left by the bookshelves."

"The woman needs to learn," Larissa said as she followed Rachel.

Ansley had occasionally gone back to the park after her disastrous maiden voyage to test cupcakes. She had learned a few things. She brought cards with the bakery's name, The Icing on the Cupcake, on it and when it was opening. She didn't make direct eye contact or seem eager to engage anyone. She held the cupcakes on a tray and they did the talking.

Rachel and Larissa had raced toward her in the park. They were in jeans that were so tight that their skin puffed out from the waist in the classic muffin top shape. The fact that their baby T-shirts left a two-inch gap of skin between their tops and bottoms only accented the jiggling fat. These girls weren't sorority material. They were enthusiastic and unguarded.

They grabbed a couple cupcakes, and instead of wolfing them down as Ansley expected, they took small bites and talked seriously about what they were tasting. They noticed hints of Meyer lime juice with a nice grating of the lime peel but none of the white pith—"The bitterness would shine through in a cupcake this delicate," one of the girls said. The other noted a slight hint of tequila, which accented the raspberry and lime.

"These are delicious," they said to Ansley in unison. "Where's your bakery?"

Ansley gave them the whole spiel and immediately both were pressing her for part-time jobs. She did need people. She hired them on the spot because she liked their enthusiasm and she knew she could learn a thing or two from these girls about being authentic New Yorkers.

"I could hook you up with a couple girls from the neighborhood," Dot said when Larissa and Rachel left the kitchen.

"I like these two," Ansley said as she heated the sugar and corn syrup to boiling and beyond on a burner. The idea was the sugar would brown and that slight browning would add a taste of caramel to the frosting.

"Why don't you, me and Thad go to dinner? I might be able to help you," Dot suggested.

"Really? You could help me figure out what to do?" Ansley said excitedly as she slowly poured the sugar into the yolks. This time it worked. The yolks didn't curdle and the sugar didn't solidify. The frosting was becoming a perfect marriage of eggs and sugar. When Ansley added the butter it was sublime. The frosting was light and airy, sugary with a hint of caramel.

"I love it. It's the best frosting I've ever had," Dot said after she tasted it.

"You think so?" Ansley asked, fishing for more compliments.

"Yes, absolutely," Dot said. "So you'll arrange a dinner?"

"Yes, great idea," Ansley said.

She didn't leave the bakery until 4 A.M.—neither did Dot, Larissa or Rachel. It felt nice to have all these people pitch in and it inched her closer to opening her bakery on time. It was like a new sorority for her, but this time she got her hands dirty when there was work to be done instead of directing everyone else while she went to the spa like she did at the sorority.

Larissa and Rachel were the clean team. They scrubbed the floor on their hands and knees like Ansley did. They wiped the bookshelves with mineral oil. They Windexed every shiny surface. They even cleaned the brass hardware on the front door until it shone. By the time they left, the front room was sparkling.

Ansley had the brilliant idea of displaying the cupcakes on the shelves as well as behind a bakery counter, so when customers walked in they'd be engulfed in frosted baked goods.

The cupcakes would have the night to set in the refrigerator and could be out at room temperature for a couple hours. If all went well, they'd turn the cupcakes on the wall over every two hours.

Picking through people's curbside trash and going to flea markets, she had found several club chairs with solid wood bases and a cute love seat that would work perfectly toward the back of the store. A few were already done by the upholsterer. The bar was stripped and stained. She installed bakery cabinets on top of it and behind it. The lights from the cabinets showed off the wood nicely.

In the little grass patch behind the kitchen Ansley planted mint, basil, fennel and rosemary. All those herbs would make it into batches of cupcakes sooner or later. She also put a chimnea, or outside clay fireplace, there for fall and winter like she had on the sorority patio. It'd be nice and warm.

Dot pulled more than her own weight as well. She baked at least four hundred cupcakes. To Ansley's delight the recipes were now working on a large scale because she was measuring all her dry ingredients by weight.

When Ansley slipped into her own bed she knew she had less than three hours to sleep. Vivian would be knocking at 7 A.M. She expected Ansley and Thad to help her all day.

The knock on her door felt like it happened seconds after she put her head on her pillow. She dragged herself into the shower, put on makeup and then poured herself a twenty-four-ounce cup of coffee. She headed to Vivian's office. Thad was already there. He seemed perky compared to her.

"You look like hell," he said as she walked through the door.

"Thanks, you're a real charmer," Ansley said as she slumped down on the love seat. "Anything you want me to review, you have to bring over here."

Thad rolled his eyes and walked over to her. He handed her a large stack of paper and markers. Then he went back to the desk. "Some Texas friends come to visit last night? You look like you have a hangover."

"Why would they be Texas friends?" Ansley asked.

"Everyone knows Texans are drinkers," Thad said, assuming he was stating the obvious.

"Have you ever been to Texas?" Ansley asked, annoyance in her voice.

"I've spent some quality time in the Houston airport on the way to South America," Thad said. "I tasted a Shiner Bock and watched the heat rise from the cement outside in waves. That was all I needed to see."

"That was all you needed to see to do what?" Ansley asked.

"To know I didn't need to venture outside the airport. Texas is a huge strip mall," he said.

"You're talking about Houston," Ansley corrected him.

"Houston, Dallas, Austin. What's the difference? Everyone in Texas thinks they're the greatest because their state used to be a country and they have a tremendous growth rate because they have no unions and few environmental regulations. It's all very parochial, don't you think?" Thad asked.

"No," Ansley said, getting a little defensive for her home state.

"Take you, for example. If you were so happy in Dallas, why did you move to New York?" Thad asked as he placed a stack of paper in the "done" pile.

"I thought I needed a change," Ansley said lamely, shifting her weight on the love seat.

There was no way she was going to explain to Thad the fact that she was dumped.

"See, Dallas didn't seem exciting to you. You thought New York was more cosmopolitan," Thad said. "I've always known I'd live in New York, because it's a part of me."

Exactly what Ansley had thought about Dallas. That city was a part of her and her heart ached for it. She longed to feel the onslaught of heat as she walked outside. She wished that just once the New York sun would beat down on her face with the strength it did in Dallas. She didn't realize it when she was there but that Dallas sun made her feel alive. It was powerful and thrust her into action. It made her cognizant of survival.

"New York is more liberal, that's for sure," Ansley said, and it didn't sound like she meant liberal in a good way.

"In some ways it is but in other ways it's much more re-served. There aren't many gold-plated things around here," Thad said as he looked at Ansley's large gold hoop earrings. She found herself fingering them as he stared. She stopped herself. They were one of her more understated pairs. In fact, all of her attire was becoming a muted version of what she used to wear. Today she had on black drawstring linen pants, a plain white T-shirt and flip-flops with rhinestones on the bands.

"No. People with means here are far more proud of the fact that they haven't redecorated their country homes since their grandparents bought them and that they've had the same pair of custom-made shoes for years," Ansley countered.

"They get better as they age," Thad said. "They conform to your foot. They feel better," he checked out his own shoes. He swung one leg up and rested his shoe lightly on the desk. It was made of a taupe-colored leather that had patinaed with age. It looked broken in, but in a good way. "That's the thing about quality. As it ages, it gets better. That's why your grandmother is such an attractive woman. I doubt you'll be viewed like her when you're her age, you think?"

Ansley seethed.

"I would think people will think of me as they do my grandmother," Ansley said and motioned at his foot. He took it off the desk.

"No, what your grandmother has isn't inherited, it's earned," Thad said.

She sauntered over to him and kissed him again.

"Do you notice I'm not kissing you back?" Thad asked through clenched teeth.

"I chalked that up to you not being a very good kisser," Ansley said.

"I'm a good kisser when I'm kissing," Thad said.

"I'll make you a deal. Come to dinner with me and my friend Dot and I'll stop kissing you," Ansley said.

"You'll stop kissing me? Let's have dinner tonight," Thad stated.

"Absolutely," Ansley said.

• Three-Alarm Chocolate Cupcakes •

½ cup shortening
¾ cup water
2 eggs, room temperature

¾ cup milk

1 teaspoon vanilla

2 cups sugar

2 cups all-purpose flour

1 tablespoon chili powder or dried chipotle powder for more spice

½ teaspoon baking powder

1 teaspoon finely ground salt, either sea or iodized

1 teaspoon baking soda

4 ounces unsweetened baking chocolate, melted

To Make the Cupcakes:

1. Preheat oven to 350° F. Place 24 paper liners into cupcake trays.
2. Cream sugar and shortening with an electric mixer until fluffy, about 3 to 5 minutes.
3. Add the eggs and vanilla.
4. Add melted chocolate.
5. Whisk the flour, chili powder, baking powder, baking soda and salt together.
6. Combine the milk and water.
7. Alternating flour mixture and milk, add them to the batter. Start and end with the flour.
8. Pour into paper liners. Fill two-thirds of the way to the top.
9. Bake for 20 to 25 minutes, or until a toothpick comes out clean.
10. Cool for 5 minutes and then transfer to baking racks.

Yield: 24 cupcakes

Ganache

½ cup heavy cream
8 ounces good semi-sweet chocolate chips

To Make the Ganache:
1. Place the heavy cream and chocolate chips in the top of a double boiler with 2 inches of water in the bottom. Put it on a burner on medium heat.
2. If you don't have a double boiler, place the cream and chips in a temperature-safe bowl and put the bowl in a saucepan with two inches of water in the bottom of it.
3. Stir until the chips are melted and the cream and the chips are combined.
4. Dip the top of each cupcake in the ganache.
5. Do not refrigerate, because the chocolate will discolor.

Chapter 16

The dinner was set. Eight o'clock at a steak house Thad had recommended.

By the time Ansley got there, Dot and Thad were already seated and appeared to be well into a bottle of wine. Both were laughing. Dot was whispering something to Thad when Ansley walked over to them. She felt like she was interrupting a very good first date.

"Hi, y'all," Ansley verbally stumbled. She was trying to remove "y'all" from her vocabulary.

"Ansley, you're right on time," Dot said, and seemed disappointed.

"Incredibly punctual," Thad said with even less enthusiasm.

Ansley sat across from the two of them in the banquette. "Do y'all—I mean, you two—know each other?"

"We know a lot of the same people. It's a crime we never met before," Thad said, and squeezed Dot's hand.

The meal went downhill from there. It was like Ansley wasn't even there. By the time the entrée arrived, she had placed a notebook on the table and was fiddling around with new recipes.

"Everyone in the South who's anyone comes out," Dot said in an exasperated tone, "Isn't that right, Ansley?"

Ansley had lost track of the conversation.

"What?" Ansley asked.

How'd the conversation get to cotillions? She could feel Thad judging Texas's backward ways. Even though she was sure if he had sisters that they came out in Paris. Somehow a cotillion in France sounded much more sophisticated than one in Plano, Texas, at the local Hyatt.

"That's right, and if you're real lucky you're from Texas and you get to do the dip," Ansley said with a smile.

"Oh, the dip. The Texas dip is amazing. Let's do it for Thad," Dot begged.

Ansley had no intention of getting up in a dining room full of adults and curtsying, until Thad looked horrified that she might. He scanned the room to see how embarrassed he'd be if she stood up. So she stood up and Dot stood beside her. In unison they lifted their arms gracefully in front of themselves and then moved them to the second ballet position and slowly bowed their heads, sliding them along their legs to the floor. The Texas dip has been compared to a swan dying in the ballet *Swan Lake*. Once their heads reached the floor, they whipped their bodies to standing from the waist. It was one long fluid movement. The Texas dip is the most dramatic of debutante curtsies. Ansley and Dot executed it flawlessly. A few diners watched, and clapped when they stood up straight again.

"That's the Texas dip," Ansley said as she sat down in her chair and allowed the waiter to replace the napkin on the table. Dot sat down again as well, fanning her cheeks delicately.

Ansley studied her suspiciously. It was odd that Dot could do such a good Texas dip when she was from Atlanta.

"How did you know how to do that?" Ansley asked Dot. Dot's face turned a deeper shade of red.

"I have friends from Texas," Dot said.

"Really?"

"You wouldn't know them," Dot sputtered.

"I would. I know every deb in the state," Ansley said.

"That's quite a tradition," Thad interrupted. He was acting like nothing had happened. It must be taking a great amount of effort for him to do so. It did for Ansley. She was horribly embarrassed that she made such a spectacle of herself. What had gotten into her lately? Normally she thrived on attention. The fact that she wasn't now was shocking. She changed.

"Yes, of course. We like to stick to the old traditions. We also believe in marrying young, not having sex until the honeymoon and going to church on Sunday," Ansley said as she took a bite of her steak.

Dot looked a bit shocked at Ansley's admission but Ansley didn't care. She wasn't going to pretend she was something she wasn't in front of this Yankee blue blood, "We also freely admit our relatives served in the Confederacy, and openly acknowledge our love of football and red meat."

"We like to immerse in our habitat," Dot said as she tried to segue away from Ansley's Texas proclamation, back to something that would include her in the conversation.

"Are you a virgin?" Thad asked.

Ansley looked at him and saw the mischievous glint in his eye that she'd observed at her grandmother's house when he thought he'd executed a particularly tedious request that Ansley was obliged to fulfill. They couldn't fritter away each other's time at dinner but they could verbally torture each other. Ansley's mood immediately improved at her understanding of the new set of rules.

"I waited until I was engaged and the next time I have sex it will be with my husband," Ansley said, and smiled proudly.

"You don't feel a little backward?" Thad asked.

"About saving myself for the person I truly love and will spend the rest of my life with? Tell me, do you feel sophisticated for sleeping with—no, let's not use euphemisms—for having sex with women you couldn't care less about?" Ansley parried.

"I don't have meaningless sex," Thad replied. His face was starting to harden. Ansley felt the same excitement she had at her grandmother's when she got one over Thad or when she kissed him.

"So the women you had sex with and didn't call the next day really meant something to you?" Ansley asked as she took another bite of her dinner. The steak tasted better than she expected a New York ribeye to, bloody and well seasoned.

"I don't have to explain myself," Thad said.

"Not to me, but you should to all those women you left crying because you never called back," Ansley said.

"I have never done that," Thad said quietly.

"Ohhh," Dot cooed.

Ansley was set to reply but Dot interjected and steered the discussion toward the recent stock market performance. Thad turned his attention back to Dot. Good, Ansley thought, *Maybe they'll start dating and I'll stop kissing a man who hates me.*

Ansley plotted a new recipe for a cupcake, inspired by Thad. The name would be Blue Blood Special and it would have blueberries and tart lemon custard with powdered sugar instead of frosting, because these Easterners are all about restraint. The custard would be so tart it would make your lips pucker.

They all walked out together. Well, Ansley walked in front and they walked side by side behind her. Ansley bid Thad and Dot good-bye, assuming they'd grab cabs and go in separate directions. She started walking toward home. She was waiting at the corner for the light when she noticed that they got into the same cab. Were Dot and Thad interested in each other?

"I'll call you tomorrow," Dot called out.

Ansley waved back and smiled brightly. But as soon as she turned around she let her mouth sink into the grimace it had been waiting to assume all evening. In the span of two months she had lost not one but two men, all her old girlfriends and possibly her one new girlfriend, Dot.

Ansley had been dead tired but the knowledge that Dot and Thad were going off together, probably to have sex, gave her an amazing amount of energy. She walked home with energetic strides and she thought, "Why is this happening to me?"

As Ansley walked she analyzed her behavior over her lifetime, trying to pinpoint when her bad karma started to accumulate. At the ripe old age of ten, she actively looked for and savored circumstances where she could make another girl cry or a boy blush and run. She was one bitchy preadolescent.

When the sneezy and whiny Amelia ran down the stairs of
Ansley's house crying because Ansley had berated her for getting her period and staining her old Care Bear sleeping bag,
Hattie had strong-armed Ansley down the stairs and into the
kitchen—"Just because you can be mean doesn't mean you
should. In fact, if you have the power to be cruel that's exactly when you shouldn't be, because your words have consequences." Ansley didn't listen. She continued being cruel,
albeit in a more nuanced and under-the-radar way.

Cruelty was a part of who she used to be. Was it still? No,
she thought, she didn't enjoy making anyone but Thad uncomfortable. She liked accomplishing things now. She loved
the feeling she got as the bakery came together. She loved
solving problems and navigating her way through difficult situations, like the health code inspection of her bakery, which
she passed with ease.

Ansley was starting to realize that she could base her con-
cept of who she was on more than how she stacked up to
other people. She could become someone she and others ad-
mired, even liked. She didn't think she was ever liked in college. She was feared.

To begin real change in her personality she needed to give
up on Thad or kissing Thad, step aside for Dot. She needed to
be a true friend instead of a competitor.

Ansley was home before she realized it. She walked up to
her room, and placed her cell phone in full view on her night
stand as she waited for Dot to call her so she could finally
know what happened. Dot said she'd call tomorrow, but
Ansley hoped Thad would leave and Dot would want to talk.
She retrieved her grandmother's diary from between her mattress and the box spring, sat down on the bed and opened it.

She paused. Did reading it make her a bad person or a good person?

She knew Vivian would hate that she read her private thoughts. She also knew that finding out why Vivian abandoned her daughter and telling Hattie was the only way to mend the relationship.

"Sometimes you do bad things for the greater good," she said to herself, and began reading February of 1964. Vivian wrote about tea parties with Hattie. She was trying out different recipes for pastry and sandwiches. Vivian thought she might have an adult tea based on what she had done for her little girl.

Another entry talked in detail about the nursery rhyme play Hattie would be in at the end of the month. Hattie had been cast as Little Bo Peep. Vivian sketched possible costumes in the book and listed what each would entail.

Asher figured heavily in the next entry. He invited a family named the Dunnes over to play bridge and made whiskey sours and joked with Barbara Dunne about having a crush on her in first grade. It felt, Vivian said, like she had lived the same evening ten times before. She didn't have to think about what she was going to say next, she merely repeated the same line from last week. Asher loved the continuity, the repetition of their life, Vivian wrote, she could see contentment in his eyes.

Ansley flipped ahead a couple more pages. Vivian wrote about going to the bar at the Hotel Adolphus and meeting Charlie Osterhaut. Vivian described him as "having the lead dog attitude with the looks to back up his confidence." She described his linen suit, wrote and then scratched out several words to capture the blue of his shirt, and she went on about his hair.

It was obvious that Vivian had a crush on Charlie and he on her. Vivian reported a day after their meeting he sent a pearl necklace, ten-millimeter uncultured pearls. Vivian hid them in her underwear drawer. When Hattie asked her what she was doing, Vivian said, "Putting these someplace I'll remember." Hattie was satisfied with Vivian's answer and left her mother with her hands in the lingerie drawer.

So far everything Ansley had been led to believe about her grandmother rang true—Vivian fell in love with a rich New Yorker and left her family. Ansley flipped the page just as Dot called. It was 8 A.M., a half an hour before Thad was due to arrive at her grandmother's house.

"So, what happened?" Ansley asked after Dot said hello. Ansley heard Dot groan slightly from the benefit of a good stretch.

"It was magical. He's something," Dot said.

That didn't clarify anything.

"What did you do after dinner?"

"We talked and talked. Did you know that his father started teaching him about the markets when he was five? Gave him monopoly money to buy stock. Now his dad is starting to hand over the reins to him and he feels so much pressure," Dot gushed.

"No, he doesn't talk to me much," Ansley said, and felt completely unloved.

"We're going out again tonight. This doesn't bother you, does it? I mean, it seemed like he and I really clicked," Dot said.

"I'm glad you found each other," Ansley managed to say with some genuine feeling.

"This won't get in the way of me helping you. I'll be at the bakery by nine tonight," Dot said.

"Thanks. We have a lot to do," Ansley said.

"What did you get done last night?"

"Nothing. I got distracted. Vivian gave me some papers," Ansley hedged. Maybe while she was reviewing Vivian's financials she could calculate the cost she should charge per cupcake and how many she'd have to sell each day to break even. She knew she had to make a minimum of $533 a day to pay for her monthly costs of rent and utilities, staff, inventory and insurance. The question was, should she charge $4, $3.50 or $3 per cupcake? The answer inventory-wise meant she'd have to sell—in order of most expensive to least—133, 152 or 177 cupcakes a day. She had to weigh how much people would pay for a cupcake against the feeling of exclusivity that people often felt when they had to pay more for an item, against how much traffic she felt the store could generate on a daily basis. It was a tricky issue that was almost as important as the quality of the cupcakes.

Ansley hung up, put the diary back under her mattress, quickly got dressed and headed downstairs. She still had a few minutes before Thad showed up and her grandmother hadn't tracked her down yet. She got out a mixing bowl. Time to make the cupcake that Thad inspired.

• *Blue Blood Special Blueberry Cupcakes with Lemon Custard* •

1 cup vegetable oil
2 eggs, room temperature
1 cup milk
1¼ cups sugar
2 cups all-purpose flour
½ teaspoon finely ground salt, either sea or iodized
2 teaspoons baking powder
1½ cups blueberries

To Make the Cupcakes:
1. Preheat oven to 375° F. Place 12 paper liners into cupcake trays.
2. Cream sugar and vegetable oil with an electric mixer until fluffy, about 3 to 5 minutes.
3. Add eggs one at a time and mix until blended.
4. Whisk together flour, salt and baking powder.
5. Alternating between flour mixture and milk, add them to the batter. Start and end with flour mixture.
6. Mash ½ cup of the blueberries. Fold them into the batter.
7. Gently fold in the rest of the blueberries.
8. Pour the batter into the paper liners. Fill to the top.

9. Bake for 25 to 30 minutes, or until a toothpick
   inserted in the middle of a cupcake comes out clean.
10. Cool for 5 minutes and then place on a baking rack.

Yield: 12 cupcakes

Lemon Curd

zest of 2 lemons
½ cup fresh lemon juice
¾ cup sugar
3 large eggs
¼ cup unsalted butter

To Make the Lemon Curd:
1. Place all of the ingredients in a double boiler.
2. If you don't have a double boiler, place all the
   ingredients in a temperature-safe bowl. Place the bowl
   in a saucepan with 2 inches of water in the bottom.
3. Bring the water to a boil.
4. Stir ingredients until they thicken into a custard.
5. Place the lemon curd in the refrigerator to cool for
   2 hours.
6. Frost the cupcakes.

Chapter 17

It was more than a surprise when Agent #1432 called Vivian. It was 9 A.M. Vivian was in her office with Thad and Ansley, going over financial papers. The three of them had spent countless hours in this room over the past week preparing for the IRS visit. They had one week left and Vivian was antsy about whether or not they would be done.

"Yes," Vivian said when Olga brought her the phone.

"Mrs. Osterhaut, I'm terribly sorry about this but . . . I'll be there tomorrow to begin the audit," Agent #1432 said, and he did truly sound regretful.

"What? Why?" Vivian barked into the receiver.

"Some time lines have changed. My superiors are eager to get this case resolved," Agent #1432 said.

"I don't understand. I'm not ready for this. I haven't been through all the papers myself yet," Vivian said as she stood up and hopped over a stack of papers.

"Well, that shouldn't matter if you've done nothing wrong," he said.

Vivian seethed.

"I believe we both are aware that I haven't done anything wrong, but my late husband may not have had a full grasp of tax law," Vivian parsed.

"I'll be at your house tomorrow at 10 A.M.," he said. "Look forward to meeting you."

Vivian pressed the END button as hard as she could and then flung the phone against the wall.

"We have to pick up the pace. The IRS is coming tomorrow," Vivian said.

"What? That's impossible," Thad said.

"It's possible. Let's get down to business," Vivian said as she sat and grabbed a large stack of papers to plow through. As she cataloged 1987 she wondered what Agent #1432 meant by "Look forward to meeting you." Was he sincere? She again started to imagine what he looked like. She envisioned tall and lean with a distinguished face—Maine patrician. She thought his hands would be long and graceful like a piano player's. He'd have a full head of hair that was completely silver and a bit long and tussled. She let out a moan.

"What? Are you okay?" Ansley asked, in a panicked tone like Vivian might have some medical issue.

"I'm fine," Vivian replied indignantly. Since when does a gasp of imagined pleasure sound like the precursor to cardiac arrest? Since she became an AARP member she guessed.

Age was a funny thing. Her granddaughter and most of the population of New York City didn't consider her a sexual being. They probably thought she never even masturbated anymore. They assumed she didn't have the working parts.

If only they knew. Vivian was more sexually awake than she had been for the past forty years. She felt sexy, too. She still thought the curves of her body were luscious, the thickness of her hair seductive and her coy smile enticing. If I think I'm sexy, then I am, she says to herself. Agent #1432 could be the one to test her hypothesis.

Pull yourself together, Vivian thought. She didn't have any idea what Agent #1432 looked like, if he was married or how old he was. They've enjoyed a mild flirtation through the mail. How much did you know about someone whom you wrote letters to? Plenty, Vivian thought. Letter writing was one of the most intimate things you could do with another person. It exposed your thoughts when you were vulnerable because it was like writing in your diary.

Ansley excused herself to take her cupcakes out of the oven and make another pot of coffee.

When she returned she asked Thad, "Shouldn't you call Dot?"

"You think? You're right," Thad said, and walked into the hallway to make a call.

On the positive side, Ansley and Thad were more friendly to each other than she'd ever seen them be. Perhaps Ansley was starting to settle into the city. On the negative, it seemed like the girl hadn't slept all night, Vivian thought, and hoped her depression over Parish wasn't making a resurgence. Vivian needed her granddaughter to rally. She prayed she would. What's life if you're broken by it before you're thirty?

As the day wore on the three of them got into a groove that was like an assembly line. Thad distributed the papers. Vivian and Ansley reviewed them, and when they found something questionable they handed the paper back to Thad, who determined if the item was shady or not. The pile of dubious investments was becoming quite large, almost a half a foot.

Vivian, Ansley and Thad stayed up well past midnight putting the papers in order, then moved the stacks down to the living room.

"He's going to be here three weeks at least," Vivian said as she surveyed the mounds of documents. There were thousands of pages, and that wasn't even half of the full amount.

"Just don't let him take advantage of you and kiss you," Thad said as he looked murderously at Ansley.

Vivian grew red. Maybe Thad had somehow sensed her thoughts. She was so embarrassed she couldn't even look at him when she told him good night and kissed Ansley on the cheek. She shot up the stairs into her room seconds after his warning.

Vivian put her nightgown on and brushed her teeth. She jumped into bed as quickly as possible. At her age her face needed all the sleep it could get. It showed the signs of tiredness too easily. She lay in bed and willed herself to sleep but it wouldn't come. She kept thinking that she looked like a fool. People picked up on her desire, her thirst for contact. Thad had made a joke of it. She needed to rein herself in.

The next morning she rolled out of bed at 6 A.M., grabbed a cold compress and laid back down for another half hour. This time when she got up she looked refreshed. She felt much better about the day.

She scrubbed her body, gave herself a glycolic peel and did her makeup as if she were going out to lunch with the ladies. She chose clothes that complimented her curves the best, a wrap dress in a vibrant red pattern. She looked like a retired model. At promptly 10 A.M., Agent # 1432 rang the bell. Vivian had Olga show him into the living room where she had a coffee and tea service ready.

Agent #1432 was shorter than Vivian by an inch. He had a full head of white and very black hair, pronounced age spots littered his face and a paunch pulled at the bottom button of his shirt. He was at least in his late fifties. He had the fragile stance of a man who never had children—a man who never had to brace himself from the daily onslaught of jumping little bodies. He greeted Vivian solicitously, gladly accepted a cup of coffee and popover and proposed they get down to business. It was like the letters they had written all summer didn't exist. He was doing his best to put a completely professional front on.

"Before we do that, tell me, why audit me now? Why did you decide to pick on me?" Vivian asked in a friendly voice.

"Mrs. Osterhaut, when an estate the size of the one you inherited gets passed down it always gets special attention. There aren't many of them in this country. You're part of the top one percent," Agent #1432 said.

"Well, Agent . . .?"

"Please call me Fred," he said.

"Fred, this is bringing up all sorts of unpleasant memories. And I thought we were handling it all so well through the mail," Vivian said, and noticed Fred blushing.

"I understand. I'll be as brief as possible. Unfortunately your late husband chose some rather inventive tax shelters. I thought the process would go easier if we did this face-to-face," Fred said as he began poring through the documents Vivian had organized on a roller cart and avoided her gaze.

"Tax shelters, I thought he had one, maybe two," Vivian lied as she grabbed her cup of coffee and added an emergency shot of Baileys Irish Cream, which was decoratively poured into a china creamer.

"No, he had quite a few," Fred said sadly. "One of the documents you sent me lists six other questionable investment vehicles. That's why I thought we should meet in person. I'm sorry, I thought you knew what you were sending me."

"That must've been one of the very first documents I sent you. I wasn't paying much attention at that point. Son of a bitch. We paid advisors to save him from himself and he screwed it up anyway," Vivian said.

Fred shifted uncomfortably on the couch. She could see he had encountered plenty of emotional people during audits and tried to make himself as invisible as possible when they exploded. She cringed at how she must seem to him, the greedy wife grateful her imbecile husband had finally died.

"I'm sorry. I didn't mean to take that out on you. You're here to do your job and I intend to help you. I've cleared my calendar for the next couple of weeks. I'll be here for whatever questions you have," Vivian said and smiled.

Fred nodded in acknowledgment. She watched as he gently pulled out the first file and started flipping through it. He had the hands of a horticulturist. He took care not to disturb the order of the papers. He read with interest. She felt strangely honored that he was being so meticulous. She excused herself and said she'd be in her study. Olga could let her know if he needed her.

When she got to her study she immediately started poring over the rest of the documents. At the same time, she called Thad and told him what the IRS agent had told her.

"Why didn't you catch the document with the list of six questionable tax shelters? It would've been nice to have been informed about it," Vivian said to Thad.

"I don't know. I must have accidentally sent him the overview of 1992. It was a very busy year," Thad sputtered.

"You didn't look at the documents before you sent them?" Vivian asked.

"Of course. But I was distracted a couple times. Ansley . . . " Thad trailed off.

"My granddaughter distracted you?" Vivian asked with a playful undertone. She was amused that Ansley had managed to throw such a dyed-in-the-wool old-school Yankee off his game.

"She can be irritating. Excuse me," Thad burst out.

Vivian smiled wide. Not only had Ansley gotten to Thad, she had exasperated him. She had never seen this young man flummoxed. He normally projected the Zen-like calm of a person whose family hadn't had anything to prove for generations. Well, if she couldn't make him fall in love with her, at least Ansley could irritate him to distraction.

"How much money is in those shelters?" Vivian asked.

"I don't know offhand," Thad said as he shuffled papers. "Here, I have a copy of the overview. In 1992 Mr. Osterhaut invested 2.6 million in questionable vehicles."

"Great," Vivian said, sounding like she meant anything but. "We need to go through the rest of the documents quickly and come up with a settlement offer. I'll have Ansley drop off any documents you don't have. I don't think it would be good for you to come to the house while Fred, I mean Agent #1432, is here," Vivian said.

"Okay." Thad paused. "Are you sure you need to send Ansley? A messenger would do."

"Ansley is more trustworthy than a messenger," Vivian insisted. "Comb your files and let's see what we can come up with."

As she said that she heard a knock on her study door. Fred, the IRS agent, opened the door shyly. "Hi, I wanted to go over your color-coding system to make sure I understand it properly."

"It's self-explanatory, isn't it?" Vivian asked somewhat haughtily. She was still a little put off that he had been so cold when they first met earlier this morning.

"It's remarkable. Advanced, logical, may even be above my pay grade," Fred said humbly.

His comments relaxed Vivian. Nothing like a man who appreciates sincere effort and organization. She got up, walked toward Fred, slipped her arm through his and walked back down into the living room with him. She spent the next two hours explaining her system and what sort of documents he'd find on the cart.

"You can see I'm trying to be as helpful as possible," Vivian said toward the end of her tutorial. "I'm very concerned about the tax shelters you alerted me to. My husband was a very wealthy man but finances weren't his field of expertise. We had many financial advisors to help him and it appears he didn't pay attention to their advice."

"Most people leave me a couple of boxes of document mishmash and throw me out in the cold," Fred said. "They hope that'll make me give up."

"But it only makes you try harder," Vivian guessed.

"Yep, I'm tenacious when people are rude," Fred said.

"If we've done something wrong, I'll pay the fine. I want to move on. That's the most important thing," Vivian said, then asked Olga to set up lunch for two in the dining room.

"Oh, you shouldn't," Fred tried to demur.

"Nonsense, we can talk about the case and eat. My cook bought vegetables from the farmer's market this morning. They'll go to waste if you don't help eat them," Vivian said as she led the way to lunch. For some reason, she didn't want her interaction with Fred to end. He wasn't attractive like Charlie or Asher, but she felt an electrical current running between them. Maybe it was their shared enthusiasm for gardening, doing the right thing and documentation. Whatever it was she hadn't felt it in decades.

Stop thinking about it, Vivian thought as for the third time during lunch she imagined kissing Fred.

• *The Devil Made Me Do It and I Liked It* •

½ cup plus 2 tablespoons (or 1¼ sticks) unsalted butter, room temperature

3 eggs, room temperature

½ cup buttermilk

1½ cups granulated sugar

1 teaspoon vanilla extract

½ cup strong, hot coffee

1¼ cups cake flour

½ cup Dutch-processed unsweetened cocoa powder

1 teaspoon baking soda

¼ teaspoon baking powder
½ teaspoon finely ground salt, either sea or iodized

To Make the Cupcakes:
1. Preheat oven to 325° F. Place 12 paper liners in cupcake trays.
2. Cream butter and sugar together in an electric mixer until fluffy, about 3 to 5 minutes.
3. Add the eggs and beat another 2 minutes.
4. Whisk flour, cocoa, baking soda, baking powder and salt together.
5. Mix the buttermilk and vanilla together.
6. Beat in a third of the flour mixture.
7. Beat in the buttermilk mixture.
8. Add a third of the flour mixture.
9. Add the coffee.
10. Add the rest of the flour and mix until combined.
11. Pour the batter into the paper liners. Fill the tins halfway.
12. Bake 15 minutes, or until a toothpick inserted in the middle comes out clean.
13. Cool for 5 minutes and then place on baking racks.

Yield: 12 cupcakes

Peanut Butter Buttercream Filling

½ cup (or 1 stick) unsalted butter, room temperature
1 cup creamy peanut butter
1¼ cups sifted powdered sugar

To Make the Peanut Butter Buttercream Filling:
1. Cream the butter and peanut butter together until smooth.
2. Add powdered sugar and beat until smooth and fluffy, about 3 to 5 minutes.
3. Fit a pastry bag with a medium plain tip.
4. Fill the pastry bag with the filling.
5. Insert the tip into each cupcake and squeeze about 3 tablespoons of filling into each cupcake.

Ganache

4 ounces semi-sweet chocolate, coarsely chopped
½ cup heavy cream
1 cup roasted peanuts, chopped

To Make the Ganache:
1. Place chocolate in a medium bowl.
2. Bring the cream to a scald in a small saucepan.
3. Pour cream over chocolate and let sit 1 minute, then whisk until smooth.
4. Let sit for 10 minutes, until thick but still pourable.
5. Dunk the top half of the cupcakes into the frosting to coat, then place on a rack.
6. Sprinkle with the chopped peanuts.

Chapter 18

Ansley wasn't sure if she was awake or asleep. For the past week she had averaged four hours of sleep a night. The IRS agent showing up had put their document-sifting efforts into overdrive and what little time she had left she had to commit to the bakery. The opening date was fast approaching. For days, she desperately wanted to return to her grandmother's diary but whenever she walked into her bedroom all she could do was collapse on her bed and sleep. Reading wasn't even an option.

On Thursday night she was determined to find out what happened next to her grandmother way back in 1964. At midnight, when she was done helping her grandmother she took a nap, woke up around 3 A.M. and immediately reached for the diary under her mattress. She turned on the lamp on her bedside table and flipped to the entry she'd had her finger on when Dot called.

"I'm sick. I'm twenty-four years old and a mother and it's time to grow up. I will be better as a wife and mother. I will cook all meals with God's love in my heart. I will look forward to bridge. I will appreciate all my life has to offer."

Ansley flipped the page to the next day. Vivian talked about the perfect pound cake, which in her opinion should be baked in a round pan not a loaf pan as the cake tends to collapse rather than crown in a loaf pan. She also recommended harshly tapping, even dropping the pan, before putting it in the oven, to eliminate bubbles.

For days the diary recorded regular daily life. There were a couple days that Vivian wasn't feeling well and that's when she started to make the French toast casserole, the rouladen, the potato salad, enchiladas and the twelve-layer cake. She thought she had the flu, though it felt more like a perpetual hangover, "But I'm not drinking a drop. I can't touch the stuff right now," Vivian wrote. But somehow she forced herself out of bed and back into the kitchen for tea party preparations.

Ansley didn't realize she had fallen asleep. She thought she was still reading but when she looked at the clock it said 5 A.M. Two hours had passed and she had read two pages. She shoved the diary back under her mattress, threw on a dirty pink tracksuit and headed for the bakery. There was a lot of work to do and she was way behind. She'd have to read more of the diary after she put in a full day of cupcake making. That is, if her grandmother didn't grab her for document duty first. She had been forced to tell her grandmother she had a job (how else could she explain her long absences when her grandmother needed her most) but she refused to tell Vivian what it was. "I want to make sure it will work out, and if it does, then I'll surprise you with it. You'll really like it."

"Can't you start it in a couple weeks?" Vivian begged.

"No, they really need me now," Ansley said firmly.

"So do I," Vivian said.

"Don't worry. I'm going to work around the clock. I won't disappoint you," Ansley promised, and she hadn't. So far she had managed to do everything that needed to be done for the bakery and her grandmother.

As soon as Ansley walked into the bakery's kitchen she set up the ingredients for making the Thad-inspired cupcakes on a grand scale. If she could replicate it she knew it would be a big seller, because the lemon curd on top instead of frosting made it look lowfat.

As she weighed ingredients, her eyelids were so heavy they kept closing. She was constantly jolting herself awake.

This is not good, Ansley thought as she finally scooped cupcake batter into the extra-large cupcake tin.

Ansley imagined getting her hand caught in the mixer or accidentally laying her face against a hot, open oven door. She felt certain she was well on her way to permanently maiming herself.

The opening of the bakery was one day away. The health inspector gave her the seal of approval a couple weeks ago but was coming back to make sure the bakery was good. She had two more recipes to test and perfect. Oh, yeah, and she needed to bake and frost at least a thousand cupcakes.

She had ordered a specialty French butter from the Poitou-Charente region. It was sweet and creamy and had the faintest taste of barley. It would set her cupcakes apart from all the other homey cupcakeries. Her cupcakes would be more delicate. She didn't want to waste an ounce of the shortening so she decided to bake everything as close to the opening as she could. A bakery secret—cakes and cupcakes will last at least two weeks in the refrigerator without a noticeable change in their texture or moisture. It's all that sugar acting as a preservative.

Ansley didn't feel right about selling week-old or two-week-old cupcakes, but she was okay with selling two-day-old ones so she was building up her store and banking them in the walk-in fridge.

She was pulling the third batch out of the oven when Larissa and Rachel arrived. She let them take over the baking and she began creating the frosting. She had been thinking whimsical and bright for the first day. She wanted people to walk by the window and see a burst of color that would draw them in. She started mixing pomegranate and beet juice into several different bowls of frosting in varying amounts. She had two more hours before she had to head back to Vivian's house. There was a lot to accomplish. She had more than four dozen eggs to crack and separate by hand for the frosting.

"Ah, Larissa, maybe y'all could help me crack and separate these eggs. I need the yolks for the frosting," Ansley said with a hint of panic in her voice.

"Going the French buttercream route? Daring," Larissa said as she stood beside Ansley and effortlessly cracked eggs with one hand. Ansley used two hands and was twice as slow.

"I need to distinguish myself. This isn't a down-home bakery or cupcakery. We're bringing cupcakes to a whole other level," Ansley said, "Cupcakes can be an art form." Ansley went over to the stove top to boil sugar and corn syrup for the frosting. She prayed the sugar didn't clump together when she poured it into the egg yolks.

The day the bakery opened Ansley planned to leave a note for Vivian in the kitchen, next to the coffeemaker. It would list the address of the bakery and instructions that Vivian be there promptly that morning at 11 A.M. She was sure Vivian would be confused and slightly annoyed by the request, but when she arrived Ansley knew it would be worth it. Her grandmother would be blown away. She'd finally be impressed by something Ansley had done.

For the day of the opening Ansley hired a host of college students and moms to hand out free mini-cupcakes at local subway stops, private schools during the drop-off period and gyms. By 10 A.M., if all went right, the bakery would have a line out the door.

Ansley finished the buttercream and poured equal amounts into bowls with varying hues of red dye in them. She whipped them together, frosted a couple cupcakes in such a way that the frosting looked like petals of a flower. She showed Larissa how to do it and left her to frost another two hundred.

At 10:30 A.M. Ansley jogged over to her grandmother's house. On the first day of Agent #1432's siege on Vivian's finances, Ansley thought her grandmother would be nervous and defensive. She assumed she would detect thinly veiled hatred emanating off of her toward the IRS agent. None of that had happened.

Vivian seemed happy during the whole week Agent #1432 had been there. She almost stumbled over herself to show Agent #1432 a new piece of Charlie's illegal activity when they found it. On two occasions Ansley put her hand on her grandmother's arm to stop her from rushing off.

"Shouldn't we study this first?" Ansley asked.

"I trust Fred," Vivian said, and sped off.

Thad, who convinced Vivian that it would be fine for him to show his face while the agent was there, and Ansley looked at each other with disbelief.

"Is this smart?" Ansley asked.

"I defer to her," Thad said.

Since the dinner with Dot, Thad had become very distracted. He was only putting in time, counting the minutes until he could legitimately leave and go rendezvous with Dot. It hurt Ansley seeing Thad happy with another woman. It's not that she liked him, but she would've appreciated it if he enjoyed even slightly being kissed by her.

"All this love and nowhere for it to go," Ansley thought.

"I'm done for the day," Thad said abruptly, and got up a little before five.

"Meeting Dot?"

"Yes, we're going to my parents' house," he said.

"Let me ask you something, you knew Dot, or at least who Dot was, for years. Two nights ago you slept with her and now it's like she's the love of your life. Is sleeping with a girl that important? Can it change how you feel about a person so profoundly?" Ansley asked more curious than challenging.

"Jesus, first you kiss me without permission and then you ask me questions like that. Where are your manners?" Thad said, and walked out.

Ansley was alone in Vivian's office, surrounded by the stacks of paper. Vivian was downstairs talking with Agent #1432. Instead of doing hours of mindless paperwork the day before her bakery opened, Ansley decided for once she would get some sleep and hiked up to her bedroom. If Vivian missed her, she'd be able to figure out pretty quickly where Ansley had gone.

Ansley laid down on her bed and closed her eyes. She should've fallen straight to sleep but the recipes her grandmother had written right before she left Dallas kept circling in Ansley's brain. She pulled the diary out from under her mattress and opened it to where she'd left off.

Vivian was still sick and perfume irritated her. She had to ask her mother to wash hers off. That's when her mother suggested she might be pregnant.

"I told her it was ridiculous. I would know if I was pregnant and I didn't feel pregnant. I felt disgusting."

It was true the foods Vivian put into the book were the ultimate foods to eat when you didn't feel good. When would a person need comfort food? When she was nauseous from pregnancy. Her grandmother had to have been pregnant. But there was no baby. Maybe she was . . . What? What happened to the baby?

The more Ansley thought about it, the more she was sure that Vivian had been pregnant when she left Dallas.

Ansley flipped through the next few days in the diary. There was no more mention of pregnancy. There was another visit from Charlie, though.

Vivian wrote, "That man from New York visited again and in the most preposterous car this time. He wants me to change my life and made a persuasive argument for it. I don't want to do it. But I don't think I have a choice."

The next few pages were filled with details about Hattie— what she looked like, what her favorite color, toy, story, song and shoes were.

Then there was a blank page. Next to it, written in black

marker, were only the words "New York." So Vivian left Texas because she was in love with Charlie—but she was pregnant with Asher's baby, so she had an abortion to make her life easier? That's the only way Ansley could logically conclude things happened, because there was no baby then and no adult half sibling of her mother's hanging around now. But what if the baby was Charlie's? Ansley was too tired to wrap her head around it all.

She needed to clear her mind. She took a deep breath and started to calculate how to turn a Sachertorte into a cupcake. Making up new recipes always calmed her.

The Sachertorte was an especially tantalizing recipe to adapt to cupcakes. It is one of the most famous cakes in the world of pastry fanatics, in part because of its magnificent story. In 1832 an Austrian prince ordered his chefs to create a new dessert that night that would impress his wealthy friends. But the top chef was ill in bed. The kitchen was in a panic. They had no direction, no creative force to drive them. Then finally a sixteen-year-old apprentice named Franz Sacher came up with the idea of creating a cake with crushed nuts instead of flour, making it moister than most cakes. The more fat in a cake the better it is—like all foods.

Ansley was carefully calibrating how much flour she would replace with ground pecans in her basic cupcake recipe when she fell soundly asleep.

• Sachertorte, or the Most Perfect Flourless Chocolate Cupcake Ever •

10 ounces good imported bittersweet chocolate, broken into pieces

½ cup (or 1 stick) unsalted butter, at room temperature

½ cup granulated sugar, divided, plus more for sprinkling

5 eggs, separated

⅓ cup finely ground pecans (done in a food processor)

To Make the Cupcakes:

1. Preheat oven to 300° F. Place 6 paper liners into cupcake tray.
2. Melt the chocolate in a double boiler over simmering water.
3. If you don't have a double boiler, place all the ingredients in a temperature-safe bowl. Place the bowl in a saucepan with 2 inches of simmering water in the bottom.
4. When the chocolate is melted, turn off the heat and leave it over the hot water to cool.
5. Beat butter and ¼ cup of sugar with an electric mixer until fluffy, about 3 to 5 minutes.
6. Add egg yolks and beat for 2 minutes.
7. Add pecans and beat for 2 minutes.

8. In a separate bowl beat the egg whites until they are light and foamy while slowly adding ¼ cup of sugar. Beat for 5 minutes.

9. Fold the melted chocolate into the egg yolk mixture with a rubber spatula.

10. Fold a quarter of the chocolate mixture into the egg whites.

11. Slowly fold the egg whites back into the rest of the chocolate mixture.

12. Pour into paper liners. Fill almost to the top.

13. Bake 10 to 15 minutes, or until a toothpick comes out with a moist crumbly coating but not wet.

14. Cool for 5 minutes and then move to a baking rack.

15. Sprinkle with sugar.

Yield: 6 cupcakes

Chapter 19

Three A.M. arrived way too soon for Ansley. She pulled herself out of bed, left her note for Vivian and jogged over to the bakery.

Her hands were shaking when she opened the door. Today had the ability to make her life or break it . . . again. She had never run a business before. She had put all her life savings into this venture. She had nothing else to cling to if the bakery wasn't successful.

"God, I hope this works," Ansley said as she weighed the sugar for coconut cupcakes.

Larissa and Rachel arrived shortly after Ansley did. They immediately started putting the cupcakes from the fridge onto the bookshelves at the front of the store. Ansley had to get over her prejudice about using "old" cupcakes. There were several reasons to do it. Cake actually tastes better after it has set for a day. The flavors marry. The icing also needs time to cool and harden.

Larrisa and Rachel arranged the cupcakes according to frosting, as Ansley instructed. The darkest red was in the center. Each successive layer, wrapping around a circle, was lighter by a shade. When they were done, the wall looked like a rose was blooming on it.

"Oh, girls, you did me proud," Ansley said as she walked into the front room from the kitchen.

"It's magnificent," they said in unison.

Ansley stood at the counter preparing the tiny cupcakes for the students and moms to hand out at schools and subway stations. They trickled in and took their trays.

The girls straightened the leather club chairs that were scattered around the room, making it look more like a posh library than a bakery.

From 8 A.M. to 9 A.M. was pure torture for Ansley. At first there were no customers. She sat, stood, busied herself with cleaning imaginary lint off of window glass. *This might not work*, Ansley thought. *Maybe the store doesn't look attractive enough. Are the moms and students handing out the cupcakes? Did people taste them and think they sucked?*

Ansley started to think all her assumptions were wrong— people didn't like cupcakes and they didn't want to go to a bakery that looked like a library. She had to make herself take deep breaths to calm down.

Finally people started to trickle in. The first customer was a banker. Obviously a banker, because he was properly dressed in a navy pin-striped suit and tie. As soon as he walked in, Ansley waved and yelled, "Hello." The exuberance of her greeting startled him. He turned slightly, like he was considering walking back out.

"Coffee?" Ansley called. "On the house."

She knew free coffee would lure him in, and sure enough he took a couple steps toward her and nodded yes to the coffee as he examined the cupcakes.

"It's our first day. You're our first customer. I'm a little nervous," Ansley prattled on.

"I got that," the man said, and smiled slightly. He was in his mid-thirties, with close-cropped hair and a reserved manner. He didn't seem like a cupcake lover, but you never knew who was going to be. Cupcakes evoke so many childhood memories that even if you aren't a person who craves sweets as an adult, you'll still crave cupcakes, because they'll remind you of a backyard birthday party or a bake sale purchase at elementary school right before you boarded your bus.

"I'll take that one," the man said, and pointed in the case to a chocolate cupcake with a pile of white icing covered in sprinkles and topped with a G.I. Joe figure.

"Good choice," Ansley said, and rang it up. She was about to put the cupcake in a box, but he stopped her.

"That won't be necessary," he said as he took the cupcake and coffee and walked out the door. He had it unwrapped and in his mouth before he walked past the bakery window.

Ansley smiled and let out a whoop. Then she turned to Larissa and Rachel. "I shouldn't wait on people. I'm gonna freak them out."

"Yeah, you're too intense right now," Larissa said.

"Let us handle it. You schmooze and hand out free coffee," Rachel said.

"There's no one to schmooze with," Ansley said, feeling incredibly anxious once again.

"There will be," Larissa assured her.

The next half hour was excruciating. Every few minutes a person would come in and buy one cupcake. There was never more than a single customer in the store. Ansley took it personally, like she wasn't cool enough to attract more people.

"You've been open for a half hour. Give it time," Larissa chided at Ansley as she complained.

By 10 there was a small line. But by 11 A.M. the line stretched out the door, Ansley was jumping with excitement. She was so happy, she started handing out free coffee in dainty mismatched china cups that she'd collected from thrift stores in small towns outside the city, instead of paper cups, because the china was more festive to people in line.

Ansley felt a tap on her back as she was handing out coffee outside the bakery. She turned around. There was Dot, with her hand intertwined with Thad's. The two of them glowed. They had gone from first date to full-blown couple in record time.

Ansley choked up. She had been hoping against hope that deep down Thad had some feelings for her. For the past couple of days he had been almost pleasant toward her as they sifted through her grandmother's papers. He even told her she looked nice one day. She felt minuscule movements on his part away from hating her and had told herself it was because he was realizing what a great woman she was. But that wasn't it at all. She was sure Dot had told him to be nice to her.

"Amazing opening," Dot said, and beamed at Ansley.

"Thanks. I'm glad it's working out," Ansley said, a little bashful.

"And the buttercream looks superb," Dot said.

"I ordered the butter directly from France so it would be a little sweeter," Ansley said as she surveyed the cupcakes.

"So this is why you were consistently late to meet me," Thad said as he scanned the bakery from the outside. Ansley had painted the window frames an azure blue that reminded her of her time in Paris and her favorite café in the Marais. She had also hung purple bougainvillea between the windows. It was a hot-weather flower that wouldn't survive the winter here, but she had to have it; it felt like home. "This is impressive," Thad said, and looked like he meant it.

"Didn't think I had it in me, did you?" Ansley asked.

"No," he said honestly, and squeezed Dot's hand. "Dot told me she was helping you but I didn't think . . . well, I didn't think you'd be this organized, not like Dot is. It's going to do very well. "

Ansley was absorbing the semblance of a compliment when she spied Vivian walking up. Vivian waved and smiled.

"So you got yourself a job," Vivian said as she took a cup of coffee.

"Yep," Ansley said, and checked out the line.

"It's a smart move. Start at the bottom and learn the business," Vivian said as she dodged people who were joining the line.

"Start from the bottom? No, I own this," Ansley said.

"What?"

"Yes, three-year lease, thirty original cupcake recipes. I even have employees," Ansley said as she greeted more people.

Vivian's face registered shock. Her eyes were open wide, as was her mouth. She looked at Thad and seemed to ask if he knew anything about this. Vivian waved good-bye to them and stepped to the back of the line.

"What are you doing?" Ansley asked as she followed her.

"I'm going to get the whole experience," Vivian said, and smiled broadly at her granddaughter.

"You didn't think I could do this, did you?" Ansley asked.

"No," Vivian said truthfully, and looked relieved to be wrong.

Ansley walked back into the bakery and wondered if her mother was the only person in the world who had faith in her abilities.

It took Vivian twenty minutes to get inside the bakery but she gasped with joy when she did. The shelves, which looked like they belonged in one of the old mansions nearby, were filled with cupcakes. The display cases contained a rainbow of colors and toppings. On one shelf each cupcake had a different face made of candy on it. If you looked from left to right you could see the faces were in the act of winking at you, every cupcake like a different panel in a comic book. On another shelf, G.I. Joe figures on top of the cupcakes looked like they were doing battle with each other. Customers were pointing and clamoring for their choices.

Vivian wedged herself inside and sat down at one of the only chairs available, right near the door. She watched Ansley as she worked the people in line, offering them free coffee and talking to them like they were neighbors. Inside the confines of the bakery the Southern charm worked on strangers. The people smiled and started to chat amongst themselves. The two girls Ansley had running the counter also seemed very good. They were young and bubbly, enthusiastic to the point that even a cranky customer had to smile. They were efficient and talked up each cupcake with a zeal that only a true food lover could muster.

"I'm not gonna sell it to you until you sample it. You can only buy it if you love it. But don't worry, you will," Larissa said, sounding like a circus ringmaster and looking like a cross between a fresh-scrubbed farm girl, with her freckles and rosy cheeks, and a girl who'd sell drugs on the corner, with jeans that could also serve as sausage casings, oversized gold-plated hoop earrings and liquid eyeliner.

"He doesn't love it enough. Yeah, well, show me the love. You have to shout it," Rachel coaxed the man into shouting the praises of the fried Snickers cupcake. Rachel had a very similar look as Larissa. She had the innocent fresh-scrubbed face thing and the tight clothing that Larissa had. But her tight clothing looked more preppy. It was like she accidentally put on her much smaller sister's outfit for the day. Her top was a striped pullover and her jeans were dark blue. Nothing but the size was particularly glaringly wrong.

Even with the girls' quirks they worked well in the bakery. Most people would've hired an Upper East Side skinnier-than-thou girl who instantly judged everyone who bought a cupcake. Sure, the Upper East Sider would be coming from the same zip code and already have imbedded in her the appropriate ways to act, but she wouldn't have loved the food like these girls did. They made you want to come back again and again. They were putting on a show at the front counter like the fishmongers at Pike Place Market did in Seattle.

"All right, what cupcake would you like to declare your love for?" Larissa coaxed the next customer, a buttoned-up white-shoe law firm type of woman. Her clothes telegraphed she wasn't to be trifled with but she smiled and laughed at Larissa. She pointed to the red velvet cupcake.

"You know, this isn't your typical red velvet, don't you? We've amped it up and added super-food to it. Pomegranate— yep, in that fruit some of the highest antioxidants you can find," Rachel said as she handed the woman a sample.

"That's amazing," the woman said loudly, obviously hoping the girls wouldn't make her shout for her baked good.

"You said that with such soul I won't make you shout this time," Larissa said playfully. This girl was possibly the best salesperson Vivian had ever seen.

Vivian was flabbergasted. She didn't think Ansley had it in her to put all this together. And where had she gotten the money? Her granddaughter obviously had a good business head on her shoulders. Ansley saw her and walked over excitedly.

"What do you think?" she asked, glowing from the high she had gotten from dealing with her customers.

"You really got yourself a job," Vivian deadpanned.

"We just opened today and if things keep going like this I'll be turning a profit within a few months," Ansley said with obvious pride.

"Including the initial amount you invested into redecorating the bakery?" Vivian asked.

"Yes. I put a lot of sweat equity into this. I predict we'll franchise by the end of the first year of business if we want to," Ansley said with confidence.

"You've made me—and I'm sure your mother—really proud," Vivian said, and smiled at Ansley. "Now, what can I do. What do you need?" she asked as she headed toward the kitchen.

Ansley followed. Vivian surveyed the mess of a bakery that has exceeded its expectations. Dirty bowls were stacked in the sink. A frosting spill on the counter had been triaged with a wet rag. Vivian rolled up the sleeves of her white silk and linen shirt and started on the dishes.

"You don't have to do that," Ansley said as she tried to wave Vivian off. Vivian just dived her hands into the dirty bowls.

"I want to do it. I've always liked to work, and if I can help you, I'm more than happy. Go tend to your customers. You have a great way with them," Vivian said, and shooed Ansley back out front.

Vivian put on an apron that said "Gino's Trattoria" and reached for a green scrub pad. She started scouring pans and bowls by hand like she did when she was a little girl. She was determined to get every bit of baked-on browned butter and batter off of the pans. Vivian was a bit obsessive when she was motivated. She could tell Ansley was too. The handiwork on the cupcake frosting was so intricate and precise, she knew it could only be the work of her granddaughter. It was in her genes. Growing up, Vivian had spent countless hours doing elaborate needlepoint for her mother for Christmas presents. The needlework was so fine her friends had to use a magnifying glass to examine it all. She wondered if Hattie used the tablecloth Vivian had stitched, or if she got rid of it because her mother had made it.

Vivian did the dishes and scrubbed the kitchen for hours. She was so happy her granddaughter had shown real strength. She had an iron will, just like Vivian. You have to be able to push past all the naysayers and do what only you think is right.

Vivian wished the other things in her life were running so

smoothly. Fred—Agent #1432—was proving to be a confusing challenge. They'd eaten lunch together for the past few days and they talked like they had been friends for years. As soon as lunch was over he reverted to a professional demeanor, which was so closed off from the person he showed himself to be in her dining room.

Last night she insisted they go out. She said it was her duty to show him New York since he had never been before. She took him to Babbo and they got the tasting menu with the wine accompaniment. They caught some late-night music and then he walked her home, since the club was only a few blocks from her house. After she opened her front door they kissed. It was a light kiss on the lips. It could easily be passed off as a cheek kiss that missed but neither one of them tried to call it that. She moved toward him—specifically, she moved her mouth toward him and his pressed into hers. Then he walked away. Almost every second she was awake she dissected the moment again and again.

The kitchen sparkled now. Vivian poked her head into the bakery. It was two P.M. and the place was as packed as it was this morning. Hearing the cash register ring with each purchase made Vivian swell with pride. Her granddaughter had the talent to create her own way in the world. That's no small thing. Vivian knew how hard it was to begin from scratch.

When Ansley looked her way, Vivian beckoned her over, then closed the kitchen door. Ansley walked in and was speechless. She looked at the gleaming kitchen and at Vivian's clothes, which were streaked with black grease marks and bleach stains. Ansley hugged her hard. Vivian hugged Ansley back and breathed in the aroma of confectionery sugar and ginger.

"Thank you so much," Ansley cried. "This kitchen has never looked so good."

"Darling, I'm so proud. Now I have to go prepare for an afternoon with Fred. I rescheduled when I was in line this morning," Vivian said as she took off the Gino's Trattoria apron.

"How's it going?" Ansley asked as she took the cloth from Vivian and hung it up next to the Saul's Bagels aprons. Ansley had inherited aprons from the businesses that used to inhabit the place and she saw no reason not to use them.

"I don't know, but I don't think it's bad," Vivian said.

"No, I would say going out to dinner with your IRS agent isn't bad at all," Ansley said.

"That's what I think. Glad to know my instincts are still working," Vivian said.

• *Everyone Likes a Cream Cheese Filling* •

1 cup (or 2 sticks) unsalted butter, room temperature
1 cup brown sugar
3 eggs, room temperature
½ cup buttermilk
1 teaspoon vanilla

4 ounces semi-sweet chocolate, chopped
¼ cup Dutch-processed cocoa powder
1¼ cups water
¾ cup all-purpose flour
¾ cup cake flour
1 teaspoon baking soda
¼ teaspoon finely ground salt, either sea or iodized

To Make the Cupcakes:

1. Preheat oven to 350° F. Place 14 paper liners into cupcake trays.
2. Cream butter and brown sugar together with an electric mixer until fluffy, about 3 to 5 minutes.
3. Add eggs and beat another 2 minutes.
4. Add buttermilk and vanilla.
5. Boil water and mix with chocolate.
6. Sift flour, cocoa powder, baking soda and salt into bowl.
7. Alternate mixing into the batter the flour mixture and the chocolate mixture. Start and end with the flour mixture.
8. Pour the batter into the paper liners. Fill two-thirds of the way to the top.
9. Drop the filling into the center of each cupcake. You will see part of it peek out of the top.
10. Bake for 20 minutes, or until a toothpick inserted into the middle of a cupcake comes out clean.
11. Let cool for 5 minutes and then move the cupcakes to a baking rack.

Yield: 14 cupcakes

Filling

4 ounces cream cheese
4 ounces peanut butter

To Make the Filling:
1. Beat the cream cheese and peanut butter together with an electric mixer until fluffy, about 3 to 5 minutes.

Chapter 20

Thoughts of the almost-kiss were driving Vivian crazy. She had never doubted her sexuality. Charlie had been attracted to her until the day he died. She took care putting herself together so she always felt the confidence and luxury of elegant things touching her body.

But Fred, Agent #1432, was vexing. An IRS agent, a lowly civil servant, had her mind spinning with uncertainty. Was he attracted to her? That sort of kiss meant something, she thought, then hesitated. Maybe it meant that he accidentally went too far and was backing away. Or it could mean he was attracted to her. It was so hard to tell.

At the beginning of the audit, Vivian felt about eighty percent certain that Fred was indeed attracted to her and had decided to audit the Osterhaut finances to be closer to her. But as the days wore on, the small doubt that he wanted her expanded to a gulch of insecurity. She was at least ten years his elder. Maybe she had imagined the attraction. Maybe she really was a silly old woman. That was one of the most embarrassing things of all. To think you were still swimming in the same race but really you were ready for retirement. The fear of seeming like a silly old woman made Vivian decide that under absolutely no circumstance would she come remotely close to what could be construed as a come-on to Fred, especially after the kiss. As soon as she arrived at her house from helping Ansley, the situation began to drive her normally very organized thought processes crazy.

Vivian customarily sat with Fred while he went through her records, in case he had questions. He usually had several. Thad was safely tucked away in her upstairs study going through the rest of the paperwork they hadn't had time to look at before the IRS came.

Vivian sat on the couch in the living room. Fred sat in an armchair across from her. She busied herself with correspondence and keeping her social calendar current. When she looked up she could see Fred's arm muscles tense and flex as he rolled up his sleeves, which he did right before he dug into the first stack of papers. She loved to watch his mouth twist and pucker as he examined a document. It was the physical manifestation of thought for him. She wished she could reach out and touch his lips, trace them with her fingers—or better yet, kiss them. But she couldn't. What if she leaned over, placed her lips on his and he recoiled? She cringed over the imagined look of disgust that might paper his face.

Almost as bad as not knowing whether Fred was attracted to her were the increasingly alarming discoveries they were making. Charlie had funneled at least ten million out of the estate and into horrible investments, like llama farms and Chinese manufacturing plants with sketchy reputations. He even put several hundred thousand into a company that built equipment that detected odors in rooms. Vivian and Fred discovered it that afternoon.

"The equipment doesn't get rid of the odors?" Vivian asked Fred as they were looking over the documentation.

"No, it only detects them," he said.

"Does it tell you what the odor is?"

"No."

"How bad the odor is on a scale of one to ten?"

"No. It flashes a red light when something stinks," Fred said.

"How about where it is in the room? It has to tell you where the odor is coming from," Vivian said.

"No."

"That is the stupidest company I've ever heard of," Vivian said, and laughed.

"Oh, I don't know. Charlie, I mean Mr. Osterhaut, seemed to have a gift for finding these things," Fred said. "The odor detector lets you know for sure, without doubt, when something stinks," he read off a piece of promotional material.

"It's based in Ohio. Do you want to bet the factory is someone's converted basement?" Vivian said as she scanned another piece of documentation. She had already been through all these papers the night before and she knew she was safe from finding any wrongdoing on their pages.

"Vivian," Fred said earnestly. She had insisted he use her first name. Vivian looked up from the documentation. Their mood had been light and jovial. It was the only way one could look at these ridiculous investments.

"Yes," Vivian said, assuming a similarly serious tone as Fred's voice.

"What happened between the two of you? I mean, it seems like he purposely did stupid things with his money so that his sole heir, you, would have to spend ungodly amounts of time to sort it out. Plus, you will probably have to forfeit a lot of this money, and, depending on your level of involvement, you might be brought up on tax evasion charges," Fred said.

Fred had finally figured out that Charlie wasn't an idiot. No, Charlie was mean. Vivian knew it almost the second the IRS contacted her. She knew this was Charlie jabbing her from the grave but she pretended that all the difficulties with the IRS were the result of her late husband's stupidity. There was no sense in everyone knowing such intimate details about her marriage.

"Try being married to someone who doesn't think you're good enough to have children with," Vivian said.

"He thought you weren't good enough? That's impossible," Fred said.

"I thought he wasn't, and I ensured there wouldn't be any accidents on that front," Vivian said, and stood up. It was time for a late lunch. She absolutely needed a glass of wine.

"Why didn't he divorce you?" Fred asked as he stood up and followed Vivian into the dining room.

"I suppose because he didn't know for a very long time," Vivian said.

"When did he find out?" Fred asked as he sat down across from Vivian at the dining table.

"In 1986, I think," Vivian said to Fred, and then turned to her maid. "Olga, please get me a pinot noir from the cellar. Something with a little spice. It'll go nicely with the coolness that's starting to creep into the air. Better make it two bottles."

"Oh, I'm not drinking," Fred said.

"It wasn't a question. You have to drink. We've both had a very tough day and it isn't even five o'clock yet," Vivian said, hoping with a little wine in him Fred might be ready for another kiss.

"Did he want children?" Fred asked.

"Badly," Vivian answered.

"I'm going to recommend they don't charge you with any criminal wrongdoing. You'll have to pay a fine," Fred said.

"That's ok. I'm happy to pay a fine. It's the least I can do to make up for Charlie's antics," Vivian said, and smiled.

"You can stop wooing me. You're in the clear," Fred said, clearly a little red around the cheeks.

"What? Do you think I've been nice to you to cut myself a good deal?" Vivian asked, confused by the turn in the conversation. She thought it was obvious, especially last night, that she was truly attracted to Fred. Now to her embarrassment, she believed it was a little too obvious.

"It's been pleasant. You're a charming person. It's not necessary," Fred said.

"Are you married?"

"Divorced."

"In a relationship?"

"Not currently."

"Gay?"

"No, I'm not sure where this is going," Fred said as he took a big gulp of wine.

"I'm honestly attracted to you," Vivian said, surprising herself and Fred with her candor.

"Really?"

"Yes. It would be very nice if you could say something other than really," Vivian said.

Fred delicately pushed away from the table and walked over to Vivian's chair. He took her hand and pulled her up to standing. Then he kissed her.

• *First Blush of Crush Cupcakes* •

6 tablespoons unsalted butter, room temperature

3 eggs, room temperature

¾ cup milk

1½ cups sugar

1 teaspoon pure vanilla extract

1¾ cups all-purpose flour

2 teaspoons baking powder

2 tablespoons potato starch

¼ teaspoon finely ground salt, either sea or iodized

To Make Cupcakes:

1. Preheat the oven to 350° F. Place 12 paper liners into cupcake trays.
2. Beat eggs and sugar together with an electric mixer until a pale yellow, about 3 to 5 minutes.
3. Whisk flour, potato starch, baking powder and salt together.

4. Add flour mixture to batter.

5. Microwave milk for 2 minutes.

6. Add milk to batter.

7. Microwave butter for 30 seconds or until melted.

8. Add butter and vanilla to batter.

9. Pour batter into paper liners. Fill three-quarters of the way to the top.

10. Bake 15 to 20 minutes, or until a toothpick inserted in the middle of cupcake comes out clean.

11. Cool for 5 minutes and then place on baking racks.

Yield: 12 cupcakes

Grenadine Frosting

1½ pounds cream cheese, room temperature

1 cup (or 2 sticks) unsalted butter, room temperature

2 cups powdered sugar

1 teaspoon vanilla extract

2 tablespoons grenadine

To Make the Frosting:

1. Cream cream cheese and butter with an electric mixer until fluffy, about 3 to 5 minutes.

2. Add the sugar and beat until smooth.

3. Add vanilla and grenadine and beat until a uniform pink.

4. Place a large star tip on a pastry bag.

5. Place the frosting in pastry bag and pipe onto cupcakes in circular pattern.

Chapter 21

When a business first opens, it's like a newborn infant. It takes constant tending. It's erratic. It brings you unbelievable highs followed by equally unbelievable lows.

It has the potential to become anything—a national chain, the root of a successful cookbook, a profitable boutique that is beloved in its neighborhood. It is a clean slate. Until someone screws with it.

As Ansley unlocked the bakery at 4 A.M. to start the day, she was confronted with several fliers plastering the door. They had pictures on them of children choking and they said in bold letters, "This bakery uses GMO (genetically modified organism), pesticide-laden ingredients." The Manhattan mothers would never stand for this. If they read these fliers they wouldn't dare walk into the bakery, even to use the bathroom. What were they doing here?

Ansley tore them down as quickly as she could, blindly ripping paper until crumpled masses were at her feet. She gathered up the mountain of paper, stuffed it into a garbage bag and immediately took it out to the dumpster in the alley. Her breath was heavy and irregular. She felt like she was caught and someone had once again branded her with a scarlet letter. The funny thing was, she'd worked hard to find upstate New York farmers who were organic and independent. She bought her eggs and butter from farms of less than fifty acres that used no pesticides. For her grand opening she even imported butter from small French farms. She had gone out of her way to be organic and environmentally friendly.

She tried to calm down. She went to the kitchen and started mixing batter. She began to reason with herself. One: Even if customers had seen the fliers it would only be a handful of them, since it was still so early in the morning. Two: She had torn down all of the evidence, so there was no problem, right? Unless the few people who saw the fliers talked about them to others. No, that wouldn't happen. The only people out at 4 A.M. were drunken club goers and serious type A runners. Neither group would be in the mood for reading fliers.

She calmed down a little. Her tugging at the huge Tupperware container of flour became less frantic. She maneuvered it out from under the stainless steel table and over to the mixing bowl with ease. As she got out the rest of the ingredients, the only nagging question was who could have done it. She hadn't been in New York long enough to build up that kind of hatred in someone. The only person who showed this level of dislike for her was the woman who destroyed her life in Dallas. She'd begun to suspect that Patty had played her for months before Parish broke their engagement. But why would Patty be after her now? Hadn't she gotten everything from Ansley that she wanted? And who had a connection to Patty and could do her bidding? Who was from the South?

In that instant it all clicked for Ansley—the Texas dip. Dot knew something. It was 5 A.M. Ansley called Dot's cell phone. She picked up.

"How do you know Patty?" Ansley asked.

"What?" Dot asked, groggy and confused.

"Don't even try it, Texas dip," Ansley warned, and the tone of her voice was a threat in itself.

"Where are you?" Dot asked.

"At the bakery, working for a living," Ansley said.

"I'll stop by this morning," Dot said, and hung up.

Ansley dialed Dot's number again and was about to press TALK but she stopped herself. It would be humiliating to call Dot and be screened. Ansley couldn't effectively yell at Dot's voice mail. She'd feel like a fool, like a stalker. No, Ansley needed to rein in her emotions and use her sharpest skills. Cut the feelings out and go for the kill—that was a number one unwritten rule of any successful society lady in Dallas.

Ansley had to prepare. She poured the flour into the industrial blender and turned it on. She watched the blades spin and imagined putting Patty's hand in it. Not nice, she scolded herself, and tried to again focus on the fliers.

Someone, either Patty or someone with a connection to her—possibly Dot—had plastered Ansley's bakery with false accusations. Why did they do it? Patty must not want Ansley to be happy in any way possible, personally or professionally, and Dot could be helping. Perhaps that's why Dot was now dating Thad. God, that was sick.

Ansley turned off the mixer and got out the ice cream

scoop. She started scooping batter into cupcake trays while thinking about Dot. The woman had been unfailingly kind to her from the moment they met. Dot had gone out of her way to help Ansley. She tracked down a pickup truck they could use for furniture shopping and woke up before dawn to sift through other people's garbage in search of club chairs and coffee tables. Who does that? Even in happier times in Dallas Ansley knew she'd have to call in serious favors to get her sorority sisters to do anything close to the things Dot had done without complaint. Ansley had taken this to mean that Dot was a true friend.

It made her nauseous to think that she may have been wrong again about everything.

"Am I that unlikeable?" Ansley asked out loud as Rachel walked into the kitchen carrying Windex and a roll of paper towels.

"I think you're as likeable as your cupcakes, which are very likeable," Rachel said. "Going through an 'I'm not worthy of this success' moment? I've read that most high-achieving people think they're frauds. Do you think you're a fraud?"

"No, I don't think I'm the problem. Someone put horrible fliers outside the bakery. They accused me of using pesticides," Ansley said, about to break down in tears.

"It's a competitor. You haven't been open a week yet and you're making people nervous," Rachel said as she finished placing cupcakes on a tray and took them out front.

Ansley followed Rachel into the public area of the bakery. She wiped down furniture and moved chairs and tables a few inches this way or that way. She wanted to make sure as soon as people walked through the door they felt like they were part of an exclusive club that was impeccably furnished.

"A bit OCD, don't you think?" Rachel said as she watched Ansley agonize over the correct position of a club chair that was near the glass display case and the giant old cash register. The cash register had been a true find. Ansley and Dot had driven more than an hour outside of the city to go junking and had found the cash register at a barn auction. It was tarnished brown and the keys were barely readable. Ansley bought it for $50. It took the two of them to carry it to the car. They spent the next two days polishing it with Brasso and toothpaste. It gleamed with a golden luster by the time they were done. You could see the intricate floral design on the sides of it clearly. It must have been from the twenties.

"I want everything to say 'This is exclusive and you belong here,'" Ansley said as she again considered all that Dot had done for her.

Until the bakery opened its doors Ansley busied herself with baking and cleaning. When the people started trickling in she served them coffee in her mismatched china and made conversation like she was back in Texas. She was already developing a reliable club of regulars. There was the slightly chubby and balding banker. He was obviously recently divorced and unaccustomed to foraging for his own food. Ansley started giving him a breakfast taco of scrambled eggs, cheese and a little hot sauce on the side to make sure he got some protein. There was a super-skinny mother who raced in as her car was idling at the curb and ordered a different cupcake to go every day. There was a high school girl who was almost six feet tall and had the body of a professional athlete. She'd order a cupcake and devour it in seconds.

Dot arrived at the bakery at 9 A.M. There was already a line of people popping out the door. Ansley was in full hostess mode, expounding on the different types of buttercreams and why they were generally superior to the basic cream cheese frosting or American buttercream (both were too sweet and better suited for children's birthday parties than adult life) but she quickly extricated herself and pulled Dot into the kitchen. Dot was wearing a trench coat and her hair was scraped up into a ponytail. Thad had kissed her good-bye out front and reluctantly walked away. It was clear they had spent every minute they could in bed together.

As soon as they walked into the kitchen Ansley headed over to a bowl of batter and started filling a two-hundred-cup tray. She had already scooped four hundred cupcakes this morning. Her wrist would ache later today.

"So what do you know about Texas?" Ansley asked, trying to sound casual.

"I know it's a state," Dot joked.

"No one knows how to do the Texas dip without having a connection," Ansley said as she continued to scoop.

"I moved from Texas, not Georgia. I don't know why I didn't tell you. Maybe I thought you'd judge me more. It was silly," Dot said.

"What about the fliers?"

"Fliers?" Dot sounded genuinely confused.

Ansley's instinct was to believe Dot. She wanted Dot to be her friend again. Ansley told her the whole story. She confided in Dot how she felt alone and hated and how scared she was that her business would fail and she would lose the $200,000 she'd committed to this venture.

"I don't understand who could be so mean," Ansley said.

"Wow," Dot said, and walked over to Ansley and wrapped her in a hug, "tough morning."

"Yeah," Ansley sniffled.

"We'll find out who did this," Dot assured her.

"How?"

"Why don't you install video cameras?" Dot said.

"I have no money to spare. I've already overspent," Ansley said.

"Sometimes you need to spend for your safety," Dot said.

"I can't handle this. I'm not cut out for it. I'm not an early riser. I don't like manual labor. I hate having a daily schedule. I don't like people being so out-and-out mean to me," Ansley said.

Dot smiled at her.

"What?" Ansley whined.

"Running a business is about a lot more than the fantasy. This isn't about making cupcakes when you feel like it and chatting with customers. It's about the bottom line," Dot said.

"I know. I calculated I have to sell 152 cupcakes a day to break even. Do you know how much I upsell now? I hate upselling. As soon as I hit that number each day I feel like I take my first breath and that's when I relax," Ansley said, relieved to be able to unload some of her anxiety.

Ansley sat down on one of the wooden chairs she had reclaimed from the streets. She put three in the kitchen so she and her employees could eat lunch together. Dot sat next to her.

"The stress of the business, my grandmother, being heartbroken is already too much. I can't handle someone actively screwing with me on top of all that," Ansley said.

"We'll get him," Dot said.

"You think it's a guy?"

"I don't know. Get the camera," Dot said, and got up to

leave. "I have my own business crisis that needs attention, sorry." She pulled Ansley up and gave her another hug.

Ansley made two hundred more vanilla cupcakes (they were the big seller) as quickly as she could, refilled the stock out front, took inventory, placed phone orders for deliveries of ingredients, did a few loads of dishes, resupplied the cash register with change and then ran back to Vivian's house. It was noon. Rachel and Larissa assured Ansley they could handle the bakery for the afternoon and told her to go help her grandmother. There was still so much to do. She hoped that jail wasn't on the agenda for Vivian.

Ansley raced up to Vivian's study in her sneakers. Thad was already there, fuming. As soon as Ansley walked into the room he looked at her with disgust.

"What?" Ansley asked as she checked out her appearance. It was a little slovenly. She was in Juicy Couture sweatpants, a T-shirt and sneakers. Her hair was in a ponytail. She hadn't showered yet today. Okay, she looked very messy but she'd been at the bakery since 4 A.M.

"Calling at 5 A.M.," Thad said.

"I needed to talk to her," Ansley said.

"Nothing is that important," Thad said.

Her bakery was that important. She was hurt he didn't recognize that and felt silly too. Maybe it was pathetic that she was so invested in her business. She could kiss him. She was that angry. She imagined how much he'd hate it, how much he'd squirm if she planted one on him right now. She took a step closer to him and was about to launch her lips at his but stopped. Thad was off-limits. Even if she was going to kiss him to make him mad, she couldn't. Dot would be hurt.

Instead she sat down and started going through documents.

"You know she was a wreck after you called," Thad said.

"Why?" Ansley asked.

"She was worried some psycho from Dallas was in New York," Thad said, and Ansley's heart plummeted into her stomach.

"Did she mention a name?" Ansley asked as coolly as she could manage.

"Patty," Thad said.

Ansley never told Dot Patty's name. The only way she would know it is if she knew Patty, and the only reason Patty would be in town was to cause Ansley pain, psychic and otherwise.

"Patty's nuts," Ansley said. It was a revelation. Patty had seemed so nice, overly nice, but that was all an act. The woman was calculating and evil to the core.

"Dot thinks so too," Thad said, and raised his eyebrows.

"So, she's in town?" Ansley asked.

"Yep, and she's after your business," Thad said as he tried to focus on the papers in his hand.

"So Patty is in New York gunning for my business?"

"Yep," Thad said.

"I have to go," Ansley said, jumped up and raced to the door.

"What are you doing? What about your grandmother?" Thad called.

"I have to warn my employees. Maybe install a better security system. I have to get over there," Ansley said as she hit the stairs. She tackled them quickly. She was outside jogging toward the bakery, running the few blocks at a fast clip. She'd get there in five minutes instead of the usual twenty.

Ansley rounded the corner to the bakery, slowed down and

crossed the street. From her view, everything at her business seemed to be running smoothly. There was a line winding outside the door. Nothing was taped to the windows.

As Ansley crossed the street relief spread across her chest. She smiled. But suddenly she felt an intense pressure on her thigh and—*wham!*

Shockingly, she noticed she was up in the air. And then everything went black. The Lincoln that gunned it's engine a few seconds before it hit Ansley was racing down the street, turning so quickly that no one caught the license plate. Everyone did hear the thump of Ansley's butt as it dropped onto the hood of the car, bounced onto the roof and then hit the pavement. Some caught the sight of Ansley's body floating in the air for a few seconds before it plummeted to the street. It looked like she was swimming. Her face registered surprise. It didn't look like she was in pain at all an eyewitness, who was also the flour deliveryman, said.

It was weird. Even though most of the people who saw the car hit Ansley had lived in New York City for decades, none of them had ever seen a hit-and-run. None of them had ever seen the spectacular image of a human being flying through the air with no strings attached.

You would think when a car hits you that you'd feel it. Ansley didn't. She was walking upright one moment and the next she was lying on the road. Her head was propped up on the curb like it was a pillow.

When Ansley woke up, Larissa and Rachel were next to her. They were talking fast and their voices were a couple octaves higher than normal. One of them was on the phone. The other one was shooing people away.

"I'm okay. Okay," Ansley said, and tried to get up. Larissa pushed her down as gently as she could.

"You're not going anywhere. Don't try to move. You could've broken your back," Larissa said.

"Why? I feel fine," Ansley said as she lifted her head and realized she was laid on the street. That caused her to jump up. She was as jittery as a fawn separated from its mother. She took a few shaky steps and collapsed.

The next time she woke up, she was in the hospital, surrounded by Larissa and Rachel.

"What happened?" Ansley said, and noticed the drip of some kind of painkiller plugged directly into her vein.

"This car came out of nowhere and slammed into you. Pow," Rachel said.

"You flew over the hood. We saw you airborne from the bakery window," Larrisa said.

"It was like it was gunning for you," Rachel said.

"Am I okay? I feel okay," Ansley said, and looked down at her body, now encased in a hospital gown. She could see her shins peeking out from the gown. One of them looked so swollen that her skin was shiny.

"You've been unconscious for hours. I'm going to go find the doctor. We called your grandmother," Larissa said.

"Great," Ansley said. "But the first thing I need to do is make a phone call of my own. Hand me my cell phone." Rachel passed it to her, and Ansley groggily dialed Parish's number, which went to voice mail. "I'm sorry to call you, but I was just hit by a car and I'm certain the driver was blond. Call me." She hung up the phone. She hadn't actually seen the driver but she knew Patty was a blond.

"Why would anyone care if the driver was blond?" Rachel asked.

"It's a Texas thing," Ansley said. Just then the doctor walked in the door.

After the doctor's examination and a nap, which overlapped, she woke up alone. There were five messages on her cell phone, which were all from Parish, begging her to call him back. There were also several large bouquets of flowers. Peonies, her favorite. By the clock on the wall, she had been asleep for six hours.

"Your grandmother was here. She went home to get some things for you," Dot said as she walked into the room.

"So what's wrong with me?" Ansley asked.

"Broken wrist, concussion, lots of bruises. You won't be wearing skirts for a while," Dot said, and smiled. She had been crying.

"What's wrong?" Ansley asked.

"I think I know who did this to you," Dot said. "I think Patty is in town. She's real pissed off."

"Patty? So you admit it, then?" Ansley said as she pushed the button to her pain medication again and again. She thought it'd be a good idea to be a little buzzed when she heard what she thought Dot was about to tell her.

"What's Patty pissed off about? She got the guy," Ansley said.

"Patty doesn't like that you're becoming a success," Dot said.

"Why? Why would she care and how does she know?" Ansley asked. She was trying to put the pieces all together. She thought that when she left Dallas her contact with Patty ended. She assumed that no one wanted anything she had anymore, because she had nothing. And how did Patty know what Ansley was up to?

"Patty and I are cousins," Dot said before Ansley even asked the question.

"What?" Ansley stated more than asked. She didn't see that coming at all.

"Patty sent me to spy on you," Dot said, embarrassed.

"Were you ever my friend?" Ansley asked.

"Not until recently," Dot admitted. "At first I was helping you just to get information to help Patty—but once I got to know you I really started liking you."

"Great," Ansley said. "Do you even like Thad, or did you start with him to piss me off?"

"I planned to get Thad away from you, but that first dinner I immediately liked him . . . and now I love him," Dot said shyly.

"Well, it's good that at least someone is happy in love," Ansley said sarcastically. She'd like a relationship to work out for once.

"I'm sorry. You don't deserve this. I thought you did, but you don't," Dot said. "I don't think you're a bitch."

"I used to be," Ansley said. "But is that a reason to destroy my business? It's a bit of an overreaction, don't you think?" Ansley said, pushing her pain medication button fast. She needed to be sedated, or she felt like she would tackle Dot, "The plumber," Ansley snapped. She'd had an ephiphany. The plumber who was responsible for two thousand dollars of damage at the bakery messed it up because Dot asked him to.

"Did you bribe the plumber to screw up the bakery?" Ansley asked.

"I paid him a couple hundred," Dot said.

"What the hell? If I hadn't fired him, he could've ruined my business," Ansley said, "I can't believe you would try to make my business fail."

"Patty and I were very close, and she convinced me you deserved it," Dot said.

"Do you understand failed business? I've put more than two hundred thousand dollars in the bakery, and I'm liable for rent for the next three years. I would've gone crazy," Ansley said.

"I know. I'm sorry," Dot said.

"You need to make this right," Ansley said.

"Don't you understand? That's what I'm trying to do. I felt bad about how much Patty hurt you, so I tried to help you. I suggested you get a security camera because I thought then you'd catch Patty in the act."

"You need to tell Parish everything," Ansley said.

"Of course," Dot responded.

Ansley pulled out her cell phone, dialed Parish's number, and handed the phone to Dot.

"Tell Parish everything," Ansley commanded.

Dot confessed to him. Ansley could hear Parish's indignation over the phone. Dot handed it to her.

"Hello, Parish," Ansley said with happiness.

"I'm sorry. I can't believe Patty would do such a thing. I'll talk to her," Parish said.

"Well, you'll break your engagement to her," Ansley said, thinking she was stating the obvious.

"Let me call you back."

Parish should be begging Ansley to come back. He was so dramatic in his decision to break off his engagement to her she figured he'd react the same way once he knew the truth about Patty. He certainly would look really foolish when everyone found out that Patty hit her with a car. The thought of being the joke of Dallas society for a few months must be killing his enthusiasm, Ansley thought.

"I can't believe that you spied on me. That you lied to me. That you were part of this," Ansley said to Dot.

"You're not going to tell Thad, are you?" There was fear in her voice.

"If there's one thing I learned from this experience—Parish breaking off his engagement with me and starting a new life— it's that honesty is the best policy," Ansley said, self-satisfied.

"I need to get a drink," Dot said.

"You're going to get smashed?" Ansley asked.

"I intend to be obliterated if there's a chance I'll lose Thad," Dot said.

Well, you have no one to blame but yourself, Ansley thought, and then felt guilty.

"Do you love him? Have you had sex with him?" Ansley asked.

"Not yet. I'm waiting. Thad is special," Dot said.

Ansley sunk back into her hospital bed. Dot's sincerity was crippling her anger.

"Did you really hate me when we first met"?

"I did—Patty had told me so many bad things about you, and she had me convinced that you'd scheme and plot until you stole Parish back. She was paranoid, convinced me that you are a terrible person. But I don't hate you anymore. You're one of my closest friends now," Dot said.

"Really?"

"Yes. I think you're great—what you've done with this bakery, for your grandmother, and stepping aside so Thad and I could be together. I want to still be friends," Dot said.

"You're my only friend. Isn't that sad?" Ansley said, and laughed.

Dot took her hand. Ansley let her. Her mind raced. There was a possibility she could get Parish back if she wanted to. And she owned a bakery based in New York, where her grandmother, who she was just getting close to, lived. And there was Thad. What did she really think of Thad? Dot loved him or was on her way to loving him.

Even though her heart jumped at the thought of seeing Parish, a part of her still desperately wanted to kiss Thad. Would the memory of kissing him ever go away?

• *Pining for the Forbidden Pineapple Cupcakes* •

6 tablespoons unsalted butter, room temperature
2 eggs, room temperature
½ teaspoon vanilla
1 teaspoon pineapple extract
½ cup heavy cream
¾ cup sugar
1½ cups all-purpose flour
½ teaspoon baking powder

½ teaspoon baking soda
½ teaspoon finely ground salt, either sea or iodized
1 20-ounce can crushed pineapple

To Make the Cupcakes:
  1. Preheat oven to 350° F. Place 12 paper liners in cupcake tray.
  2. Cream butter and sugar together in an electric mixer until fluffy, about 3 to 5 minutes.
  3. Add eggs and beat another 2 minutes.
  4. Add vanilla and pineapple extracts.
  5. Whisk together the flour, baking powder, baking soda and salt. Add to batter.
  6. Whip cream in cold bowl to soft peaks, fold in batter.
  7. Drain pineapple. Make sure to remove as much liquid as possible. Gently fold the pineapple into batter.
  8. Pour into paper liners. Fill three-quarters of the way to the top.
  9. Bake 20 to 25 minutes.
  10. Cool for 5 minutes and then place on a baking rack.

Yield: 12 cupcakes

Frosting

1 cup sifted powdered sugar
2 tablespoons unsalted butter, room temperature
2 tablespoons milk
½ teaspoon vanilla
Pinch of salt

To Make the Frosting:

1. Cream the powdered sugar and butter together in an electric mixer until smooth, about 3 to 5 minutes.
2. Add milk, vanilla and pinch of salt. Beat until smooth. If frosting is thin, let it sit for a few minutes. It will thicken. If too thick, add more milk.
3. Frost cooled cupcakes.

Chapter 22

D ot left. Vivian hadn't arrived yet. Ansley was alone in her hospital room. She felt only a dull pain pulsing through her body. Her mind was filled with the foggy thoughts painkillers create—not necessarily incoherent, but assuredly nonsensical.

When Patty walked into the room, Ansley wasn't sure how to react. She wasn't hallucinating, but Patty's calm demeanor and her ability to breeze into Ansley's room was out of sync with the fact that not such a long time ago, Patty had hit Ansley with a car.

Ansley casually wondered if her life was in danger. She grabbed her nurse call button but didn't press it, deciding that would be rude. She should hear Patty out first.

"How are you liking New York?" Ansley asked in a fake nice voice.

"It's been eventful. I have lots of projects on my list and

have only crossed off a couple," Patty said as she took a seat next to Ansley's bed.

"I think you've done your part here," Ansley said, and motioned to her bruised body.

"I don't know. There's always room for improvement," Patty said in a way that unnerved Ansley. Ansley checked to make sure the door to her room was still open. It was.

"You took my fiancé. You tried to ruin my life in New York. You ran me over with a car. What more could you want to do to me?"

"I don't know. None of it is as satisfying as I thought it would be," Patty confessed in a friendly manner. "I thought I'd feel a lot better about myself. I thought I'd have this big emotional high that would last for days."

"But . . . ?"

"But it only lasts for a few hours, and then the bad feeling comes back," Patty said.

"Do you love Parish?"

"Absolutely."

"Then you need to focus on building up yourself and building that relationship. Truthfully, Patty, it's pathetic that I still play such a role in your life. Get over me," Ansley said with much more bravado than she was feeling. Though she was beginning to get pissed off that this woman was complaining because Ansley wasn't feeling bad enough.

"Maybe you're right. Maybe this was never about you. Maybe it was about low self-esteem," Patty mused.

"I think it's time you work on that, without me," Ansley said.

"The thing that bothers me is that you've recovered from all of this so fast. You don't even seem fazed by my engagement to Parish. A person could argue you've built a better life here," Patty said.

"I don't think my happiness should concern you. Your happiness should," Ansley said.

"You won't tell Parish about any of this, will you?" Patty asked.

Ansley stalled by pretending to straighten her IV. She had to think fast. If she lied and said she wouldn't, then Patty would leave. If she told the truth, she wasn't sure what Patty would do. Ansley could see her trying to choke her to death. Of course, if Ansley lied and Patty found out later, it might make things even worse.

"Christ. Patty, I've told Parish everything, which in the long run is probably healthier for your relationship," Ansley said. "He didn't say he was leaving you. He said he wanted to talk to you, that's all."

"What's your angle? Are you trying to be nice for once in your life?" Patty asked.

"Oh, I'll be honest, nothing would make me happier than to have Parish dump you, come running back to me, and then he and I could operate my business together until I start having kids. Then I'd let him take over everything but creative control," Ansley said, feeling more and more like a woman who was in control of her life.

"He'd never go back to you," Patty said.

"Hope is a powerful thing, and so is finding out your fiancée is insane. Let's see what he says after he and I talk more," Ansley said, sitting up straighter. She was going to be ready to take on Patty if she tried to hurt her.

"I've got to call him," Patty said as she dug in her purse for her cell phone.

"Please take it outside. I need my rest. I got hit by a car today, in case you didn't hear," Ansley said, hoping to play on Patty's guilt.

Patty stood, nodded her head and left the room quickly. The girl was several cards short of a full deck. What did Parish see in her? For that matter, what had he seen in Ansley? She and Patty couldn't be more different, Ansley thought as she replayed her sorority days in her head. Some of her actions did have shades of deranged drama queen, like when she insisted a couple of her younger sisters bring her breakfast in bed every morning for a week before her birthday or when she demanded one girl get her hair color redone because it was too close to Ansley's own shade.

"High maintenance," Ansley said to herself. She was about to drift off to sleep. Before she did she needed to talk to a nurse and let everyone know that Patty was not allowed back into her room.

She called Dot as well, to let her know that Patty had paid her a visit.

"She's not staying with you, is she?" Ansley asked.

"No, we've grown apart since this whole thing with you started," Dot said. "Maybe I should call the police. Patty needs to own up to what she's done."

"No, don't do that. I don't want to ruin her life."

"Look at you. That was nice, genuinely nice," Dot said proudly.

"Don't get all mushy yet. If she comes after me again, I will call 911. Let's see how this plays out," Ansley said, hoping that Parish would come to his senses.

Ansley fell asleep and dreamed about her life five years from now. She dreamed the business was still going but it was in Dallas and she was in the kitchen making cupcakes with her two young daughters. Both had bright blond curly hair, just like Parish's. This is the way things were meant to be, she thought, and woke up strangely dissatisfied. The dream didn't sit well with her.

I don't want to live in Dallas anymore and I don't want Parish, she thought as she opened her eyes. But there he was, sitting in the chair beside her bed. He looked tired and depressed.

"Hi," Ansley said, and turned on her side so she was facing him. She curled up as gracefully as she could considering that she was in a hospital gown and painted with bruises.

"I'm so sorry," Parish said, and tried to smile. Instead, he broke into tears.

"It's okay. I'm gonna be okay," Ansley said.

"You don't understand," he said, and explained everything in one long sentence. There were no periods, commas or any punctuation marks to indicate a pause. Parish kept talking until he got everything out. How he was so confused. He flew to New York after Ansley called and he couldn't get Patty on the phone. Finally Patty called an hour ago. She was in New York and she confessed to everything—putting up the fliers and hitting Ansley with the car. He was mad, who wouldn't be, and he did the dutiful thing and broke off the engagement.

"I want us to get back together," he said, and looked Ansley directly in the face for the first time since the start of his monologue.

"So, you want to get reengaged?" Ansley asked, confused.

"Yes. I know it's going to be embarrassing but I'm willing to brave it. You're worth it," he said.

"I am," Ansley said.

"Absolutely," Parish said.

"No, I know I am. Parish, I can't go back. I've started something here and I have to see it through. I can't go back to Dallas," Ansley said.

"Okay. Well, then I'll move here," Parish said, though the thought of it obviously was killing him.

"I'm not ready for this. I can't get married now," Ansley said, and felt how true those words were. She didn't feel like a completely real adult yet. How could she function in a marriage? "Besides, are you sure you don't have feelings for Patty?"

Parish put his head between his hands and ran his fingers through his hair like he always did when he was in deep thought. He didn't talk for a few minutes.

"I know she smashed into you with a car and tried to destroy your bakery, but she did it all for me and for our relationship. I don't know . . . it shows commitment," Parish said.

"Commitment?" Ansley asked, confused by what he meant—should Patty be committed or was she committed to him?

"Would you ever do all that for me?" Parish asked.

"No," Ansley said, and thought sarcastically, *But I'm sane.*

"It was an intense summer. I've never loved anyone more than Patty," Parish said. That hurt Ansley deeply. She had been in love with Parish once she was sure of that.

"So, did you love me at all?" Ansley asked, pushing the pain even deeper into her heart.

"I don't know. I had a huge crush on you. Come on, you're beautiful. Gorgeous. You know how to work a crowd. Everyone wants you. I think part of me dislikes you. You're so perfect," Parish said.

"I thought people envied me," Ansley said.

"They hate you," Parish said.

"Patty does."

"She hates and envies you," Parish said, getting up.

"Where are you going?"

"To find Patty. She must be really freaked out. She hit you with her car and now she's all alone in a strange city," Parish said. "I'm sorry for what Patty did but she needs me now. I'll be back." He quickly walked out the door.

Ansley analyzed what had just been said. She had told Parish no. He had finally come back to her, even if it was out of guilt, but she had turned him away. She said no to the fairy tale. She knew that she had changed too much to go back to her old life. She didn't want to get married, lunch and have babies. She wanted to work at something she loved. She wanted to make her mark on the world so when she had children they would know that life has more possibilities than you could ever anticipate. She wanted to build something that would grow and thrive. She had started and she couldn't walk away from that.

• *Baby, I Don't Love You Cupcakes* •

1 egg, room temperature
½ cup vegetable oil
½ cup sugar
½ cup molasses
2 teaspoons freshly grated ginger
1½ cups all-purpose flour
1 teaspoon cinnamon
½ teaspoon finely ground sea salt
⅛ teaspoon ground cloves
½ cup water
2 teaspoons baking soda
2 tablespoons potato starch

To Make the Cupcakes:
1. Preheat the oven to 325° F. Place 12 paper liners into cupcake tray.
2. Whisk together oil, sugar and molasses.
3. Add egg, and mix until smooth.
4. Stir in ginger.
5. In a separate bowl combine flour, cinnamon, salt, potato starch and cloves.
6. Add to the wet mixture and stir until just combined.
7. Bring water to a boil in small saucepan.
8. Remove from heat and stir in baking soda.
9. Whisk the hot water into the batter until combined.

10. Pour batter into paper liners. Fill three-quarters of the way to the top.
11. Bake 25 to 28 minutes until toothpick comes out clean after inserted into the middle of the cupcake.
12. Cool cupcakes for 5 minutes and then move to baking rack.

Yield: 12 cupcakes

Orange Flower Cream

1 pint whipping cream
1 teaspoon orange flower water
1 tablespoon powdered sugar
Pinch of cream of tartar

To Make the Frosting:
1. In a chilled bowl mix whipping cream with the orange flower water.
2. Add the sugar and cream of tarter gradually.
3. Beat with an electric mixer until stiff.
4. Frost cooled cupcakes.

Chapter 23

This wasn't the way it was supposed to happen—Ansley hooked up to an IV and Hattie forced to come to the city. This didn't make Vivian look very good.

Hattie had called her shortly after she got home and gave her the details of her flight and then hung up. Vivian hadn't even known that Hattie had her phone number. Ansley must've called her from the hospital. Ansley must be awake again. Vivian called the hospital to see; the nurse she talked to assured her Ansley was asleep and that she'd call Vivian when Ansley was ready for visitors. Vivian reluctantly hung up. She'd had a more pleasant conversation with the nurse than she had with Hattie.

You have to make do with what you have, Vivian silently said to herself as she prepared to see her daughter for the first time in decades. Hattie's plane would land around 11 P.M. It would take at least forty-five minutes for her to get to Vivian's house from the airport. Vivian had some time to kill.

She walked around the house adjusting pillows and cleaning imaginary lint. After the fifth lap, Vivian couldn't stand it anymore. She needed to do something. She went to Ansley's room, got the book and brought it to the kitchen. She opened it up to the entries she'd made. The first entry she was allowed to write in the book was inspired by Hattie. It was the vanilla cake she made for her daughter's first birthday, and every birthday after that. Vivian had read through dozens of cake recipes, combined them and tweaked the ingredients until she created a cake that was moist, flavorful and sweet, but not too sweet. It was the perfect cake. Now, it brought back all the memories she had of being a mother. She decided she would make it, but change it to cupcakes in honor of Ansley.

Vivian got out her butter and eggs. She let them warm up while she placed all the other ingredients and bowls on the counter. She measured her dry ingredients all into one bowl.

She remembered Hattie's face covered in frosting as she tried to eat her birthday cake. It had been her first taste of sugar, and she'd loved it. She dove right in with her mouth and tried to eat it all at once. It wasn't just her face that was covered—her whole body was crusted with frosting and crumbs. Vivian had to strip her down and dunk her in the bath to get all the sugar off of her.

Vivian smiled at the memory as she dumped the butter in the stand mixer and turned it on. "My daughter is coming," she said, and still couldn't believe it was true. After all these years, she was going to see her daughter again. She had waited and fantasized about this moment. She had crafted hundreds of different scenarios in her head. Vivian had imagined she would fly to Dallas and knock on Hattie's front door. When Hattie opened it she'd cry and hug her mother fiercely. They wouldn't need words to express all the emotion. In another fantasy, Hattie came to New York with her whole family and invited Vivian to dinner at a fancy restaurant. Vivian walked into the restaurant, and before she even sat down, Hattie said, "I want you to know I understand."

Vivian was frosting the cupcakes when she heard the front door open. She raced to the foyer. She was so excited to see Hattie, and so scared. Her heart fluttered and her hands were sweating. She skidded to a stop in the doorway. Hattie looked just like the framed photos Ansley had in her room, with a strong and sophisticated air. She stood tall in a crisp white shirt with exaggerated French cuffs, and wide-leg pants. She projected timeless chic.

She smiled at Vivian. "I thought you might've skipped town." Vivian pulled her in by the wrists and wrapped her in a hug.

Hattie instantly stiffened and pulled back. "I'll leave my bags here. Let's go to the hospital."

"Don't you want to change? Freshen up? Eat?" Vivian asked.

"No, I need to see Ansley," Hattie said firmly as she looked around the foyer. She didn't hide the appraisal. Vivian had done well for herself. Hattie walked over to the clock and touched its face.

"Let's go," Vivian said, and called for her car.

They stood uneasily by the front door waiting for the black Lexus to pull up to the curb. The excitement of seeing her daughter for the first time in years was being held in check by fear. Hattie was so self-possessed and serious, Vivian was afraid if she let her own emotional needs show, Hattie would squash them like ants. She didn't trust her daughter to treat her with tenderness or even decency. Though truly, she thought, she didn't deserve either. This wasn't the meeting she imagined— but then, fantasies were just that, fantasy. They never took into account the resentment and anger that must've built up in Hattie for the past forty-six years.

Vivian examined her daughter's face. It was pale, with faint freckles that never had time to darken in the sun. Hattie had lines around her eyes and mouth. Her face looked lived in but well taken care of. *She looks like me*, Vivian thought, and felt proud.

"It's late. She'll be asleep. She was barely awake when I was there a few hours ago," Vivian said, hoping Hattie would walk back in the house and they could talk over cupcakes in the kitchen. Kitchens and food always relaxed people. She knew she'd have better luck with her daughter if they could start to unwind all the hurt and years of absence.

"It doesn't matter. I need to see her," Hattie said.

"You're a good mother," Vivian told her.

"It wasn't hard, I just did the opposite of what you did," Hattie shot as the car pulled up. The ladies got in. *This is going to be a very long night*, Vivian thought.

The hospital was old. Ansley's room with its gray linoleum floor and Pepto-Bismol-colored tile walls gave the impression it was twenty years ago. It made Ansley, tucked into an old hospital bed, look frail and in need of a mother's protection. Hattie ran to her bedside.

"Baby," Hattie said as she gingerly hugged Ansley, "who would do this to you? You're such a sweet girl. I don't understand why anyone would want to hurt you."

"Momma, I'm not that sweet," Ansley said.

"Yes you are," Hattie purred. "I've only ever seen you be mean to people who deserved it."

"No, she wasn't sweet. She was a bit of a spoiled brat," Vivian said, and smirked at Ansley. The two women had developed a strong bond. Vivian could criticize her and Ansley would listen.

"Ansley is perfect," Hattie pronounced.

"Aw, only my momma would say that," Ansley said, and squeezed her mother's arm.

"Are you okay? You seem a little out of it," Hattie said as she felt Ansley's forehead.

"I'm fine," Ansley said.

"She's fine," Vivian repeated, and leaned into the doorway. She hadn't decided whether or not to fully come into the room.

"If she were fine she wouldn't be in the hospital," Hattie said, and gave Vivian a cold stare. Hattie's attitude was getting more and more hostile.

"It's a bump on the head. They keep you for observation if you get a bump on the head," Ansley said.

"How could you let her get a bump on the head?" Hattie cried as she stared at Vivian. She was silently saying to Vivian, "How could you screw this up too?"

There was so much Hattie didn't know. She didn't realize that Vivian loved Ansley completely and had come unhinged when she heard about the accident. As soon as she got the call, Vivian rushed to the hospital. She didn't even bother to tell Fred why she was leaving in the middle of reviewing taxes, didn't call her car because she didn't want to waste the time. She just walked out of the house and hailed a taxi. She raced to the hospital and stayed with Ansley for hours. Larissa and Rachel shooed her away by telling her Ansley would be really freaked out if she saw a mascara-streaked and crumpled Vivian, since normally Vivian never had a hair out of place. They told her Ansley would think the injuries were worse than they were, so Vivian needed to go home and make herself presentable. She grudgingly did.

Hattie had no idea how Vivian felt about her granddaughter or the hell she had been through in the past few hours, waiting for Ansley to wake up. Vivian didn't know how to respond to her daughter's criticism, so she remained silent.

"You can't even defend yourself, can you? Typical. You have no feelings." Turning to Ansley, Hattie said, "This is why I didn't want you to move to New York. She doesn't care about anyone." Hattie's voice rose with each word.

"All right, let's get to it. Let's get to what this is really about," Vivian said as she walked into the room and stood on the opposite side of Ansley's bed, claiming equal space with Hattie. "I left you. I left my little girl alone. I didn't call and I didn't write and I didn't visit. I was a horrible mother, I was worse than a horrible mother. I was no mother. And you have a right to be furious about it. But before I left, if you remember, I was a great mother. And isn't it strange that a great mother would all the sudden stop being a mother, all at once?"

Vivian stared at Hattie with the cold anger of a woman who has had enough of being called every dirty name in the book behind her back without the benefit of a confrontation.

"I know why you left. Because you loved that man, Charlie Osterhaut, more than your child and husband," Hattie said, and Vivian burst out laughing.

It wasn't the most appropriate response to a heated

mother–daughter fight forty-six years in the making. Vivian tried to stifle it but the laugh only rose up stronger. She snorted out a burst of full-throated laughs that evolved into a long belly laugh. Ansley and Hattie looked at her with shock, surprise and then they both started laughing too. Though Hattie tried to stop hers from coming out and made the same snorting sound that Vivian had.

"You think I loved Charlie Osterhaut?" Vivian coughed out in between giggles.

"Why is that funny?" Hattie asked as she continued to laugh and wipe the tears away from her face.

"You didn't know Charlie Osterhaut, that's for sure," Vivian said, and began to tell them what happened, how she had made the biggest mistake of her life.

It was 1964. Vivian was a young wife with a five-year-old daughter. She was smart, popular and financially well-off. She was part of Dallas society. She had established her signature look—a smart take on Sophia Loren despite the minimalist craze. She was truly in love with her husband, Asher. Once their daughter was in bed, they would sit out on their porch, drink gin and tonics and he would read books to her. They were so close that she even told him the things she didn't tell her closest girlfriends—her fear that she wasn't a good mother, her worry about what her life was about.

She had it all, and that's when a woman is at her most vulnerable.

"I was cocky in my happiness," Vivian said. "I was happy, but a little bored too, and I took a stupid chance."

Vivian started going to the Adolphus Hotel bar once a week. That's when she met Charlie Osterhaut. They drank together, slept together and slept together some more. Vivian was in lust.

She had only had sex with Asher before Charlie. She and Asher had had the same sex twice a week for the past six years. She was bored and curious. She wanted to feel something new, she wanted to feel like she was sexy. Charlie made her feel she was worldly, luscious, more than a wife and mother.

"My God," Hattie breathed.

"It was lust—petty, unadulterated lust—mixed with a lot of alcohol," Vivian said matter-of-factly.

"Charlie was attractive?" Ansley asked as she pulled her blanket farther up her chest.

"Charlie was a beautiful man. He was charming, rich, confident," Vivian said.

"And Daddy?" Hattie asked.

"Asher was a beautiful, beautiful man, but I couldn't imagine having sex with the same man for the next forty years of my life. It'd be like eating rice pudding morning, noon and night, without an end in sight. It sounded unbelievably boring to me. Though now that I understand how things work, I know Asher and I could've been very happy together if I had grown up sooner," Vivian said. "Ansley, I do recommend having lots of sex before marriage."

"Do you see why I didn't want you to have anything to do with her?" Hattie asked Ansley.

"I realize I was wrong. I realized I was wrong the day after I slept with Charlie, but I was too young to get out of the way of myself," Vivian said.

The morning after sleeping with Charlie, Vivian said, she was hungover and full of regret.

She turned away from Charlie in bed and started to chart the quickest exit. Charlie got up and ordered room service for two, including Bloody Marys. He walked over to her side of the bed and sat down next to her.

"It's not the end of the world," he said.

"No, just the world as I know it," she said, and ended up telling him everything about her life. They drank their Bloody Marys and ate their eggs. Charlie listened intently. Every now and then he'd pat her hand. Vivian was starting to feel better.

By the third Bloody Mary they were in bed again. Vivian wasn't sure how it happened. Charlie and alcohol were a persuasive combination. He was so different from Asher. Charlie and Vivian tried multiple positions. Vivian felt so free, she was even on top—something she'd never do with Asher. She kept pouring drinks from the pitcher, kissing Charlie and giggling. It was like she was single and only had herself to worry about. She could do anything, and anything felt really good. Coming up for air after her fourth orgasm of the morning, Vivian looked at the clock. It was noon. Vivian rushed out of bed. The feeling of freedom was quickly replaced with embarrassment, worry and complete responsibility. "I have to get going. My daughter will be really upset."

"Wait," Charlie said, and grabbed her hand. "Once more?" And she did.

Because when would she ever have this feeling again? She was about to plunge back into the world of predictability, routine and servitude to others. She wanted to grab the last bit of seduction and excitement that she could.

About a month after the incident with Charlie, she was in her kitchen having a tea party with Hattie and creating a guest list for her husband's birthday party.

The doorbell rang. It was Charlie. He stood before her with a cockiness Vivian wasn't sure he had a right to. Parked at the curb was a ridiculously expensive import of some kind. It was showy for the sake of showiness.

In her living room Charlie kissed her and it felt wrong but also right. It felt passionate and sexy. It made her feel like she wasn't just a wife and mother locked into the suburbs of Dallas. It promised her there was a plan for her, a life outside of her own life that she could have if she grabbed for it.

"I'm here until tomorrow," Charlie had whispered.

"Why are you doing this?" Vivian asked, creeped out by his intensity. They'd had a one-night stand. A really great intense session of sex, but it was absolutely finite. Was he fuzzy on the definition of "one night"?

"I like you. I like your fieriness, I like . . . there's something about you," Charlie said.

Vivian liked him too. In the past month her mind often slipped back to their time together. She replayed the seduction and the feeling of letting go so much it was starting to drive her crazy.

They arranged to meet at the Adolphus later.

Vivian laid her arms on Ansley's legs and put her head on her forearms.

"So that's why you left? You were tired of being a wife and mother," Hattie asked.

"No. I wasn't going to leave at all," Vivian said.

"And then? What happened?" Hattie asked.

Vivian met Charlie one more time. They had a couple of drinks and took a bottle of champagne upstairs with them. They drank and kissed and took each other's clothes off. They took their time having sex in that slow excited way you do when you want it to last a long time. When they were done and lying next to each other in bed, naked, Charlie tracing his fingers along Vivian's back, Vivian suddenly bolted toward the bathroom to throw up. She stayed in there for a while because she couldn't shake the nausea. Charlie walked over to her and stroked her hair. "You're pregnant aren't you?"

"Probably," Vivian conceded, accepting for the first time that pregnancy could be a distinct possibility. She wasn't on any birth control.

"It's mine," Charlie said.

"No, it's not," Vivian flatly stated.

They spent the next hour going over dates and counting backward to her menstrual cycle and ovulation date. Scientifically he was right. But Vivian also had sex with her husband on a regular basis, which she pointed out to Charlie. What she didn't tell him was that Asher could no longer have children. After Hattie, he had gotten into a bad car accident. He made a full recovery, short the ability to have more children. In their circle, most people knew that Asher could no longer procreate—why else would Hattie be an only child?

So passing this baby off as Asher's would be tricky. Vivian could claim it was a miracle, some of Asher's sperm must have escaped and found Vivian's egg. Fortunately she hadn't slept with anyone in Dallas, so there was no one who could counter her claim. She might be able to fold the new baby into her existing family, she thought.

"Marry me," Charlie said.

"I'm married," Vivian said, hoping to stay that way after she told Asher about her condition.

"I'll tell him everything," Charlie threatened. Vivian knew he would too. She could tell Asher Charlie was lying, but why would a rich New Yorker come to town and lie about sleeping with her? Asher would be crushed, heartbroken and ultimately shamed because he would think he hadn't been enough for her.

"Why would you do that? Why would you break up a happy family?" Vivian had asked, infused with anger over the things she was about to lose.

"Because that's my child and no one else is going to raise him," Charlie said. There wasn't a trace of empathy in his voice. When Charlie wanted something it was obvious that other people and their emotions weren't part of his calculus.

"I need some time. I have a life here, a daughter," Vivian said.

"Take her with you. The more the merrier," Charlie said as he walked away from Vivian, who was still crouching over the toilet, and started to get dressed.

"Asher would never allow that. The courts would never allow that. I'm the guilty party in a divorce. I'm the embarrassment," Vivian said.

"I could pay him off," Charlie said nonchalantly as he buckled his belt.

"I need time," Vivian repeated.

"Two weeks. I'll be back in two weeks to pick up you and whatever you're bringing," Charlie said as he sat down on the edge of the tub by Vivian. "You should get dressed. I need to take you home."

Vivian quickly put on her clothes while Charlie made a phone call to some business associate. She felt used, like sex was just another transaction for Charlie. The excitement that was so powerful a couple hours ago had evaporated. She felt like a woman she didn't want to know, a woman who would open her legs for the first man who asked her to. She wasn't in love with Charlie. She didn't know Charlie.

She sat on the bed and waited for Charlie to finish his call. When he did he walked over to her and sat down beside her. He took her hand in his and gently kissed it. "We'll have a wonderful life together. You'll see."

He got up, graciously helped her up and kept his hand resting on her back until they got into the elevator. His tenderness gave Vivian a slight glimmer of hope. She was about to ruin her life in Dallas, maybe a life with him in New York would be okay.

After he dropped her off, Vivian tried to pretend nothing had happened. It was easy if she didn't think about the nausea. Asher and Hattie acted like they always did. Charlie didn't call her for ten days. Maybe he had given up.

On the eleventh day he did call, with instructions. He would pick her up in three days at 11 A.M. She was to have everything ready because they would leave an hour later on Charlie's company plane. He had a dinner meeting in New York that evening.

Vivian told Asher everything that night after a couple gin and tonics. The alcohol didn't cushion the shock. They had been lying together on the chaise longue on their back porch. Vivian could feel his body tense as she got deeper into the story. When she got to the part about being pregnant with another man's child he pushed her off. She landed on the cement.

"I know this seems like the end of the world, but it's fixable," Vivian said.

"How on earth is this fixable?" Asher screamed.

"I can tell Charlie that we're not getting a divorce. We're

going to raise the child as our own, and if he wants to see him or her occasionally we can work something out," Vivian explained. She had been working on this plan for hours.

"I don't want to raise another man's child," Asher said.

"But we'd still be a family. It would still be us. It would be us and two little children who don't know any different," Vivian said as she sat at the foot of the chair.

"*Us* isn't what it used to be," Asher said. "Besides, people know about my accident—I'd be the laughingstock of Dallas. Face it, Vivian, it's over between us."

Over the next few days Vivian tried to sway Asher to go along with her plan. She thought she was getting close every time they had sex, which they had a lot, but he never budged. It was like he was having sex with her to say good-bye, getting all he could out of their last hours together because after she left he was going to cut her off. The night before Charlie was supposed to show up they were lying in bed after a very physical session of making love. Asher had moved her on top of him—the first time ever   grabbed her breasts and used them to guide her in and out of him. When he did it she felt so turned on, and saddened because she knew this wasn't making love, this was fucking—that was what Asher had distanced her to.

"Do you really want me to go?" she asked as she watched him lying there with his eyes closed. She didn't dare touch him—she was afraid he would flinch.

"No, but there isn't much choice," Asher said.

"There is a choice if you take it," Vivian said.

"That's not something I'm going to do. When you leave tomorrow, don't tell Hattie anything. I'll do it," Asher said.

"But I want to tell her she'll see me real soon. She can take trips to New York anytime she wants. I will miss her so much," Vivian said.

"None of that is for her, it's for you. I know what's best for my little girl. You go worry about your own family," Asher said. There was so much venom cutting through his words that Vivian got up from bed and slept on the couch. She knew their marriage was over. Asher had been cutting the ties to her systematically over the past few days. Sex was another way to make her not his wife but some woman he could do what he wanted with and not care.

The next morning Vivian did what any impulsive woman making all the wrong choices would do. She didn't tell Hattie anything. She went to New York with Charlie and married him as soon as her divorce was final.

"I've regretted what I did almost every single day. But what was done was done," Vivian said.

"You see, she's not all that bad, Momma," Ansley said as she stroked her mother's hair.

"Jesus," Hattie uttered, "how is she not all bad? What happened to the baby?"

"I miscarried and then I got my tubes tied," Vivian said.

"Oh, Charlie must've been pissed," Ansley said.

"I think he found a way to get back at me."

"The IRS," Ansley said, everything clicking into place.

Vivian grabbed her hand and Hattie's. Hattie let her.

"So Daddy was the one who didn't want me to see you?" Hattie asked softly.

"I wanted to take you with me. I wanted to give your grandmother a credit card to use whenever you wanted so you could fly to New York. I wanted to be your mother so much. But the times were different. I could never have gotten custody of you after the affair," Vivian said, "and I didn't want your father to fall any farther off the wagon. I loved him too."

"If you'd only known," Hattie said with tears running down her face.

"Known?"

"How much I needed you. I needed my momma to tell me I was perfect, to tell me I was special, like I did with Ansley," Hattie said.

"You might've told me that too much, Momma. I wasn't very nice for years," Ansley confessed.

Hattie smiled at her daughter. Ansley was always trying to do better. Say what you will about how Ansley treated her friends at college, in the past few weeks she had grown up beautifully. Hattie smiled at Vivian too. It was hard to hear how normal and flawed your parents are. It was difficult to accept that her father had let his anger at Vivian get in the way of any mother-daughter relationship, but it was so gratifying to know that she had been wanted. Vivian hadn't cast her aside for Charlie, at least not on purpose.

"Why didn't you try to contact Momma? You should've tried," Ansley scolded.

"I tried several times, but Asher or my mother told me to stop, and then I did. I should've never given up. It's one of my biggest regrets. I knew what was best for my little girl, and that was having me in her life."

"I understand. I understand," Hattie said quietly.

"I don't," Ansley insisted. "You try and you try, until you break through."

"Ansley, I love you, and I am proud of what you've accomplished here—but, baby, you need a hell of a lot more life experience before you lecture me on this," Vivian said.

Ansley kept quiet. She looked bashful, like she was actually taking what her grandmother said to heart.

"We need to talk to you about Parish," Hattie said.

"That man doesn't deserve you," Vivian said, and then realized Parish was standing in the doorway. Both Vivian and Hattie became instantly quiet, nodded to Parish and marched out of the room together, their arms linked. "I made you some cupcakes," Ansley heard Vivian say to Hattie.

"What was that?" Parish asked as he took the seat next to Ansley's bed. Her covers were a crumpled mass from the past couple hours. Her face was tear-streaked and glowing, until she saw the expression on his. He seemed on the verge of tears again.

"What's going on?" she asked.

"I talked to Patty."

"And?" Ansley asked.

"She needs understanding. If you could forget all this happened, I'll take her back to Dallas tomorrow," Parish said.

"Don't I at least get an apology?" Ansley asked.

"She's in a fragile state; seeing you again could agitate her. She knows how close she was to losing me to you. It upsets her a lot. She loves me so much," Parish said.

"So if I let you take her back to Dallas quietly, I don't talk to the police here and I don't tell my sorority sisters in Dallas that she hit me with a car, you and she will let everyone know that I am not a horrible bitch?" Ansley asked. She had switched to her businesswoman mode.

"I don't see how we can do that. You were a horrible bitch," Parish said.

"But I'm not anymore," Ansley said, then she gestured to her body, "and I think this more than makes up for any cruelty I inflicted."

"We'll figure out a way. We say we made a visit to New York and talk up how much you've changed," Parish said, changing his sentiment as soon as he surveyed Ansley's injuries again.

"I would appreciate that. I plan on visiting my family and I plan on holding my head up high," Ansley said, and gave him a mean stare.

"All right," Parish said.

"And you and Patty are going to give me some fabulous Christmas gift that I can wear in public and talk about to show how well we all get along," Ansley said.

"Do you want us to go out together one night?" Parish asked.

"That's pushing it. I might try to trip her or something if I get too close," Ansley said.

"I'm not sure if I can trust Patty, to tell you the truth," Parish said, thinking about the scenario. "Best if we don't see you."

He gave Ansley a warm but careful hug, and said, "I know you're going to have a great life, with a great guy. Met any contenders in New York?"

Ansley paused, realizing that while there were parts of Parish as well as Thad that fit, neither man was really the right one for her. "No. Not yet anyway. I guess I still don't know what I want."

"You'll figure it out. You'll find a guy who's perfect for you," Parish said.

"I hope I'm smart enough to hang on to him when I do,"

Ansley said, remembering her grandmother's story. Vivian had
let the love of her life, Ansley's grandfather, slip away because
she didn't realize how valuable love was.

"You will be. You're always the smartest one in the room,"
Parish said genuinely.

"Thank you," Ansley said, and felt buoyed with confidence
about the life she was diving into. It wasn't the marriage she
had anticipated, but with luck her business would survive
longer than the typical marriage.

"You are still the most beautiful sorority sister from Baylor,"
Parish said as he got up from the bed and kissed Ansley gently
on the lips.

"Nice breaking up with you," Ansley said, and then immediately wished she hadn't. She waved as he walked backwards
out of the room. This could be the last time she ever saw
Parish. She felt sad, but not destroyed like she had back in Dallas. She knew there was more in the world waiting for her. She
was making the right decision.

• New York Vanilla •

1 cup (or 2 sticks) unsalted butter, room temperature
1 cup heavy cream
4 eggs, room temperature and separated into whites and
  yolks
1½ teaspoons pure vanilla extract

½ teaspoon pure almond extract
2 cups sugar
¼ teaspoon cream of tartar
3 cups cake flour
½ teaspoon salt
2½ teaspoons baking powder
2 tablespoons potato starch

To Make the Cupcakes:

1. Preheat oven to 350° F. Place 28 paper liners in cupcake trays.
2. Cream butter and sugar together in electric mixer until fluffy, about 3 to 5 minutes. Add extracts. Beat 1 minute.
3. Add egg yolks to batter and beat another 2 minutes.
4. Whisk flour, potato starch, baking powder and salt. Add to batter.
5. Whip cream in cold bowl until soft peaks form, fold into batter.
6. In a separate bowl beat the egg whites with cream of tarter until bubbles appear, about 1 to 2 minutes. It's better to underwhip than overwhip, because that will make the cake more moist.
7. Fold the egg whites into the batter.
8. Pour batter into cupcake liners. Fill two-thirds of the way to the top.
9. Bake for 21 to 24 minutes, or until a toothpick inserted in the middle of the cupcake comes out clean.
10. Cool for 5 minutes and then transfer to baking racks.

Yield: 28 cupcakes

Jennifer Ross

Vanilla Frosting

1 cup (or 2 sticks) unsalted butter, softened
2½ cups powdered sugar
2 teaspoons vanilla extract

To Make the Frosting:
1. Cream the butter with an electric mixer until fluffy, about 3 to 5 minutes.
2. Add the powdered sugar and vanilla and beat until smooth.
3. Frost cooled cupcakes.

Chapter 24

Ansley poured vegetable oil into the batter and blended. Recently she had become a convert and loved using oil and butter in cupcakes. Oil makes a moister cupcake. Butter makes a better flavor. Being in New York for a year had taught her something.

She scooped the batter into cupcake tins, careful to make them appear as neat as possible. These were wedding cupcakes after all and she felt honored to be making them. They would be a nod to Texas, with their Mexican vanilla batter—a must-have for any Texas girl.

She still longed for Dallas. She missed the searing heat and the bright sun. The sorority would never be her support group again. Some girls had contacted her after they heard about what Patty did (it couldn't remain a total secret after all), but it wasn't the same. A rift had formed. Some of the girls even went to Patty and Parish's wedding. That had hurt Ansley. She hadn't forgiven either one of them yet and she didn't think Dallas society should.

Hattie was the one part of Dallas that Ansley couldn't live without. Fortunately Hattie was now taking regular trips to the city and staying at Vivian's house in the room across from Ansley's. It was like a slumber party when she was there. The three of them had stayed up far too late last night talking, planning and writing in the book. Ansley finally put the Sachertorte cupcake recipe in it. It was her first one to go in. Her hand wobbled a little as she was writing because she was so nervous about printing everything correctly. She imagined her daughter and granddaughter carefully following each step she wrote down.

Vivian was the one to break up the party. She said good night and met Fred in her bedroom. They weren't married, but he stayed over a lot, commuting from his home in Washington, D.C. Ansley doubted that her grandmother would ever marry again. Charlie had given the institution a bad reputation. But she and Fred were having fun.

Ansley liked him. He treated her grandmother like she walked on water and that went a long way in her book toward him being a great guy. Vivian paid the IRS a five-million-dollar fine and they agreed to not press charges against her. Charlie's revenge from beyond the grave had been costly, but it was his money that was spent to make everything better. So in a way, the joke was on Charlie in the end.

Dot stopped by the bakery at 6 A.M. to keep Ansley company as she frosted the cupcakes.

"These are beautiful," Dot exclaimed at the sight of the frosting flower petals.

Dot and Ansley had grown closer and closer over the past

year. They really did have a lot in common. The morning Dot confessed her role in Patty's plot had stripped away any layers of superficiality between them. After that they built their bond on honesty and trust.

Thad had initially been upset to hear about Dot's duplicity, but he understood and forgave her and soon after proposed to her. It took some convincing, but ever-traditional Thad finally agreed to let Ansley substitute cupcakes for wedding cake. After all, who doesn't love a cupcake?

• Tex-Mex Vanilla •

½ cup (or 1 stick) unsalted butter, room temperature
½ cup vegetable oil
4 eggs, room temperature
1 cup whole milk
2 cups sugar
3 cups sifted all-purpose flour
1½ teaspoons baking powder
2 teaspoons ground cinnamon
½ teaspoon finely ground salt, either sea or iodized
1½ teaspoons vanilla extract

To Make the Cupcakes:
1. Preheat oven to 350° F. Place 24 paper liners into cupcake trays.

2. Cream the butter and sugar together with an electric mixer until fluffy, about 3 to 5 minutes.
3. Add oil. Mix another 2 minutes.
4. Add 1 egg at a time, beating well after each egg.
5. In a medium bowl sift together flour, baking powder, cinnamon and salt.
6. Combine milk and vanilla.
7. Alternating between the flour mixture and milk mixture, add them to the batter. Start and end with the flour mixture.
8. Bake for 20 minutes, or until a toothpick inserted in the middle of a cupcake comes out clean.

Yield: 24 cupcakes

Coconut Buttercream

6 egg yolks, room temperature
¾ cup sugar
½ cup light corn syrup
2 cups (or 4 sticks) unsalted butter, room temperature, cut into small pieces
1 tablespoon vanilla extract
½ cup sweetened coconut milk
2 pounds (or 2 cups) flaked unsweetened coconut

To Make the Frosting:
1. Beat the egg yolks with an electric mixer until pale yellow, about 5 minutes.
2. Heat the sugar and corn syrup in a saucepan over

medium-high heat. Bring to full boil without stirring. Cook until mixture reaches soft ball stage, or 238° F.

3. Pour the mixture into a buttered measuring cup to halt cooking.

4. Gradually add the corn syrup mixture to the egg yolks, being careful not to cook the yolks.

5. Add the vanilla and the coconut milk.

6. In a separate bowl, cream the butter with an electric mixer until fluffy, about 3 to 5 minutes.

7. Add the corn syrup mixture to the butter mixture. Blend until smooth and creamy.

8. Fold in the coconut flakes.

9. Frost the cooled cupcakes.

Acknowledgments

Thank you to Kathy Anderson for fighting for this book, Jill Schwartzman for encouraging me to emphasize the entrepreneur fantasy that most of us have, Kim Ross for enduring endless baking and lots of late nights writing, Jeff Sharlet for getting me into this profession, Troy Campbell for general contagious enthusiasm, Judd for helping me further my baking techniques, and to everyone who loves to eat cupcakes.

About the author

JENNIFER ROSS is an avid baker. She learned
from watching her grandmother's covert
business—selling cookies to her friends for the
holidays so that they could have "homemade"
treats when their families visited.

About the type

This book was set in Berling. Designed in 1951 by Karl Erik Forsberg for the Type-foundry Berlingska Stilgjuteri AB in Lund, Sweden, it was released the same year in foundry type by H. Berthold AG. A classic old-face design, its generous proportions and inclined serifs make it highly legible.